ROBIN SCHADEL

Crossroad Blues

Cursing Raven Books

This book was professionally typeset on Reedsy.
Find out more at reedsy.com

To my Found Family. The best and truest family in existence.

Chapter 1

"Your dad will keep calling unless you answer, Sam," Destiny Grimm said as she dumped half a dozen case folders on my desk.

She was right, of course. My fucking father, Donal James Hain, Esquire, esteemed barrister and Arch Magus for the Hermetic Order of the Astrum Argentum, was nothing if not stubborn. A growl escaped my victory red lips as I exhaled. Destiny plopped into the new brown leather-cushioned chair in front of my desk and glared at her blue-blocking glasses as they slid down her nose. A singular lavender ringlet bounced along with her blonde bob. Her pink and white *Ghostbusters* insignia pin sparkled against her gray blazer.

Yawning, I opened the first folder, Liz Jefferson's mystery stalker case, and read through our notes. Without looking up, I shrugged and said, "Then he can fucking keep calling. We have nothing to talk about—not since what he pulled in Bannagh and especially not since he demanded I break up with 'Milla."

My voice had a nasal tone today. I stifled a sneeze and blinked rapidly. My eyes were heavy, and a fog filled my head. I coughed twice. March always did this to me. It was one of the main reasons I considered leaving Butcher's Bend.

But I loved this city, *my city*, both despite and because of its flaws. Sure, the old plantation-owning families still governed the town and whitewashed their legacies with televised displays of colorful generosity while keeping their power through backdoor bribery and subtle slander. Several churches joined and boasted plans for a "Christian Pride Fest" for the second week of June to coincide with our own Pride celebration. Our new mayor ran on a platform of increasing police spending, removing the homeless from public view—I mean, "ending homelessness," beautifying public spaces, and decreasing funding for schools and mental health services. All in the name of boosting the economy and gaining tourist dollars.

Despite all that, or maybe *in spite* of all that, Butcher's Bend, South Carolina, was a nice place to live. Laura Kelsington and the rest of the Arts Council fostered a thriving, multicultural art scene. Our minor league baseball team, the Butcher's Bend Bobcats, won their third consecutive Double A Championship. Blues and bluegrass musicians flocked here, finding inspiration in the mix of cultures and environments from the city to the forest at the foot of the Appalachians to the lonely dirt roads south of town, flanked by the ruins of old sharecropper shacks. Butcher's Bend also boasted the largest per capita population of NHMs, or Non-Human Mythics, as our government labeled the supernatural and folkloric beings who have gained citizenship and merged their lives with the human world, south of New York City.

That's where I, Samantha Hain, Private Investigator, entered the picture. After dropping out of college, I got my P. I. license and started helping both humans and supernatural creatures with their problems. I started accidentally while still in college, helping a leprechaun named Flann Mac Magnus, and then things took off. The first years, well, all the years were struggles. Destiny and I scraped by. Sure, we could have made more money, but I refused to not help those who needed our help if they couldn't pay or if they couldn't continue paying. I couldn't fix the broken system, but I could keep its gears from crushing a few innocent souls.

But things are looking up. Since the new year started, we've had an upsurge in normal business. Even the Full Moon Specials, which is the name Destiny gave to our supernatural cases, have been easy and well-paying. I replaced my ancient Honda Civic with a Subaru Forester, and we got new computers and furniture for the office. I also moved into a small house in the Veiled Heights. As basic as it sounds, I almost posted photos of our new office decor on my Instagram with the hashtag "New Year, New Me." But I resisted.

Destiny handed me a tissue. "Hay fever setting in again?"

I coughed again and nodded. "Yeah. All the work's been great, but the long days and late nights have worn me down. Guess I should've expected this. I'll see if Rayna has something on the way home."

Destiny giggled. I glared, and she covered her mouth. "Sorry, but we both know that most of those *late nights* have nothing to do with work. All those Zoom dates with your nocturnal lover. It's like you've just started dating all over again. Oh, don't look at me like that, Sam. It's cute. And we're all happy for you—even if you didn't help me win the betting pool. Christmas Eve? I didn't think you had it in you."

I rolled my eyes and then beamed, allowing my voice to drift "Yeah, but no Zoom dates for a while." My eyes shot open, and I jerked upright in my chair. "Shit! Destiny, 'Milla should be here sometime today to finish setting up for her gallery exhibition. I've got to get ready."

Destiny shook her head. "I honestly can't believe you talked her into showing her watercolors. She's as stubborn as her Irish mule of a girlfriend. But I don't think we have any after-hours work that needs doing tonight, so you go through those case files, make a list of any actionable steps we need to take in the next week, and I'll run to White Wolf to get coffee and sandwiches for the afternoon."

"No use. White Wolf is closed for a few days. Derek broke his foot during baseball practice, and with a few other kids off on spring break, the Albinors decided to close shop while he heals instead of making him work through the pain. Imagine, caring for your employees' health. If only Anna Jackson would do that for the ladies working at Jackson Java. Let's do tacos, and Rogers Ranchero delivers."

Destiny rose. "Gotcha, boss. I've been a citizen for five years, and I still don't understand American healthcare. I'll go put the order in and hold down the fort."

I sighed in exasperation as I looked at the massive stacks of paper, photographs, and documents in the case files. How was I going to move through this in a few hours? "Thanks, Des. You're the best. Do me a favor and keep everyone out of my office while I work. I need to focus."

"Gotcha. No one gets in. Take all messages. I'll only bug you when the tacos arrive."

She closed the door as she left my office. Time sped since December. 'Milla and I rekindled our relationship when I spent most of that month with her in Austria. I tried to convince myself—and her—that we worked better as friends than we did as lovers, but I realized what she and everyone around me already knew. We made each other happy. I needed her in my life despite the challenges our relationship posed.

I smiled and bounced. 'Milla was my girlfriend again. I was in a relationship—Facebook official even—with Countess Carmilla Karnstein, Matriarch of the Karnstein-Bertholt clan of vampires. Over twenty of our friends bet on what day we would get back together. The winner, Carmilla's estate steward Martin, gained over four hundred bucks. They were right.

I worked through our late lunch. An hour passed before Destiny slipped in with our tacos. We always divided a six-pack containing two Big Top Carnitas, two Lamb Pastor-Al, and two Wurst Tacos on the Planet. Des usually claimed the two Wursts "in the name of the Fatherland," which was fine. They were good, but I didn't mind. I loved all tacos, and I was happy to have either an extra pork or, usually, an extra lamb taco.

A few more hours passed, and we both worked in relative silence. Destiny had a Spotify playlist of current Eurovision entries playing softly enough that I could hear the songs but not make out any of the lyrics when they were actually in English. I slid the eighth folder to the other side of my desk as I finished making notes from its contents. My phone revealed my father had called twice more and texted me three times. I sighed. The clock read twenty past three. No word from 'Milla. With a stretch, I opened the next folder—the Devereaux creeper case.

The doorbell chimed. I continued working while overhearing bits of the conversation.

"Welcome to Hain Private Investigations. Give me one moment, and I'll help you." I could see Destiny kept her face focused on her computer through the crack in the door. There was a figure in black. I checked the calendar and saw it wasn't a full moon, so I shrugged it off and went back to work.

"Is Miss Samantha Hain available?" The person asked. She

had a German accent. The person's voice sounded familiar. It couldn't be. It was too early in the day. I mean, she *could* be here, but it wouldn't be safe.

"I'm sorry, ma'am," Destiny said. It appeared she still wasn't looking up from her monitor. "Miss Hain has asked not to be disturbed this afternoon. She's trying to get a lot of work done before an important visitor arrives this evening. Is there something I could help you with?"

Destiny giggled. Really, Des? This is a client. I sighed and walked around my desk. As I reached my door, the person said, "Oh, I suppose I can arrive later, but I thought *Samantha* would have time for one who has come all this way to see her."

'Milla! My eyes brightened as I rushed through the door and hugged Carmilla, raising the black veil she wore so I could kiss her. Her arms held me by the waist, and I threw my arms around her neck. "I didn't expect you until after sunset."

She smiled. Her plum lips tasted of blood and wine, and green flecks danced in her red eyes. She kept her black hair in a bun, and she covered her skin, head to toe, in a black skirt and coat resembling Victorian mourning attire. "My final preparations for the gallery exhibition begin at sunset. I thought perhaps I could arrive early and spend the afternoon with you, my dear one."

I blushed. "I'm so glad to see you. And this outfit is a bit more formal than your usual attire, 'Milla."

"Is it unflattering? Martin suggested I wear this to the gallery as part of my persona. I am an ancient vampire in mourning of my deceased former lover."

Destiny snorted and guffawed. I snickered. "That's what he came up with? The man who led the defense of your castle and who predicted the date we'd get back together came up with *that* cliched story?"

She ran her fingertip along my jawline. I sucked in air as every hair on my body leaped to attention. "And what, my dear one, would you have preferred for my fictitious narrative? Something more modern, perhaps?"

I wanted to suck her finger into my mouth. She knew that; her eyes told me so. As I opened my mouth to speak, Destiny blurted out, "She'd prefer you to dress in something classy but sexy and tell the story of chasing your lover through the candlelit halls of your castle and how you use art to stave off your hunger because you feed off sexual passion. Also, the reds in your art are blood, and you complete the last strokes of your work during orgasm."

Carmilla and I turned toward Destiny. Carmilla searched Destiny's eyes to gain an understanding of what made her tick. I shot a gaze that screamed how I did *not* want her blurting that out to Carmilla. Destiny beamed like a proud child who didn't realize that the "rocket ship" she found in her parents' bedroom was her mom's vibrator. I lowered my gaze and brushed my hair behind my ear. "Anyway, 'Milla, why not tell Martin that I'll drive you to your hotel. I think I'll clock out early."

She nodded. "That sounds lovely, but do you not have work to complete?"

"It can wait until tomorrow," I said. "Des, you know the drill."

"Yep. Put away the folders on the right side of your desk and lock your door. You love bats go have some fun. I'll see you tomorrow, Sam." She winked and then turned to Carmilla. "*Gräfin, ich sehe Sie am Eröffnungsabend Ihrer Kunstausstellung.*"

Carmilla smiled and nodded. "*Ich erwarte unser nächstes*

Treffen mit positiver Vorfreude, Fräulein Grimm."

I grabbed my purse and slid my arm inside the crook of Carmilla's elbow, and we left my office.

* * *

A minute shy of an hour south of Butcher's Bend, near the crossroads of Highway 178 and Old Highway 76, sat the small town of Fiddlers' Ford. A blue, dual cab Ford F-150 drove north on 178 into what remained of the town. As the car traveled along the pothole ridden Main Street, it passed the empty storefronts with broken windows, chipped paint, and rotten wood panels. The owners resided in Holy Rest Cemetery, and their families had moved to either Butcher's Bend or Greenville over a decade earlier. Turning left on Maple Street, the truck passed the skeletal remains of Fiddlers' Ford High School, once home of the Fighting Wild Cats, which stood as a testament to the ravages of both fire and hurricane.

Two people rode inside the truck. Craig Wellington, a young man with a shaven head, kind green eyes, three-day stubble on his chin, and a scar on his left cheek, drove with his left arm on the wheel. His right arm cuddled his wife, Amy, a tall and slender brunette whose charcoal tank top highlighted her well-defined shoulders and arms. An empty car seat sat in the back seat. A plastic milk crate filled with toys and books sat on the floor beside the car seat. George Strait promised to be in "Amarillo by Morning" over the truck's speakers. Otherwise, they traveled in thoughtful, heavy silence.

Thick black clouds covered the crimson sky as the sun descended below the western horizon. Craig took a right turn on Egret Drive and drove beyond the dusty gray antebellum homes, still inhabited after a century and a half. They passed the Fiddlers' Ford Southern Baptist Church toward the edge of town. Houses, smaller and more rundown than those closer to downtown, gave way to fifty-year-old mobile homes. Trucks and tractors in various stages of disarray stood on blocks in front yards. Tattered, weather-beaten Confederate battle flags hung limp from poles beside ripped screen doors. Lightbulbs flickered from behind ripped blinds.

Craig turned onto an unlit, narrow dirt road with an illegible sign. Elm and myrtle trees lined the road. Their reaching branches slapped the windshield as the truck bounced over rocks and rough patches. Through her window, Amy noticed the shadowed outline of a small cemetery beyond an iron cattle gate. A handful of stars poked through the clouds as the waxing crescent moon hung in the black night sky.

They drove through the gate in a chain-link fence and pulled into the driveway of an old wooden cabin that once served as a sharecropper's shack. Its peeling robin egg blue paint revealed a dirt-stained white layer. A small garden was all that remained of the once heavily cultivated farmland. A white 1997 Chevrolet Silverado, dented in three places and with the front bumper hanging lower on the passenger side, rested beside the house. An old man, tall and powerfully built, rocked in a wooden chair on the porch. As Craig stopped the truck, the old man rose to his feet and hobbled toward them.

Small patches of curly gray hair dotted his wrinkled head. He wore a brown polo shirt and tattered Levi's 505 jeans over his dark, sun-leathered skin. A wrinkled and worn pack of Lucky Strikes poked from his breast pocket. After three heart attacks, this man refused to give up "the cigarettes that helped beat the Nazis." The man, Johnny Wellington, shook Craig's hand before pulling him in for a bear hug. He then greeted and hugged Amy, who smile radiated affection and concern, before inviting them inside.

John Wellington's home had sparse decorations, allowing visitors to see the natural wood walls and floors. Family photographs, in both black and white and color, adorned the walls, testifying to the family that has lived and worked on this land for many generations. They walked into the kitchen where chipping yellow paint created open wounds revealing mismatched wallpapers. Craig and Amy sat at the wooden table John's father made immediately after marrying. John put on a pot of coffee and poured everyone a glass of sweet tea while the percolator worked.

As John sat down after pouring everyone a cup of coffee and bringing sugar and milk to the table, Craig asked, "I'm glad to see you up and about, Grandpa, but mom says the cancer's back. Guess you haven't started chemo again?"

John stirred the milk into his coffee with a slender-handled silver spoon and sipped. "No, Craig. Not doing it. Too much of a hassle these days what with my knees, my arthritis in my hands, and the old truck's engine not being what it used to be. Mine's not either. Think I'll just see if I can ride it out."

Craig clenched his left fist and his jaw. "Grandpa, cancer ain't like a storm or a tornado. And you're still smoking. You've always said how important taking care of your health is, so what's up?"

John looked into the darkness beyond the window behind the sink. Amy stared into her heavily milked and sugared coffee, contemplating anything she could say. John focused his gaze so his gold-flecked brown eyes stared through Craig's brown-flecked green eyes. He sighed and sipped his coffee again.

"You know I've never drank a drop of alcohol a day in my life. Smoking's my one vice. I ain't giving that up—not for a doctor, not for anybody. Truth be told, I've been thinking it's time to try and see your grandma again, God willing."

Craig and Amy blinked. Amy swallowed hard. Craig gasped. He slammed his fist onto the table and winced. "Damnit! Ouch! Don't say that. You're barely seventy. And you've beaten cancer before. You've got decades left in you."

John shook his head and chuckled. "Nah, boy. This old body ain't what it used to be. I've lived a good life, a hard life, but a good one. I've worked hard tending fields, bailing hay, and tilling the soil. I lost my best friend outside of Saigon to a shit-covered punji pit. Sure, I married later than most my age, but I got to meet and love the best woman in the world. And she loved me back. Not everybody is fortunate to say that part. Raised a family, got to see my grandkids and even some great-grandkids. Now I creak when I walk more than a screen door with rusty hinges. Ain't trying to die, Craig, but it's coming soon. Doctor said last week I might have a month. Chemo might give me two."

Amy drained a third of her coffee and then took John's calloused hand in hers. She smiled and nodded. "Is this why you asked us to leave Justin with my parents, Grandpa John? He's only two, so I doubt he would understand."

John nodded. "He probably wouldn't, Amy, and I want to see the little fella before I die. But the real reason..." He paused and sighed as he drained his glass of sweet tea. "The real reason is something I need you to do for me, Craig."

Craig tilted his head and raised his left eyebrow. He leaned forward, both hands gripping his coffee cup. "Uh, sure, Grandpa. What do you need?"

John Wellington's face darkened as he nodded. He stared at his left palm where three dime-sized burn marks rested. His voice dropped half an octave and lost most of its inflection as he said, "I need you to convince your dad, your Uncle Roger, and your Aunts Gwennie and Jonnie not to hold a funeral. I don't want *him* knowing I'm dead as long as can be."

Craig took a long sip of his coffee. *Him? Who is this 'him' that Grandpa doesn't want to know about his death? He's had some feuds with neighbors over property lines and with Edison Oil over mineral rights, but I can't say he'd be that upset if they knew he was dead.* He exhaled. "I can try, Grandpa, but you know Aunt Gwennie will be hellbent on you having a funeral in the church, right? So, what's this about? Who don't you want to know about your death?"

"The Devil himself." John's face remained devoid of emotion as he spoke those words with flat intonation.

Amy jumped back in her chair, and Craig rolled his eyes. He waved a dismissive hand and snorted. "I thought this was something serious, not that old story you always told when we were little. You never met the Devil at the crossroads. It was just some drifter who scared the hell out of you."

"You weren't there, Craig Aaron." John wagged his index finger a mere inch from his grandson's nose. "I know who I fought, and I know what we said. Anyway, I ain't asking you to believe me. I'm asking you to promise me you'll do something for me. Can you do that?"

Amy opened her mouth and tilted her head. She reached a hand and held Craig's thick, rough hand. "Grandpa John, what are you talking about? The *devil?* As in the *Devil* devil?"

The old man nodded. Craig waved his hand and said, "Don't get him riled up, Amy. It's just an old family story that *is not true.* Just his old age talking. You've heard us talking about it."

"Yes," she said. "I've heard you mention Grandpa John's tall tales and how he fought a devil of a man, but I don't think—I know I wouldn't forget this story."

"I wish there was a beer here." Craig waved his hand as he muttered. Amy was curious, and John Wellington was going to tell the story anyway. Craig knew he could do nothing to prevent that.

John Wellington recounted the story of how when he was a young man, just a few years older than Craig, he enjoyed getting into fights. "I didn't drink then, and I don't drink now. But I would go to the local bars and saloons, wait for some big asshole to get three sheets pissed, and then pick a fight with him. Why would I do it? I wanted to test myself. I didn't kill anybody in the war—especially not any babies like that damned liberal media accused us of, but everyone thought that made a man out of you. I needed to prove it to myself. Your grandma, God bless her angelic soul, tried to talk me into the way of peace, but all the men in our family are stubborn mules."

"Ain't that the truth," Amy said. Craig rolled his eyes.

John snickered and sighed. "Anyway, one night when there was a full moon or something close to it, I was at the crossroads south of town. You know, the one where One Seventy-Eight and Old Seventy-Six meet up. I was walking back to town after losing my bus money in a game of poker. I was playing some slick city folk in Greenville, and I got in over my head. I was a bit sore at losing.

"Anyway, as I reached the crossroads, there was this strange man leaning on the streetlight post. He was scrawny, pale, and dressed all in black. As I approached, he asked if I knew the time. I told him, and he asked why I was walking from nowhere to nowhere. We talked. Conversation got heated. He said I must not love my wife if I was out so late losing my money. I told him I'd beat his ass if he didn't take that back, and he said—and I'll never forget this—he said, 'I bet your soul you can't.'"

"See, Amy," Craig said. "Do you see how he tells this story? That's how it always goes, and if it were real, the Devil wouldn't be damned cheesy."

Amy reached out and placed her hand on Craig's arm. She glared at him, saying, "Hush, Craig." She then turned to John and said, "Go on, Grandpa John. I'd like to hear the rest of the story."

The old man smiled. "She's a spitfire, Craig. That's what the men in our family need. Anyway, that's when he grabbed my hand and burned these three spots into it. Hurt like hell, so I punched him. We fought, and eventually I beat his ass hard into the ground. Promised him if I ever saw him in South Carolina again, I'd beat his ass again and send him back to Hell with a bloody nose. Promised if I couldn't, my kin would take care of it. Well, now I'm at the end, and I don't want him to know I'm dying. Don't want the burden to fall on you."

"Do you see," Craig said, point a finger at his grandfather. "Do you see how stupid it sounds? How crazy? I can't tell anyone this—not even family."

Amy sat in silence, processing what John said. John sipped his coffee and said, "I'm not asking for much, Craig. Just promise me you'll do what you can to keep the funeral out of the papers."

Craig sat motionless for a few moments; his eyes bored through the bottom of his coffee cup. He scratched the back of his neck, and Amy shot him a pointed glance. He sighed. "I can try, Grandpa. I'll promise you that."

John David Wellington passed away from what doctors diagnosed as pancreatic cancer three days later. Save for Jonnie, his children, grandchildren, and great-grandchildren were at his side when his eyes dimmed, and the final, hollow rattle gurgled from his throat. In his last moments, he turned from his son Daniel to his son Roger and then to Craig. A trembling, knowing smile crept over his face as he closed his eyes and said, "Be strong. I'm sorry."

On the following Saturday, the Wellington family and dozens of friends gathered at the Hunter Funeral Home to pay their final respects and to bid farewell to John David Wellington. Zeke Daniels, the pastor of Fiddlers' Ford Southern Baptist Church, praised John Wellington as a man of faith and family who fought hard, loved hard, and prayed hard. As the assembled crowd of mourners sang "Onward Christian Soldiers," John's favorite hymn, Craig looked around the funeral home's chapel. He recognized everyone apart from one bearded man in a long black coat—too long and heavy for the weather—sitting at the end of the last pew. He brushed it off, thinking the man to be a distant friend or acquaintance. As the eulogy ended, Craig turned back again, but the man in black was gone.

The smaller crowd seated before the grave sang "Just as I Am" as they lowered the casket into John Wellington's final resting place. Friends hugged the family and promised prayers and casseroles as they left. The pastor shook hands with each man, reminding them of the importance of continuing in John's legacy of faith and family. Craig remained behind, even as his wife and son returned to their truck. Resting his hand on the polished marble headstone that now bore the names and epithets of John David and Margaret Anne Kimble Wellington, he allowed the tears to drip from his eyes.

"I miss you, Grandpa. You tell Grandma I miss and love her too, okay? I know it ain't always been easy, but you rest now. I'll come visit soon, I promise."

He turned to leave, but stopped. That strange man in black stood before him, dark eyes focused on Craig. They flickered with a pale green light. He was thin, some might say gaunt, and pale. A blond Van Dyke goatee adorned his face. He smelled earthy, with a hint of sulfur and ash. Craig excused himself and moved around him. He blocked Craig's path. They repeated this interaction, with Craig growing progressively angrier, three more times. The man in black smiled a lean and hungry smile.

"Look, man, I'm trying to hold it in, but this isn't the time." Craig's words contained the growling rage of a cornered dog.

The man in black smiled and nodded. He lowered his head. "Forgive me for angering you, but we needed to speak. I apologize for your loss, but your grandfather has a debt that must be settled."

He had a German accent. Craig snorted. "Then get in line. My dad's the executor. He'll handle the bills."

Craig pushed past the man, hitting him with his shoulder. The man in black spun and grabbed Craig's left hand. He had a powerful grip, and his touch sent icy spikes through Craig's nerves. Craig pulled his hand away and saw three burn marks on his palm. His jaw dropped, and he stared at the man in black.

"Who the hell are you?"

The man in black smiled. "Thirty years ago, your grandfather swore on his soul that should I return to South Carolina, his descendants would beat me back to Hell. I have given you the same gift I gave your grandfather, but your body isn't as strong as his. Neither is your soul. I will always know where you are.

Meet me in six days at the location of your grandfather's fight with me. Midnight. Defeat me, and I will leave peacefully. Lose, and your soul is mine."

The man in black bowed and disappeared, leaving only a ring of ash behind. Craig blinked and stared at his hand for a moment in disbelief. He walked to the grave and stared at the headstone. "Damn, Grandpa. You weren't lying."

* * *

On that same Saturday in early March, Sam and Destiny arrived at Steinway Women's Goldstar Gym and Fitness Center. Sam dressed in a black tank top that matched her oversized cat's eye sunglasses and leopard print leggings. She carried her water bottle that bore an "I violate the Hays Code" sticker. She had her hair in a ponytail. A pink headband held Destiny's blonde curls in place, and she wore a gray and white tee shirt and purple and black leggings. She carried a Pikachu-shaped water bottle that doubled as a wine flask.

They entered the massive concrete building, populated by a handful of middle-aged women on elliptical machines, three women on the free weights, and two women in their twenties working the leg press machines. The televisions throughout the gym played one of the more insipid celebrity dating shows where an aging, no longer relevant rockstar tried to find true love with a woman easily half his age. Sam rolled her eyes as she stepped onto a treadmill, and Destiny chided her for not doing her stretches. Sam nodded. They stretched, and then they began their warm up walk.

After a few minutes of walking, Sam yawned. Destiny turned her head, smirked, and asked, "Hungover or up all night *on a case?"*

Sam sighed and shook her head as Destiny laughed. "I'm not hungover. You know exactly where I was."

Destiny faced forward and placed an AirPod in her right ear. She shrugged and beamed. "I wanted to hear you say it."

Sam smiled as her mind drifted to last night's events. She increased her pace to a light jog. She sighed. "I like having her close. Long distance is hard as it is, but when you add in the worries we have, the stress eating and sleepless nights take their toll."

Destiny quickened her pace to a brisk jog. Her breaths came quick and shallow. "Yeah. Austria is nice at Christmas, but they attacked you. And her."

Sam nodded. A stabbing pain shot through her left knee. She winced. Pushing through, she matched Destiny's pace. Her heart quickened. "Yeah, and given her history, they'll try again—maybe even while she's here. Especially if they resurrect *him*. If not the Order of the Dragon, the Astrum Argentum may try."

Destiny nodded and fell silent, listening to *The Magnus Archives* podcast. Sam exhaled. *Christmas in Austria was wonderful, and after the shit I went through in Ireland, I needed that vacation. The snow in the mountains, spending evenings with 'Milla in her study and library—her amazing library with antique first editions—and sure, the cuddling, kissing and eventual sex were amazing. It wasn't all relaxation and pleasure, though. The Order of the Dragon sent an operative to frame 'Milla for murders and either incite a mob or get us to kill each other. All because of the role she played in the execution of her torturer, Vlad Dracula. Then I kind of almost fucked things up by breaking a promise to stay out of the castle's dungeon, which, while it helped me prove her innocence in these murders and murders from almost two centuries ago, I knew how important oaths and promises were to vampires when I did what I did. I was a mess and led with my head instead of my heart. Fortunately for both of us, Destiny and Martin, Carmilla's estate steward, were there to keep us in check and remind us of what mattered—and still matters—to us.*

I still don't know what's going on. The Order of the Dragon has joined forces with the Hermetic Order of the Astrum Argentum—with my father being centrally involved—for something. I know they summoned a demon named Zozo for some purpose, but the High Bard of the Bardic College of the Duilearga and I interrupted the ritual and sent that goat fiend packing. Zozo isn't dead. I don't know if that's something I can even do, but I banished it. Donal and I have never had a good relationship, and he hasn't involved himself in my life since I was six. But I thought nothing could be worse than the way he treated Mom, but I think this comes close.

Sam sighed and drank water. She stretched her arms and tripped over her shoelaces. Sam backed off the treadmill, tied and double-knotted her shoes, and then returned her focus to the run. She sped up to a brisk jog. Sam's heart thundered in her chest. She focused on regular, deep breaths. A stabbing stitch shot through her left side. Sam winced, stumbled, and returned to her jog, albeit at a slower, limping pace.

They finished their workout, showered, changed, and headed to Blended Pleasures Smoothie Cafe. Destiny, a regular customer, ordered the Berry Blast with a blueberry Greek yogurt granola cup. Sam searched the menu board for a few minutes before choosing the Pomegranate Passion and a Belgian waffle with strawberry rhubarb compote. Half a dozen other diners sat at their tables as Charlie Christian's "Six Appeal" played in the background of the cool, well-lit dining room next to the open kitchen.

After finishing half of her granola bowl, Destiny pointed her white plastic spoon at Sam and asked, "So, you ready to play the socialite girlfriend on Monday night?"

Sam rubbed the back of her neck and blew a lazy raspberry. "I'm going to have to Spanx and corset to be safe. We may close on Monday so I can rest enough to be perky and social. I don't want to blow this for her, since I kind of pushed her to do it."

Destiny sipped her smoothie and nodded. "I know you've heard Aaron Saltz is going to be there."

Sam stabbed into her waffle. She chewed and swallowed. And then she sighed, staring into her smoothie. "Yeah. And with everything else going on, at least Martin's in charge of security. He bluffed that story about vampire hunters chasing 'Milla because of a centuries-old grudge between her and their family over the death of her former lover."

Destiny checked the notifications on her phone. She rolled her eyes. Turning her attention back to Sam, she leaned closer. "I mean, he's not *wrong*. It's just he altered some major details and then left out a few specific details to let imaginations run wild."

Sam rested her chin on her palm and nodded. "So, are you and Jeremy coming?"

A sound similar to an annoyed cat escaped Destiny's lips. She scratched her head and looked around the dining room. "Of course, I'm going to be there, Sam. You're my best friend. Besides, as nervous as you are, it'll be fun to watch."

Sam glared as Destiny grinned. Sam laughed. "Fucking bitch!"

Destiny shrugged. "I'm German. We have the word *Schaden-*

freude for a reason. And yeah, Jeremy will be there. We're going suit shopping this afternoon."

Sam tilted her head and softened her face. "You don't seem excited. What's up, Des?"

Destiny shook her head and removed her headband. A toddler screamed as her scrambled eggs splattered on the floor. Destiny snickered as the flustered mom scampered to the floor and cleaned the mess. She calmed herself. Destiny said, "And that's why I can't have kids. Ugh, but no. I don't know, Sam. Jeremy's a great guy. He's fun to hang out with. My overprotective parents seem to love him. His overbearing parents love me. He knows I'm demi, and he's patient and accepting. That deep connection isn't there for me to be intimate with him. It's almost there, like just hovering out of reach, so I don't know."

Sam reached across the table and held Destiny's hands. She smiled. "Whatever you decide, I support you. You know yourself, and you know your heart. You also give the best advice. Now it's my turn. The first time 'Milla and I dated, you know how I skirted around admitting my feelings and then I put off ending it due to..."

"The fact that you weren't ready to handle the complexities of human-vampire relations beyond the fantasies of cheap and tawdry romance novels you buy second hand for five bucks."

Her voice was flat and pointed. Sam frowned. Her eyes narrowed and met Destiny's challenging gaze. Sam sighed. "I wouldn't have said it *that way*, but... yeah." She waved her hand. "Anyway, the point I was making is that I didn't trust my heart. I knew I needed 'Milla in my life, and I knew I wanted her in my life. Everyone knows what a mess I was for the last five years. So, whatever your heart tells you, follow it."

Chapter 2

"You're breaking my fucking ribs, Martin!"

That scream rasped from my throat as Martin, Carmilla's estate steward, yanked the lacing on my black overbust corset covered with a delicate blue lace with a floral pattern. Destiny cinched tightly, but this ancient—I assumed, ancient—vampire with his white tonsure and matching fluffy mustache flattened my lungs.

"You will survive, Miss Hain, and stop trembling. Your nerves have made this more challenging than it needs to be. I am being far more gentle with you than I have been with the women of the Karnstein family."

That wasn't quite as comforting as his even-toned voice wanted it to be. I was certain he could go tighter, but I also wanted to breathe at dinner and during the opening night festivities. Yes, I was nervous. So many things could go wrong tonight for 'Milla, and I had so little power to prevent or mitigate many of them. Also, fear of embarrassing her formed a mental ear worm.

"Easy for you to say." I glared at him, and he remained visibly unafraid. Fine. As I got used to the corset's tightness, breathing became easier. "You don't have to worry about embarrassing your girlfriend on a night you begged her to allow you to make happen. I just want things to go well."

Martin turned me to face him. Even in my six-inch stilettos, he stood taller than me, and he had a strong build. Centuries of being a soldier and defender of the Karnstein family paid off. He softened his features and placed his calloused hands on my bare shoulders.

"Forgive this old man's failing memory, but you did not seem worried about failing when Order of the Dragon mercenaries attacked Castle Karnstein. Nor did you show fear when that assassin staked the Countess and the only way to save her meant giving her four pints of your own blood. Why does spending an evening with art afficionados and critics terrify you?"

I sighed. "Because I can't just shoot them or tell them to fuck off when they upset her. I can't control their reactions to 'Milla's work. We both know she's got an amazing talent, and I want the world to know that. I want *her* to know how talented she is."

He smiled and nodded. Raising an eyebrow, he asked, "And they will. And *she* will. Is that all, Miss Hain?"

I exhaled. He was perceptive. Sure, it helped me see through the walls of bullshit I set up to keep me from admitting my feelings, but his Saxon smugness was fucking annoying.

"What about the Order of the Dragon? They've been quiet since mid-January. Have you heard anything and not told me?"

He shook his head. "I have not. Their silence concerns me, but your friend Miss Kelsington proved quite amenable to private security patrolling both the building's interior and exterior. She did not balk when asked to replace all modern mirrors in spaces where the Countess may enter with silver-backed ones for the duration of our stay here. That surprised me.”

I chuckled. “Laura’s dealt with eccentric artists for years. She’s told me some requests that make ours seem like we just asked for coffee to be served lukewarm. Plus, she also works with NHM artists and knows who and what ‘Milla is.”

He folded his arms across the chest of his black tailcoat that bore the Karnstein family crest, a badger slaying a dragon, on his right lapel. “And she is trustworthy, I take you to mean?”

“She is. I wouldn’t have suggested this if she weren’t. When ‘Milla and I started dating the first time, she noted the coincidences between the beautiful, black-haired, Austrian countess holding my hand and La Fanu’s fictional account of a lesbian vampire. She asked.”

He nodded. “Then let us join the Countess at our hotel. If fortune favors us, she will have dressed and readied herself for the evening.”

I took his offered arm, and we left my house. He opened passenger door on the black Mercedes S-coupe. As we drove to the Westmont Hotel, I asked, “Martin, one more thing. Is ‘Milla comfortable with the plan to bite my neck publicly this evening?”

He shot a brief glance through the rear-view mirror. “The two of you should have time to discuss that before your fashionably late entrance, Miss Hain.”

An hour later, Carmilla, Martin, and I drank an 1887 San-guinovese. Maybe I’ve been drinking it more frequently in the past few months than I did the first time ‘Milla and I dated, but the iron aftertaste of the blood wine didn’t bother me any longer. Martin fiddled with his cuff links. Carmilla wrapped her free arm around me, and I ran my hand along the outline her thigh made in the fitted black lace Morticia Addams dress she wore. My three-tiered ruffle skirt that matched my corset bustled in the back; adding my lace opera gloves, I felt like a heroine in a Victorian-inspired romance. Destiny would have a field day with this.

As we approached the Butcher's Bend Modern Art Museum, I said, "You know, Martin,this is the first time I've ridden in a vehicle with you, where you're not the driver. Are you enjoying the break?"

He scoffed while loading a Desert Eagle and holstering it beneath his tailcoat. "Driving is far more relaxing, Miss Hain, than running security detail for an event when one has no access to security cameras."

"Tell me, dear one," Carmilla asked, "how is it again that you have certainty that my vampiric persona will alert neither the Grimms nor their American counterparts?"

I drained my wineglass. "Well, Destiny and I set up a website where a stalker who believes you really are a vampire tries to out you only to uncover your birth certificate, details of how you fabricate everything, receipts for fake fangs, and fake photographs of you applying makeup to make your skin deathly pale. We even set up images and videos from your 'apartment' in Hanau. Also, I have empty stage blood capsules in my purse that I'll conspicuously drop after our kiss on the balcony. All you have to do is be yourself, and Martin, Destiny, and I will handle the rest."

Carmilla nodded; I doubted the answer satisfied her concern. I wasn't sure it would satisfy either the Grimms or the S-Ts. A few minutes later, the limousine stopped before the entrance to the Spring Hill Street Fire Station. This historic building resembled the one used in *Ghostbusters*, but after being decommissioned in the late 1990s, it found new life as our modern and contemporary art museum. The Butcher's Bend Arts Council hosted guest and local artists in the Jackie Dee Parker Gallery on the second floor. 'Milla and I attended the Erin Zed exhibition here on our second date. I smiled, remembering we had our first kiss that night.

Martin opened the door and helped both of us descend onto the sidewalk, where Laura Kelsington greeted us. Always smartly dressed in one of her pencil skirt suits, Laura's copper eye shadow and red lipstick brought out the bronze undertones in her umber skin. She shook Carmilla's hand first and then Martin's. She then hugged me before leading us into the museum and up the elevator to the gallery.

I've never seen more tuxedos and sequined gowns in that gallery than I did tonight. Servers dressed as Gomez and Morticia Addams passed trays of various hors d'oeuvres, chocolate-covered strawberries, pomegranate sorbet, and red wine. A string quartet played in the background as rose and violet scented candles perfumed the room. 'Milla's art adorned the honey oak walls.

A few eyes noticed us as we entered, but all turned their attention to us when a server approached, presented 'Milla and me each a glass of wine, and bellowed, "Welcome, Countess Karnstein. Here is the special blood wine you requested." A few laughed. And a few more rolled their eyes. Cheesy meant they didn't believe she was a vampire. Good.

We walked the gallery, admiring 'Milla's watercolors and speaking with various attendees. These brief conversations focused on 'Milla, her inspirations, techniques, and attendees' interpretations of her work. I exhaled and relaxed. On the rare occasion, someone asked me a question or two, the inquiries focused on our relationship. My answers were descriptively vague. Three years toward an English degree means I know how to use a lot of words to say little. All that changed when Senator Danforth Planter approached.

Senator Danforth Planter resembled a cross between Colonel Sanders and Ebeneezer Scrooge. This patriarch of the wealthiest old money family in Butcher's Bend had spent the last fifty years serving in either the state or national government. He and his third wife lived in the plantation that has been in the family since the Monroe administration. When not sitting in his Senate seat and blocking bills that would provide economic relief, healthcare, and education for all his constituents—not just the ones who donated to his campaigns—he spent his vacation days as a slum lord lobbying for more eviction powers.

"Well, Miss Karnstein," he said, extending his hand to kiss the back of Carmilla's. "I am Senator Danforth Planter, and it is my distinct pleasure and honor to welcome you to the fair city of Butcher's Bend."

"Thank you." Carmilla bowed before offering him a measured smile. "My title, as you know, is Countess."

"Of course, ma'am, but this is America. We don't do fancy titles here. All are equal. How are you enjoying your first visit to our city?"

Carmilla's lips tightened. Destiny and her family made the same expression when they needed to avoid ripping a moron's ass out through their throat. A practiced smile returned, and she said, "I see, *Senator.* However, this is not my first visit to your fair city. When Samantha and I first dated, she invited me to your zoo and to an exhibition here."

Planter smiled, oblivious to the point she made. Typical. To my chagrin, he turned to me as a smile slithered across his wrinkled face between his white mustache and that stupid, oval-shaped goatee. He extended a hand and said, "Samantha, I do not believe we have had the pleasure of meeting."

No, we have not had the *pleasure* of meeting, Danforth. We haven't had the pain of meeting before tonight either. I smiled and accepted his gesture. To my relief, he only shook my hand. I inhaled and smiled. "Hain. Samantha Hain. And no, Senator. We haven't met; although we have traveled in overlapping circles."

"Hain. Samantha Hain." He paused, taken aback. I held my breath, and then a light entered his eyes. "Ah! I think my grandson mentioned your name for some nasty business last year. You're a detective or something, yes?"

"I'm a private investigator, Senator."

Last year, I found evidence that his grandson Henry had repeatedly molested his preteen daughter and whored her out to his business associates in exchange for favors. His ex-wife, whom his daddy had blackmailed and bullied during the divorce, hired me to help her gain custody. We won, but family money and influence kept the case out of the news. Humiliation would've been great, but winning against that type of perverse corruption felt good.

And last month, we helped the S-T's arrest his great-nephew Augustus who had kidnapped six children and used them as models for his art. The young man was possessed by a demonic entity that possessed his father and grandfather. We caught him before he could replicate the full nature of their crimes, and then I exorcised the entity within him while the S-T's had him in custody. We got a conviction; he was sentenced to life in a mental health facility, but family money and power kept his name out of the news.

A look of disgust colored his pasty face, and he said, "Private investigation? That's such a nasty business. A woman such as yourself would be better suited to a more domestic profession to support your husband. Don't you think?"

Carmilla wrapped her arm around my waist and smiled. "Samantha has no need of a husband, Mister Planter. As her *girlfriend*, I say that with confidence. And her reputation for success is known internationally."

"And someone, Senator," I said with a forced smile, "has to protect the innocent from the monsters in this world. Standing up for what's right isn't the exclusive province of any one group but a responsibility for all."

He nodded and shoved his hands into his pockets. "So true, Miss Hain. That's why it always surprises me at these events when people try to convince me we don't need stricter punishments for marijuana users, illegal immigrants, and those who choose to live in sin."

"Yes, that must be so terrible for you."

My fist trembled as I sneered my words through a fake smile that wouldn't win any pageants. He opened his mouth to reply, but Laura appeared and diverted his attention. We bid him farewell, and each of us grabbed another glass of wine.

Carmilla sipped the wine, leaned close, and said, "Well, he was a rather unpleasant man."

I exhaled and drained half my glass. "You know how you've made it a habit to never ask about my mundane clients? If I told you what I know, you'd rip his head off, and that would be an unhelpful scandal."

She nodded. Given what Dracula put her through in his twisted attempt at conversion therapy after he set her up to be accused of multiple murders and endangering the safety of the vampiric community, Carmilla would slaughter the

Planter family. We milled about the gallery, chatting with other attendees. The crowd grew larger and louder than when we entered. I kept an eye out for Destiny and Jeremy. Sure, we'd talk to them, but I wanted to see how they acted together, given Destiny's expressed concerns.

Carmilla began placing her hand over one of her ears. This happened during the last exhibition we attended here. The reverberation from all the chatter overwhelmed her heightened hearing. I smirked and subtly led her through the gallery, pausing to talk to attendees or to admire her art, and onto the balcony.

The balcony, a recent addition to the building, featured a waist-high railing supported by a row of Ionic columns. Red LED candles flickered atop it. Butcher's Bend was quiet tonight, and the waxing gibbous moon shone through the clear sky. 'Milla's eyes fixed on the moon. A deep sigh glided through her crimson lips. She smiled.

"It happened again, and you remembered."

She wrapped her arms around my waist. I blushed and brushed a loose strand of hair behind my ear. Her rose and violet perfume graced my nose while her natural scent of honey spiced with warm gingersnaps cut through, comforting me. 'Milla smiled. My heart quickened as our eyes locked. I bit my lower lip. I closed my eyes and sighed before looking at the moon and then returning my gaze to the amazing woman before me.

"The moon is lovely tonight, no?"

Her eyes scanned my body, and her smile grew wider. My breathing became rapid and shallow. Carmilla brushed my cheek with the back of her fingers. My body tensed and then relaxed.

"Not as lovely as you, my dear one."

Without breaking eye contact, Carmilla closed the narrow gap between us. My heart jackhammered in my ears. Her breath felt warm, like a September morning, against my neck. My head fell back. She caught it in her hand, raised it, and slid her hand forward to cup my cheek. I blushed as her delicate fingers traced my cheekbone. She licked her lips, raising them slightly to tease with a little fang.

She brushed her nose against my ear as she said, "May I have your permission to kiss you now?"

"You have my permission to kiss me." I beamed every time she asked for permission.

She pressed her warm, wet lips to mine. I tasted the wine she drank through the night. Her tongue brushed against my lips. My body beckoned it deeper; she teased. The back of her hand stroked my chin. I whimpered a sigh into her lips. She wrapped her other arm around my waist. My breaths raced from my lungs. I threw my arms around her neck, and her tongue slid between my lips and danced with mine. My hands slid down and gripped the back of her dress. She growled into my ear.

"May I have your permission to taste you in the most intimate way I can?"

I melted. Words died in my open mouth. I nodded. Carmilla asked again. My heart thundered. I took a single deep breath.

"Yes."

'Milla nibbled my earlobe and then planted a trail of gentle kisses down my neck. The hairs on my neck rose. Blood raced through my veins. Air sped through my lungs. My chest rose and fell. She wrapped her arms around me and brushed the tips of her fangs against my skin. I moaned. Carmilla's fangs pierced my neck; I squealed. Then euphoria replaced the pain as I felt her heart beat cradle mine, calming it until the two beat as one. I moaned again. When she finished, Carmilla pulled away, her cheeks flushed. Our eyes met.

"You didn't lick the wound," I said as warm blood drizzled down my shoulder.

She smiled and held my hands. "My dear one, you know we need the image for our narrative."

I nodded.

* * *

The remainder of the exhibition's opening reception was a blur for Sam. She felt less self-conscious about the blood trailing from her neck, over her shoulder, and down the curve of her breast, as the euphoria of the small bite, just a snack for Carmilla, left her head in a fog. Time slowed in a dreamlike manner. Conversations happened, but Sam had no memory of the content. Destiny handed Sam a bottle of water, and Carmilla fed her meatballs. As midnight struck, Martin escorted them to the limousine.

Martin handed Sam a thermos and said, "Here, Miss Hain. Cool broth to help you regain your strength. The euphoric impact of the bite is still an unfamiliar experience for you, but you handle it better than most."

Sam nodded and sipped the broth. She rested her head on Carmilla's shoulder. Carmilla kissed her forehead. Sam blinked. After a few more sips, her head cleared.

"Thank you, Martin. We agreed to a small bite, and I just hope I wasn't too embarrassing after the fact."

Carmilla chuckled and stroked Sam's hair. "You were wonderful, dear one. Your natural reactions proved convincing, and your narrating when you handed the empty blood capsules to a server was adorable. It reminded me of when you have too much to drink."

Sam blushed. "I felt drunk. It also felt like we just had a quickie. I mean, we did, but you know what I mean."

The vampires laughed. Carmilla said, "This is the danger of the bite. While we gain pleasure from the bite, ours is more akin to enjoying a fine meal. Mortals react as you do, and some find it addictive."

Sam nuzzled Carmilla's neck, nibbling and kissing it. "I mean, I've only let one vampire bite me, but I could get used to it."

Carmilla laughed and then kissed Sam deeply. They laughed, talked, and cuddled as the ride continued. Ten minutes passed, and the limousine pulled into Sam's driveway. The two story, white brick Charleston single had a balcony and a side porch on its western wall. Sam and Carmilla hugged and shared another kiss as Martin opened the door.

"You're not coming in with me?" Sam asked.

Carmilla smirked. Fire danced in her crimson eyes. "You need your sleep. I will see you soon. I promise you."

Saddened, Sam took Martin's outstretched hand, and he helped her to her home. She unlocked the door. Martin asked if she needed assistance removing the corset. Sam declined; he bid her a goodnight.

Sandy Paws paced at the door, meowing plaintively as Sam entered. Sam kneeled and stroked the calico's fur, apologizing for being late. She removed her heels, and Sandy weaved between Sam's legs as she walked. Sam stopped as she reached the staircase, unclasped her corset, and removed her skirt. Dressed only in a white chemise, she ascended the stairs to her bedroom. She tossed her clothing onto the chair in the corner, removed the chemise, and added it to the pile. Sandy leaped onto the clothes and started kneading. Sam laughed.

Sam walked over and scratched Sandy's eyebrows. The cat purred. "Well, Sandy, let me remove my makeup, and then I guess you'll be the only one sleeping with Mommy tonight."

Sandy Paws meowed. She followed Sam into the bathroom next door to her bedroom and jumped onto the toilet, watching as Sam removed her makeup and moisturized. Sam saw no new notifications on her phone; she sighed. Sam pulled down the gray comforter and revealed the lavender sheets. The balcony light flickered. Sandy stared as a shadow moved on the balcony. Sam stretched and rubbed her neck. Naked, she crawled into bed, pulled the covers up to her neck, and sank into her pillow top mattress.

An hour passed, and Sam's mind quieted enough to sleep. Sandy leaped onto the bed and stared at the balcony door. A knock came from the door. Sam grumbled and waved it away. Sandy meowed. The knock grew more insistent. Sam wrapped her pillow around her ears. The knock grew louder. Sam growled, grabbed the Rawlings bat she kept under the bed, and walked to the balcony door.

"The fuck is going on? I just want to go sleep."

This is stupid. Everything I know says this is how you get killed, Sam. Why are you doing this? Here we go.

Sam held her breath. Holding the bat in one hand, she inched the curtain covering the door's oval window. The outline of a face, framed by either long, dark hair or a dark hoodie, slowly revealed itself. Sam cocked an eyebrow and squinted. She tensed. As she pulled the curtain away, Sam's eyes burst wide. A scream escaped her lips, and she stumbled back as Carmilla's smiling face stared into her bedroom.

Sam dropped the bat and gathered her wits. She unlocked and opened the door. "'Milla, what are you doing here? I thought you were a burglar."

Carmilla, wearing only a black lace robe, sauntered into Sam's bedroom. Sandy Paws meowed, and Carmilla sat on the bed and scratched behind the cat's ears. Sandy licked Carmilla's fingers. She smiled at Sam. "Did I not promise you that I would see you soon?"

"Yeah." Sam locked the door. She sat next to Carmilla. "Why didn't you just come inside when you dropped me off? I'm not complaining. I'm glad you're here. Really glad."

Carmilla leaned forward and planted a gentle kiss on Sam's lips. She turned her gaze to the books on the nightstand and said, "I researched the books you keep by your bed, but hide when I ask about them. *Blood/Lust. A Bite to Remember.* I thought you might enjoy this."

Sam blushed. Carmilla's hand slid up Sam's inner thigh as the vampire nibbled on her earlobe. Sam inhaled sharply. Carmilla kissed Sam's neck, her lips planted on the site of her earlier bite. Sam moaned. She shot upright, and her jaw dropped.

"Oh."

Sam smiled and returned Carmilla's kisses.

The next morning, Sandy Paws woke Sam by pawing her eyelids. Sunlight, softened by white curtains, illuminated the room. Sam groaned and rolled over. Icy spikes shot through her body. Sam's eyes shot open. Perched atop Carmilla's side, Sandy begged for breakfast. Sam smiled. A soft moan followed by a groan escaped her lips as she stretched. She rolled to face her nightstand and two message notifications from Martin on her phone screen.

Miss Hain, I will arrive at precisely four in the afternoon to collect the Countess. Please ensure her safety and happiness until then. Thank you. I will also deliver blackout curtains to you.

Sandy whined. Sam patted her head. She whined again. Sam sighed and chuckled. "Alright, baby. Let's get some breakfast going. Looks like I'm taking the day off."

Sam kissed Carmilla's frigid cheek. The vampire did not stir from her death-sleep. Sam slipped into her blue and silver terrycloth bathrobe, checked the locks on the balcony door and bedroom windows, and descended the stairs to the kitchen. Sandy Paws trotted alongside her.

Sam blew stray hair from her face as she grabbed a honey macadamia coffee pod and shoved it into her Keurig. Sandy Paws, who knew better, jumped onto the yellow and white checkerboard counter top when Sam popped the top on a tin of turkey and gravy cat food. Sam's nose wrinkled. She glanced at her reflection in the tablet screen she affixed to her refrigerator and lamented her lack of sexy bed head. She grabbed a sausage, egg, and cheese biscuit sandwich from the freezer, heated it, and ate in her breakfast nook. Sam sipped her coffee.

"Well, Sandy, guess I should let Aunt Destiny know I won't be in today."

Devouring her breakfast, Sandy Paws ignored her. Sam scrolled her Twitter for a moment before dialing her office.

"Hain Private Investigations. This is Destiny speaking. How may I help you?"

"Des, you're earlier than expected," Sam said while chewing.

"Traffic was light, Sam. I take it you're running late after your hot and sexy night?"

Sam paused. "How did you know about 'Milla showing up

on my balcony?"

Destiny screamed. Sam held her phone at arm's length. Destiny calmed herself and said, "Well, *now* I know about it. I meant your hot balcony make out and snack session last night. So, feel the need to confess your naughtiness?"

Destiny laughed. Sam narrowed her eyes and shook her head. She sipped her coffee, giving Destiny time to stop cackling. With a sigh, Sam said, "You're going to have to use your imagination for that. But I'm not going to be coming—stop laughing—I'm not coming *in* today. Martin wants me to stay with 'Milla until he picks her up this afternoon. So, if you want to take the day off, go for it."

"Got it, boss. I'll finish organizing things and then head home to finish playing *Swansong*. You eat lots of red meat and fruit today. You're going to be a snack tonight."

Destiny cackled as Sam ended the call. Sandy Paws snuck onto the table and stole a bite from the biscuit. Destiny was right, and Sam knew it. She sipped her coffee and smiled. She stroked Sandy's fur, eliciting loud purrs. Having Carmilla close made for a great day.

* * *

On Saturday evening, Justin Wellington sat on the beige shag carpet, stained with coffee and beer, in the living room of the family's modest house in Fiddler's Ford. The toddler giggled and blew raspberries as he drove his oversized red and blue truck across the carpet. Craig, a Bud Light in his hand, sat in his brown leather recliner and split his attention between his son and syndicated reruns of *Reba*. He smiled. Justin's mother, Amy, dried the dishes from the evening's dinner. She kicked the broken Maytag dishwasher.

Craig Wellington kissed his son Justin on the crown of his curly-haired head. He chugged the last sips from the amber bottle as he walked into the kitchen. Amy smiled weakly as he wrapped his arm around her and kissed her cheek. She set the soapy rag on the counter and the water glass in the sink. Amy turned and wrapped her arms around him, burying her head in his chest.

"You don't have to do this, Craig. Stay here tonight. Nothing good can come of this."

Craig squeezed her butt and tossed the empty bottle into the trash. "I've got to, Amy. Grandpa wanted me to handle this."

Amy squeezed her husband. Her hands clenched the folds of his black and white Buffalo check flannel shirt. "John never asked you to fight anyone. He asked you to keep his funeral out of the news."

Craig pulled away and grabbed another beer, flipping the cap into the sink. Amy glared. He walked to the folding table where they ate and sat. He swigged the beer, ran his fingers through his hair, and sighed. His eyes focused on the blue vinyl of the table.

"And I failed. I tried, and I failed. Both Aunt Gwennie and and Aunt Jonnie demanded a funeral. Hell, they even paid for everything just to get their way. And then that creepy, skinny as fuck man in black showed up at the funeral."

Craig looked at the three marks on his hand. Since his grandfather's funeral, they had turned black, and jagged lines spread from them. At least once a day, they oozed puss and blood for a few minutes. He sipped the beer. Amy sat beside him and clutched his hand with both of hers. Tears glassed her eyes.

"It's just a coincidence, Craig. John was known for his stories, and we all loved listening to them. But this one—fighting the devil at the crossroads—is nothing but a story, and it wasn't even one of his better stories. Come on, please."

Craig shook his head and sipped his beer. Amy smiled and ran her fingertips along his arm. She looked through the door and saw their son crawling and playing. Justin giggled, looked toward his mother, and smiled. She said, "What about Justin? You're going to fight this stranger, because it's what you think your grandpa would want. You could *die*. Did you think of that? He needs you. I need you. We love you."

"I love y'all too, Ames." Craig kissed her hands. He turned and watched Justin play. He smiled. *This is stupid. I'm going to fight some scrawny ass stranger just because he knew Grandpa's dumb story. But the marks on my hand. They're like the ones Grandpa had on his hand. They even bleed like his. None of this makes any sense, but I have to do this.*

Craig chugged the beer. He closed his eyes and clenched his jaw. He rose and said, "That's why—look, this is just something I have to do. And look, I've been in plenty of fights. Only lost one in County, and he wasn't no scrawny stranger. I'll be fine."

Craig Wellington grabbed his keys and left the house.

Craig drove south from Fiddler's Ford on an empty, unlit stretch of highway. Sheer gray clouds obscured the waxing moon. Craig's hands choked the steering wheel, whitening his knuckles. His forearms trembled. He passed the rotting, roofless skeleton of the old Mobil Oil station that lightning set on fire three years ago. When the fire department doused it, they found the bodies of three drifters—all black men and homeless Operation Enduring Freedom veterans—burned inside. No one touched the land after that.

The radio played "Symmetry of the Cemetery" as Craig pulled to the side of the road at the crossroads of Highway 178 and County Road 2713. He arrived half an hour early. A single street light hanging from a weathered wooden pole flickered. All was quiet. Craig's heart pounded, screaming how terrible and dangerous this was. Amy texted him, begging him to return home. He remained. His mother texted she was praying for him. An arid, blacksmith forge-hot wind blew from the south. Midnight struck.

Craig's nose wrinkled, and his stomach turned. The rotten egg smell of burning sulfur filled the air. The light flickered. He coughed, and his eyes watered. The windshield on his truck shattered. The street light switched off. Craig jumped and cursed. The light clicked and flickered before it switched back on. A shadow slid across the grassy dirt the streetlight illuminated. Craig spun around. The shadow's source was the man in black.

"The stars foretold you would come. I commend you, Craig, grandson of John Wellington."

The man in black's voice echoed. He stroked his mustache as he circled Craig. A pale blue flame flickered in his eyes. Craig cracked his knuckles and shifted into a loose boxer's stance.

"Can't go making Grandpa a liar. Funny, though, you know my name, but I don't know yours."

The man in black offered a mocking bow. "Well then, Craig of Fiddler's Ford, know me by the name John of Helmstadt."

Craig narrowed his eyes eyes and slammed his right fist into the side of John's face. The man in black grunted. He reeled. John rubbed his cheek.

"I've only lost one fight, Johnny boy," Craig said. "And it

wasn't to a pasty ass, scrawny motherfucker like—"

John's right jab and left hook interrupted Craig's taunt. A knee followed, slamming into Craig's stomach. Craig grunted. He doubled over.

Craig's heart raced. A quick jab snapped John's nose. Blood spurted. *He bleeds. Good.* Craig slammed his steel-toed work boot into John's skull. The man in black staggered. Craig pushed the attack with a left jab, a right hook, and an uppercut.

Craig hurled his fist toward his reeling opponent, but John caught the fist in his hand. He squeezed. Craig grimaced and grunted. John flicked his wrist. Craig screamed; his wrist snapped. John yanked Craig forward and shoved a knee into his chest. An elbow to the back of the neck thrust Craig into the dirt.

He crawled toward his truck and rolled over. John pounced and pummeled him, slamming his head into the Ford's front bumper. Craig grunted and groaned. Blood streamed from his nose. Swelling forced his left eye closed.

Craig covered his face with his forearms and said, "Please. Please stop. I've got a wife and kid. I can't die. Please let me live. I'll give you anything."

John pulled back and stroked his goatee. His laugh was hollow, brittle, and mocking. He snapped his fingers and a golf ball–sized crystal that glowed with an amber light. He peered into the crystal and smirked. John pressed the crystal's point to Craig's forehead. Craig winced as a sigil burned itself into his head. Tears fell from his eyes as he looked up at John's eyes that glowed with the same amber light.

"Your grandfather swore on his soul that you would beat me back to Hell. If you fail in your quest, I will collect both his soul and yours. I will offer you this, Craig of Fiddler's Ford. Prepare.

Return here in one month and face me again. The next time we fight will be to death and damnation. Fail to defeat me once more or fail to return, and an eternity in the fourth bolgia of the Malebolge, where fiends will twist your face onto the back of your head and force you to walk in circles backward for all eternity, ripping your flesh and snapping your bones each time your path deviates from perfection."

The street light's globe shattered. And then the man in black, John of Helmstadt, sank into the darkness and disappeared.

* * *

On the Ides of March, the crowd at the Gin and Jukes, a dive bar in Fiddler's Ford, roared with laughter. Crushed pretzels and spiced nuts littered the floor as the smells of stale lager, sweat, and cheap cologne perfumed the air. The clack of pool balls cut through the antique jukebox playing "Crossroad Blues." Craig Wellington sat alone at the end of the splinter-laced oak bar, drinking Bud Light. A slender man in a beige cowboy hat rubbed Craig's bald head and tapped his wrist cast.

"Cone on, Craig," the man said. "Tell us the story again. What do you say, boys? Want to hear how the devil beat Craig's ass down at the crossroads?

The crowd roared. Craig focused his gaze on the amber bottle. The man's teasing became more insistent. Craig pushed him away without saying a word. The man went back to his pool game. Craig finished his beer and ordered a double bourbon on the rocks. He swigged the oak-scented caramel liquor, sighed, and stared into the glass. After a few moments lost in his own thoughts, a gruff but affable voice boomed over his shoulder.

"Drink never has the prophetic properties we so often ascribe to it."

Craig heard the thump of someone sitting on a bar stool. He ignored the man. Craig sipped his bourbon. He swirled the glass in his hand, heaved a sigh, and resumed his ineffective scrying. The bartender sold the man beside him a Shiner Bock, and Craig glimpsed the man's thick, coarse arm hair.

"It may taste good, but it rarely helps," the man said.

Craig's nostrils flared. His fists clenched. A growl escaped his lips. He spun to face this unwanted conversant, but blinked at the sight before him. The seated man loomed over him. His black skin was rich and warm. A ponytail of long locs crowned his head, and his thick, graying beard gave his massive but gentle grin an almost lupine quality. His eyes sparkled.

"Look, man,"Craig said. "I don't need—"

"Janus Johnson." The man extended his hand to Craig. Taken aback, Craig shook it reflexively. Janus patted his shoulder. "I just walked in and saw how you're getting ribbed by, well, everyone. Didn't seem like you liked it, so I thought you could use a friend. What's up?"

Craig drained half the remaining bourbon and snorted. "Like you care, stranger. You just passing through town or something?"

Janus nodded and sipped his beer. "Sort of. I live up in Butcher's Bend. On my way home from a haul down to Tallahassee. Thought I'd stop in for a cold beverage and to rest a bit before the last hour or so until home."

Craig nodded and fell silent. They sat, drinking, in silence as the jukebox played "Restless Sinner." Craig exhaled and ordered another round. Janus told the bartender to put it on his tab.

"Thank you, er... Janice? Strange name."

"Janus—with a 'u.' My dad named me for the Roman god of beginnings, transitions, and doors. Proved pretty prophetic. I didn't catch your name."

"It's Craig. Craig Wellington, but might as well be just Craig the Loser."

Janus clapped Craig's shoulder, causing the man to wince. "Nice to meet you, Craig Wellington. Tell me, with a name as four star as that, what makes you a loser?"

"You wouldn't believe me if I... Wait. You're a trucker, you said? Probably seen some strange shit, right?"

Janus nodded. He gazed at the flickering lights above the bar for a moment, sighed, and then chuckled. "Yeah. We all seen some strange shit the last few years, but I've seen things most people haven't. So, why don't you tell me your story?"

Craig scanned the room. The bartender cleaned glasses at the far end. Engrossed players filled the four pool tables. No one listened to them. His muscles tensed; Craig released them with an exhalation.

"The whole thing started thirty years ago. I wasn't born, but this started with my grandpa. He was known for getting into fights. I inherited that trait, I guess. Anyway, he was at the crossroads of One-seventy-eight and County Twenty-seven thirteen, walking from Greensville to here after a bad night of poker where lost his bus money.

"Anyway, he met this man in black, says it was the Devil himself. They exchanged words—words changed each time he told the story—and then got into a fight. Grandpa won. As the story goes, he told the Devil to get the hell out of South Carolina, and if he didn't, Grandpa promised to beat his ass back to Hell. If he wasn't alive, then one of us would do it.

"As his life ended, he begged me to keep his death out of the papers so the Devil wouldn't come back. Well, I couldn't. My aunts were too stubborn and demanding. The Devil showed up and eyed me. At Grandpa's grave, he challenged me to a fight, giving me the same mark as he gave Grandpa."

Craig showed Janus the three marks on his hand. They oozed yellowish puss and watery blood. Janus whistled, and his eyes widened.

"That's something strange," he said.

Craig nodded. "Yeah. So, I met him at the crossroads last Friday at midnight, just like Grandpa had. He was a scrawny dude, but he beat my ass. Broke my wrist and nose, and gave me this black eye. I begged for mercy, and he gave me one month to train until our rematch. He burned some symbol into me and said he'd take my soul and Grandpa's soul to Hell if I lost. Now, my wife took our son, and they're staying with her parents. Probably going to lose them too."

Janus exhaled. "Heavy. That's rough, buddy."

Craig drained his glass and pushed it forward. He threw open his hands. "Go ahead, make a joke. Everyone else does."

Janus shook his head and swigged his beer. "How do you get a country girl's attention? A tractor! No? Nothing? My kids don't like them either. I got nothing funny to say, but dad jokes. But I do know something that might help, if you're interested."

"You planning on teaching me to fight?" Craig snorted. His words grew slurred. "I learned that the hard way. And I've already got religion, accepted Jesus as my savior at ten, and I go to the Baptist church every Wednesday and Sunday when it's open. What, Mister Janus Johnson, do you have to offer me?"

Janus sat in silence. He felt Craig's anger. The younger man had been through a lot more in the past week than most people twice his age. Something about the story seemed off, but Janus did not know what. He sighed.

"Craig, you've been through some shit. I can teach you how to fight. I can give you some strengths and skills you don't have, but that might take more than a month. And there's paperwork involved. What I can do is give you a name. She's a private investigator by day—damned fine one at that. But I'm giving you her card because once a month, she takes on cases like yours. She's been doing this for ten years, and, to my knowledge, she's only failed once. If she can't help you, I don't think anyone in South Carolina can."

Janus handed Craig a small card with Sam's logo, Hain Private Investigations in Helvetica curved over a full moon, and business contact information. Craig thought for a moment. His hand traced the embossed text and image. He exhaled hard and looked at Janus.

"You really think she can save me?"

Janus pulled his stool closer to Craig and wrapped his massive, hairy arm around his shoulder. The hair on his arm felt like a dog's fur. He leaned close and said, "If anyone can, it's her. Two years ago, my family ran into some government trouble when reports of a dog described as a cross between a wolf and a pit bull attacking and eating children drew a special government agency's attention. We're registered with that agency because of a genetic condition, so we came under investigation. Almost lost both our businesses and got sent to jail. Sam proved our innocence and stopped a firefight before anyone died. She'll figure it out."

Janus checked the time on his phone and whistled. "Well, Craig, I got to get home to family. Think on what I said, but be quick. Tomorrow, she'll be expecting this."

Before he answered the question in Craig's mind, Janus settled his tab, rose, and left.

47

Chapter 3

"Are you certain you are well enough to drive yourself to work, Miss Hain?"

Martin kept his voice level as he watched, arms crossed over his chest, as I drank coffee in the sitting room of Carmilla's hotel suite. He only used that vocal tone when he knew that either Carmilla or I knew he was right, but wouldn't admit it. While 'Milla and I had another late night, I felt rested, but not. Pressure throbbed around my nose and watery eyes, making me drowsy. The fog inside my head didn't help. Martin handed me his silk handkerchief after I sneezed five times.

I walked to the desk and prepared another cup of coffee. I'd have to pick up more on the way; at least White Wolf was open again, so I could avoid Jordan Java or one of the chain shops. I nodded and coughed. "Look, Martin. I'm not going to lie and say I feel good. You've already figured that out. I have to go to work. The moon goes full this afternoon."

He placed a black mug bearing the stylized "W," the logo of the Westmont Hotel, on the BELLA single-pod machine. The fragrant, light brown liquid drizzled into the mug. Martin returned the Styrofoam cup to the stack.

"Be civilized, Miss Hain. No Styrofoam, please. Also, I am not suggesting that you take the day off from work and rest.

Were the Countess awake, she would, however, suggest that you remain with her. What I suggest, and what I offer, is that you allow me to drive you to work and to return you here—or to your home, should you wish—so you may prepare for your date this evening."

I sipped the coffee, hacking up another lung at its watery, mild flavor. I pinched my nose to stifle a sneeze from escaping. If we still had Benadryl at the office, I'd take one—maybe two—take a nap at lunch, and be well enough for the date. I'd be fine.

"I'll be fine, Martin." Another sneeze shot from my nose; I blushed as my snot floated atop the coffee. Martin took the mug from my hand and smiled. "I will stop at White Wolf Roasters, if you grant me permission to drive you."

He was good. I folded my arms across my chest and raised my right eyebrow. "Can you guarantee 'Milla will be safe while you're gone and I get coffee?"

"I am not the sole member of the Countess' security detail. She will be well guarded. I have served as the guardian of the ruling family—"

"Of the Karstein-Bertholt clan since 'Milla's grandfather was the clan patriarch. I'm not questioning you, Martin. It's just..." My gaze turned to 'Milla's bedroom and sighed. "It's just that I'm concerned with all we know about the Order of the Dragon. They want her dead. They probably want me dead for what happened in Bannagh. All evidence points to them working to resurrect Dracula, and that would be a disaster for everyone. I just want her safe. I love her."

Martin placed his hand on my shoulder, and I wrapped my hand around as much of his massive hand as I could. "As do I, Miss Hain. It is my most sincere hope that either you, your allies, or our allies will uncover the Order of the Dragon's true desires, especially as they intersect with those of your father and his hermetic order."

I nodded.

An hour later, I stepped into the Oberon Center, where we rented office space. The hall lights flickered again; the property manager preferred to bandage the electrical issues rather than fixing them. We had plans in place to move to another location, but that wouldn't happen for at least three months. I walked into my office, sunglasses covering my eyes and a forty-four ounce black coffee from White Wolf in my hand. Destiny typed at her desk. She removed an ear bud when she saw me enter.

"Sunglasses and a giant coffee? Hungover? Oh wait! You violated the Hayes Code, right? How is the Countess?"

I rolled my eyes and smiled. "All night long. And she's making a beautiful, naked corpse as she sleeps. We still got any Benadryl?"

Destiny grabbed a cloth mask and a can of Lysol she kept in her desk. She sprayed the air. As she slipped the mask around her neck. "I figure it's just allergies, but I'm not taking chances. My boss only gives me two weeks of sick leave, and I might need that when skooma season hits in five weeks."

I chuckled and sipped my coffee. "Des, just say you're taking time off when the new *Elder Scrolls* game comes out. I know it'll take you five hours to create your character. Honestly, I think it's just a cold."

Destiny responded by sticking out her tongue. "All those late nights you've had with little sleep have worn you down. When your girlfriend's in town, you might want to adjust your hours to get some sleep. You know what today is."

"Yeah." I removed my sunglasses. "That's why I didn't let

Martin talk me into calling in sick today."

As I said that, the door opened.

Maria Johnson, dressed in a mustard and black plaid fit and flare dress with a white Peter Pan collar, entered our office. Her key chain dangled from her right wrist, and a giant canvas bag with a red and black plaid thermos poked out. She pulled her tight black braids behind her ears and chose copper highlighter to accentuate the reddish undertones in her sepia skin. She smiled.

"Hey, Maria," I said, punctuating my works with guttural, mucus-laden coughs. I yawned. "How are you this too early morning?"

Her warm brown eyes smiled as she said, "I'm tired, but okay. With Janus home, I can run a few errands while he and the kids play in the yard. Can't stay long; got a show a few homes to a pair of clients this afternoon. More importantly, how are you? Seems you have a cold."

I nodded, blinking as my eyes watered. "Perceptive as always. But is everything okay? Full moon later today and all."

She walked to the counter and set the thermos and a mason jar filled with tea leaves and herbs beside the microwave. She pulled this amber bottle with a blue wax stopper from the bag and handed it to me. "From Rayna. She was out gardening when I was leaving, and she reminded me how you always get sick around this time of year. So, I thawed a few blocks of my chicken and garden veggie soup, put them in a thermos, and grabbed a mason jar of tea and a bottle of Rayna's special medicine. You've done this enough, so I don't have to explain the process."

"Mix half the bottle with a jigger of bourbon, warm, and drink. Thank you. I'm lucky to have friends like y'all."

"Especially given your current living situation," Destiny said.

Maria cocked her head. She turned to me and asked, "Sam, is everything okay at home? You're not back in that tiny apartment, are you? And after I helped you find that lovely house."

I opened my mouth, but Destiny cut me off and said, "Her girlfriend's in town, so she's basically living out of the Westmont and raiding the crypt."

Maria laughed. I shook my head and grumbled. Destiny beamed. I filled one of our tea balls with the herb and black tea while heating water in the microwave. Tea was better for my throat, but coffee was better for my mood. As the tea steeped, I said, "Look, I know 'Milla's like ten times my age, and it can make things weird at times and hard to navigate—Destiny, no TikTok psychoanalysis—Trust me, it's a downer when your girlfriend shreds any romantic notions you have about certain decades, fashion trends, or historical figures. And helping her with new technology can be frustrating. Also, I'm sure I don't always behave how she expects."

"And then she spanks you. What?" Destiny's face screamed she didn't think she said that aloud. She shrugged and said, "We *all* know."

Maria nodded. "It's true, Sam. And we're happy you're happy. Oh! Before I go, Janus said he gave your card to someone he met at a dive bar on his way home. Thinks you could help him. Cookout's this Sunday. You're both invited, and bring the Countess if she's still in town."

A sneeze shot from my nose. I sighed. "She leaves before dawn on Saturday. Probably won't see her in person until summer."

Maria left, and I sipped the hot tea. Destiny and I discussed our mundane case files. The Devereaux creeper case just got weirder. The person leaving her random gifts and messages just left a pair of boxers with the crotch cut out inside a hollowed coconut shell on her porch. About an hour after Maria left, a bald white man with a broken wrist and a black eye entered. He looked like he hadn't slept in three days. He doffed his hat.

"Is either of you ladies, Miss Samantha Hain?"

"I'm Samantha Hain," I said, waving. "I'd shake your hand, but I've got a cold. How can I help you?"

His eyes scanned my body. Not in a creepy way. I knew this difference. This was the look of someone who didn't believe a plus-sized woman in a blue 1940s-style A-line dress with a cropped burgundy sweater, seamed stockings, and stilettos could handle whatever he needed. His eyes trembled in desperation. Destiny grabbed a notepad, and I sat on the corner of her desk.

He ran his hand over his head and sighed. "Well, I don't have any other option right now, so I guess I'll take a chance."

Destiny said, "We've got coffee, tea, and water if you need them."

"No whiskey?"

Destiny snorted, and I laughed. "Sorry," I said. "I finished the bourbon I kept in my desk last month and haven't replaced it. So what can I do for you, Mister...?"

"Craig. Craig Wellington. Well, let's see what you can do."

Craig told us a wild story of his family's multigenerational fight with the Devil at the crossroads about two hours south of Butcher's Bend. I listened and asked questions. Destiny took notes. His halting and trembling voice suggested his honesty. Even for what we dealt with, this was one special Full Moon Special. I examined the three marks on his left palm. He claimed they oozed puss and blood at times, but they were still now. Some information was missing, but I wasn't sure what. And I didn't recognize the name John of Helmstadt. Destiny noted Helmstadt was a town in Bavaria.

He finished and said, "Honestly, I'm just glad y'all aren't laughing at me. You're the third and fourth who aren't. Well, my wife didn't laugh, but she yelled at me, took our son, and left for her parents. Can you do anything?"

I thought for a moment and then looked at Destiny. She shrugged and said, "Your call, Sam. I'll draw up the contract in five minutes, but I don't know what's going on. And you can't even play a fiddle."

Something is wrong here. This didn't sound like Nick Scratch's *modus operandi*. Fist fights? That posh asshole got more manicures than I did. There's no way he would do this. But who would? And why the name John of Helmstadt? I'd have to find out. I ran my fingers through my hair and exhaled.

"Draw up the contract, Des. Mr. Wellington, my standard fee for a supernatural case is fifteen hundred. I need half up front for expenses. This is local, so I can cut you a deal. So, five hundred down, and then you pay the remainder once the investigation is complete. Is that acceptable?"

Craig exhaled and shifted from one foot to the other; his hands remained in his jean pockets. After a minute or so, he shrugged. "Not like I have much choice, but sure. I'll pay that."

* * *

The Arch Magus' daughter is distracted and with the traitor. Enter through the west door and retrieve the grimoire.

James Carlson read the message Knight-Commander Paul Bertalan sent to his cell phone. He nodded. Carlson stood taller than average height with a strong build, but his features, when not hidden by a black ski cap with red stitching and a black face mask, were unremarkable. His brown eyes and tanned skin peeked through the opening in the fabric.

As the moon shown on the clear night sky over Butcher's Bend, the white van emblazoned with the South Carolina Electric Cooperative logo he drove parked across the street from Sam Hain's new home. Her Subaru sat in the driveway. Cars passed as he surveyed the area. Patience and protocol dictated that he wait until her neighbors' children reenter their house. Five minutes after that moment, Carson, dressed in a black sweater and gray-scale camouflage pants, walked around her home to the door on her back porch.

The wooden door with a square stained glass panel at eye level was locked. Carlson slipped his lock pick set from his wallet and set to work. His hands moved with a surgeon's precision, and after a minute, Carlson heard the distinctive click of the last spring. He turned the knob, but the door resisted his force. A chain rattled as he slid a pen along the crack formed when he pushed on the door. He tied string to a rubber band, opened the door, looped the band around the chain, slid the string over the crack on the top of the door, and released the chain. The door opened.

Carlson switched on his flashlight. Sam kept her home cold. Sweeping the room, the beam revealed him to be in Sam's kitchen. The paper sacks and piles of cans on the yellow and white granite-topped island revealed she had not put away her groceries. Carlson crept along the wooden floor. His combat boots muffled most of the sounds from his steps. Turning his light-led gaze at right angles, Carlson swept the kitchen, moving toward the alcove next to the opened French doors that led to the dining room. As he reached the alcove and placed his right foot on the first ascending stair, the lights from the den switched on, their beams pushing through the archway connecting the den to the kitchen. Carlson froze.

He backed against the wall as Sandy Paws trotted into the kitchen. *Motion sensors. Of course, the Arch Magus' daughter had them on the first floor.* The calico cat's eyes glimmered as she stepped into the darkness. Carlson watched the cat make her way to her water bowl and lap. He took a single step back, ascending to the second stair. Sandy's ears twitched. Carlson turned and ascended two more steps. Sandy raised her head and meowed. Carlson froze.

Sandy trotted to the base of the stairs, tilted her head, and stared at Carlson. He remained motionless. Sandy leaned forward, her eyes searching the stranger on her stairs. Carlson kicked a foot forward. Sandy reared back and hissed. Carlson kicked again, taking care not to hurt the cat or leave any boot marks on her. The cat scurried into the living room. Carlson remained still until the motion sensor lights switched off.

Carlson stood at the end of a hallway that ran the length of the floor. Two doors stood closed, and one hung open on the hall's left side. Three doors stood closed on the right side. He crept along the oak floorboards to the open door at the far end. These floorboards creaked. Carlson slowed his pace and his breathing. As he approached the open door, his back touched the wall.

He ran his gloved index fingertip along the handle of his Beretta 92. No one should be home. Reconnaissance was never wrong. There existed no reason this door should be open now. Carlson shook his head, inhaled, drew his firearm, and spun into the open doorway.

Sam left her bathroom door open. Carlson cursed the undisciplined nature that revealed itself both in an open door and in the disorganization that plagued her master bathroom. Residue from a purple, blue, and red bath bomb remained in the claw foot bathtub. A washcloth, soaked and dripping, hung from the faucet. Multiple hairspray and dry shampoo bottles, brushes, tweezers, and a pair of nail clippers littered the wash basin. Sam even left her toothpaste tube uncapped. Carlson shook his head and left the bathroom.

Carlson searched the remaining five rooms on the floor. He rifled through the closet, dresser drawers, and nightstand in Sam's bedroom. Carlson slammed the photograph of Sam and Carmilla on the nightstand, shattering the frame's glass. He repeated this process in her guest bedroom. Neither contained the grimoire. As he searched the makeshift storage room filled with unopened boxes, he ripped through both the heaviest box and its contents, mementos belonging to Sam's deceased mother. He opened the door to Sam's office and paused as a woman's voice came from downstairs.

"I'm fine, Martin. You don't have to stay. It's probably just someone checking the meters," Sam said as she entered her den.

"I shall not remain long, Miss Hain," he replied in his Saxon baritone. "However, the Countess extends her protection and her resources to the one who is both her lover and her champion. As such, I would be remiss if I allowed you to enter an empty home alone."

Sam shot a knowing look his way. She sighed. "Fine. I won't

say I don't appreciate it, but I don't see any direct need to worry."

Sandy Paws descended from atop Sam's oversized chestnut brown leather library chair and rubbed her human's stocking-clad leg. "Hi, baby. Yeah, 'Milla has a work meeting tomorrow, so we had to end our date earlier than Mommy hoped. Let me get you a little snack before Mommy reads in bed. Okay?"

The bitch is home, and she brought the estate steward with her. This complicates matters. Jim Carlson cursed under his breath. He checked his phone. Knight-Commander Bertalan sent another message; this one warned him of Sam's return. Nothing mentioned Martin being with her. He fired a quick text requesting guidance, and backup considering this development. Sam's stilettos clicked on the floorboards, and Martin's boots clamored. Carlson waited.

Sam grabbed and shredded some roasted turkey breast leftover from her lunch and placed it on a porcelain appetizer plate. Sandy raced to the plate and started eating the moment Sam set it on the floor. Martin opened every closet and cabinet door. He scanned the floor. Neither of these searched proved fruitful. He approached the door to her back porch and ran his fingertips along the door. Martin turned the knob.

"Miss Hain, do you normally leave this door unlocked?"

While petting Sandy as she ate, Sam shook her head. "No. I keep that door locked at all times. I barely use that porch. Shit."

Martin produced his Desert Eagle. "We are not alone."

Jim Carlson's phone illuminated. *Backup will not arrive. This is a covert operation, not a pitched battle. Continue with mission. Do not engage unless necessary. Out.*

Carlson cursed again. He prepared to fight a mortal woman.

And to kill her if necessary. The Order issued him no vampire-slaying equipment for this mission. Carlson's heart thumped faster. He grumbled. Carlson switched off his flashlight. He unholstered his pistol and switched off its safety. Standing behind the door frame, Carlson closed the door, leaving a slivered crack through which he observed the hallway.

Martin finished sweeping the ground floor. He noted the basement door remained locked. Sam fished a can of pepper spray and her keys from her purse. She hoped her Walther remained locked in the safe under her altar. Martin shifted a hand to guard her.

"Remain behind me, Miss Hain. You have proven yourself capable in a fight; however, I can survive a bullet better than you."

"And what should I do if something happens to you?" Sam's glare stated she would not back down.

"Then I expect there will be a period of mourning and flagellation, a hiring of my replacement, and a move to Austria to live in Castle Karnstein." Martin moved toward the stairs.

"Wait. What?" Sam grabbed his arm.

Martin flashed a smile. "Or pick up my gun and shoot back. The intruder is likely a mortal. They die easily."

Sam rolled her eyes and sighed. Jim Carlson heard heavy steps ascend the stairs. The vampire led. That meant the Arch Magus' daughter followed behind. A plan formed in his mind. Only one complication arose. He had yet to acquire Donal Hain's traveling grimoire. Carlson cursed again.

As his head rose above the railing, Martin signaled to Sam. She glared but nodded, and she crouched so only her eyes rose above the floorboards. Her heart pounded beneath the white blouse she tucked into her black pencil skirt. A gargantuan horned figure's shadow loomed at the end of the hallway. Sam blinked. The figure was not there. A thin layer of sweat formed on her palms and on her forehead. Her breaths became rapid.

Jim Carlson held his breath. Vampires had heightened senses, and he watched as Martin sniffed and listened while moving into the hall. Carlson crouched, waiting for his moment. His heart raced. His eyes darted side to side. A single breath slipped through his lips. Martin remained calm, his face devoid of emotion.

Come on, you fucking treasonous dog. Pick a door. The bitch is in my sight, and all I need is for you to keep walking and to stay... over... Fuck!

Martin kicked the closed door; it flew open, and Carlson tumbled backward. A coffee table's corner slammed into his shoulder. His plan failed to account for a vampire's speed and strength. Carlson scrambled to his feet, but Martin slammed his right fist into the intruder's jaw. Carlson staggered. He responded with a lunging jab to Martin's stomach.

Sam sank onto her rear. She trembled. She blinked. When her eyes opened, she was outside of Bannagh. She smelled the torches' flames, the gunpowder, her father's incense blend and cologne, and the burning flesh. Zozo's brittle, bleating, demonic laughter reverberated through her ears. Tears and eyeliner ink flowed down her cheeks. She took slow, meditative breaths and swallowed hard. She narrowed her eyes and crawled.

While Sam scurried the length of her hall, Martin kneed Carlson in chest. He followed with an elbow to the back of Carlson's neck. The intruder dropped. He crawled toward the door, and Martin kicked his ribs. Carlson screamed. Sweat beaded on his forehead. Martin's red eyes glowed, and he appeared unphased.

Carlson scrambled to his feet and threw a trio of punches at Martin's chest. The vampire dodged the first. The second connected, and the third staggered him.

"You feel pain." Carlson laughed, wiping blood from his own lip.

"I am not a machine," Martin said.

Carlson spat and charged. Martin transformed into mist. Carlson tripped over the coffee table. As he regained his balance, Martin reformed behind him and applied a rear naked choke hold. Carlson gasped. One second passed. Martin increased the pressure on the Adam's apple. Two seconds passed. Three seconds passed. Carlson blinked and swayed. Four seconds. Carlson slammed his boot heel into Martin's foot. The vampire winced, loosening his grip. Carlson pushed through and escaped the hold. He bolted into the hall; his phone fell from his pocket.

While the fight raged, Sam crawled to the room opposite the master bathroom. The door was still locked. With a trembling hand, she slid the key into the keyhole and unlocked the door. The keys fell from her hand. Sam cursed, grabbed the keys, and scurried into her magical work room. Although they disagreed on most aspects of life, Donal Hain persuaded his daughter to learn a few basic esoteric principles and protective arcane rituals. She crawled into her magical circle and kneeled at the western side of the altar that stood immediately west of its center. Sam opened a small panel and slid a tiny silver key into the now-revealed lock.

Two objects rested inside the compartment. The largest was her father's tattered, leather-bound traveling grimoire she recovered from the Bannagh incident. The other was her

Walther P-38. She grabbed her gun, locked the cabinet, and returned the panel to its place. She winced. Sam took three deep breaths, rose to her feet, and returned to the hall.

Jim Carlson bolted into the hallway the moment Sam stepped into the hall. He glimpsed her from the corner of his eye, stopped, and turned. She leveled her pistol at him. Panic spread over his face. Sam narrowed her eyes and slid her finger onto the trigger. Carlson's gaze shifted as Martin loomed in the doorway. Sam's arm trembled. Her shallow, rapid breathing rattled her chest. Carlson's heart thundered. Sam froze.

Carlson bolted for the stairs. Sam tensed and fired. The bullet grazed Carlson's right shoulder. He winced and grunted. Carlson stumbled down the stairs, landing on his face. Martin gave chase. Sam screamed and fell to her knees. Her cry froze Martin, who spun and raced to her side. Carlson rushed through the kitchen door, around the house, and into his van. He sped away.

Through her glassy eyes, tears, and eyeliner-streaked face, Sam looked at Martin. With a trembling lip, she said, "I saw Bannagh. I saw Zozo. I was there. But I'm here. He got away. I'm sorry."

"He was a thief, Miss Hain." Martin helped her to her feet. "His life is unimportant. Let him flee. Your life and your safety are my primary concerns. Are you hurt?"

Martin considered this. He nodded. "Allow me to draw you a bath. While you relax, as best as you can in this moment, I will sweep the house once more."

As Sam soaked in the hot water, Martin searched Sam's house. He noted the opened drawers and cabinets in her bedroom. He then folded and put away the clothes Carlson scattered over the floor. Martin returned to Sam's library, the room where he fought the intruder, and searched. None of the books in the rustic oak shelves built directly into the walls appeared out of place. The coffee table suffered minor damage. And then he saw the cell phone.

The phone was a newer model, but it was not the most secure. Martin did not have the skills to enter the phone, but he knew those who did. He opened the case but found nothing promising information. He clicked the phone's side button, illuminating the lock screen. The image of a dragon with its tail coiled around its neck like the ouroboros with a cross on its back. Martin pocketed the phone, unlocked his own, and made a call.

"My Countess, I apologize for my delay in returning, but there has been a complication."

"How is she, Martin? What is wrong?" Carmilla's voice was frantic.

He nodded. "She is physically well. There was an intruder—a burglar—who appears to be either an agent or a contracted mercenary of the Order of the Dragon. The interaction triggered a flashback to the events in Ireland. The thief appears to have failed in his mission. She is currently in the bath, and once she has finished, I will return. Yes, she will be with me."

* * *

On the following evening, Jeremy Meadows pinched the bridge of his nose and sighed at the laughter coming across the table from him. It was Thursday night, and he was on a date. Jeremy ran his meaty fingers through his short, red hair. He covered his beer belly with a blue and white striped polo shirt and khaki pants. He sipped the light beer in his pint glass and shook his head.

"Will you ever not laugh at this place's name, Destiny?"

Destiny Grimm cackled and snorted, drawing the attention of nearby patrons. The bartender shook his head and smiled. Her blonde ringlets bounced as she shook her head. She clipped a red and black miniature top hat left of center on her head. She tucked a red blouse with French cuff sleeves into a black pencil skirt.

"Nope." She choked on that word. When she calmed herself enough to converse, she said, "It was funny enough as Veritas Vino, but when those Brits with the posh accents bought it and changed the name to The Uncorked Bottle, all I hear is 'The Uncocked Butthole.'"

The Uncorked Bottle was Butcher's Bend's newest gastropub and wine bar. The rustic chic interior blended raw oak and iron with antique lighting. Jeremy surprised Destiny when he first suggested this as a date spot, not because of the quality of the food, the drink, or the ambiance—both proved superb—but because of The Uncorked Bottle's location. The gastropub sat on Crowley Lane, two blocks from Sam's new house and within the Veiled Heights neighborhood. Most humans avoided the area, claiming a vague feeling of unease, but Jeremy seemed oblivious to the supernatural presence.

Destiny glanced around the room as she sipped her Riesling. The dining room was full, and their server had yet to return with the Banging Banger Board. Jeremy drummed his fingers on his knee. He said, "I'm glad we could make it out tonight. Sorry your raid got canceled."

Destiny shrugged. She smiled. "Well, Garthax had surgery this morning, but he's doing okay. Anyway, I'm not tanking Paradigm's Breach without my best healer. And this is nice."

Their server, a perky young woman with a blonde bob and hazel eyes, returned with their appetizer on a rustic board resembling a slice of freshly hewn maple. Five bias-cut sausage links, three cheese wedges, a bunch of grapes, a sliced green apple, pickled squash, stone ground mustard, and baguette slices tossed in herbed butter and toasted topped the plate. Destiny's eyes sparkled, and her trembling legs shook the table. Jeremy braced to keep the glasses upright. Destiny blushed and clasped her hands.

"What? I'm German. We love our sausages."

I wish she loved other types of sausages. Jeremy smiled. As a girlfriend, Destiny was a breeze to buy gifts for. Sausages, cheeses, and anything connected to any of her fandoms—even something kitschy—made her happy. Keeping up with her interests and current anime obsessions proved daunting. Certain interests, like online gaming, devoured time, making date nights few. He smiled.

"And it's cute seeing your excitement, honey."

He reached across the table and held her hands. His rough hands reminded her of her father's, a fact that provided both comfort and homesickness.

The server smiled. "We've changed the board a bit, so let me go over things. You'll find two traditional bangers, two andouille links, and one Thuringer—"

"A Thuringer Rostbratwurst?" Destiny bounced in her seat. "Katie, that makes me ecstatic."

Katie smiled. "Edgar and James have noted comment cards asking for these always coming in the same handwriting. So, while trying to source a local butcher to make a proper one, they decided to import some wurst—primarily for you. Anything else? Oh, for cheeses, we have a smoked Gouda, a creamy goat's milk Brie—pairs nicely with the apples and andouille—and a Manchego."

Jeremy shook his head. "This looks amazing."

"This is perfect, Katie. Remind me to thank Edgar and James. And you got our entrée orders, right? Did we give them to you?"

Katie nodded. "Yeah. Miss Grimm, you're having the Crispy Chicken Sando with double pickles and a side of sprouts and bacon. And your date is having the French Kiss, easy on the horseradish on garlic brioche instead of hoagie. I'll grab a pitcher and refill your waters. Okay?"

Katie left their table. Destiny forked half of the Thuringer onto Jeremy's plate before taking the other half for herself. As she spread Brie on a slice of bread, Jeremy asked, "Are you sure? You've made up a love song to Thuringer brats. Don't you want all of it?"

Destiny set an apple slice and a Thuringer slice on her bread. She tossed the bite into her mouth. Her shoulders relaxed, and she moaned as she chewed. She swallowed and then sipped her wine. She smiled at Jeremy.

"First of all, yes, I do. Second, I don't even..." She giggled. "I don't even share my sausage with Sam." Her laughter intensified.

Jeremy shook his head and chuckled. That was funny. He ate one of the sausage slices. "It's a really good saus—It's very flavorful. Caught myself."

Destiny giggled. "You're getting good." She softened her gaze and leaned forward. And I do like you."

Jeremy nodded.

They dined and conversed, finishing their meal with The Uncorked Bottle's signature dessert, the s'mores pot de creme. Experience taught Jeremy that, while Destiny would share, ordering two meant he could enjoy this artistic interpretation of his favorite childhood dessert at his leisure.

After dinner, they returned to Destiny's townhouse. Hundreds of manga volumes littered her den floor, laying siege to her empty white bookcase. Jeremy recognized a handful—*Inuyasha, Fruits Basket, Black Butler, Hellsing, xxxHolic, Vampire Knight, Rosario Vampire, Trinity Blood, Ouron High School Host Club, Nana,* and *Skip Beat.* Destiny scooped a stack of manga from the white sofa's Tiffany blue cushions and added them to the stacks on her coffee table. She kissed Jeremy's cheek as he sat, and then she went to the kitchen to get them drinks.

Destiny returned with two Flensburger Dunkels her father sent as part of a care package. They drank in silence, save for the noises made by the ceiling fan, for what felt like an hour. Four inches of empty air hung between them. Jeremy held his breath for a moment, exhaled, and then asked, "Rearranging your manga shelves?"

"I'm deciding what stays on the shelves here and what goes to the attic. Then I can take the new ones out of the boxes on the dining table and put them on the shelves here. See something you want to read?"

Jeremy smirked. "No, but there's something else I'd like to do."

He wrapped his arm around Destiny's shoulder. She slid closer and sipped her beer. Destiny closed her eyes and listened to her body. Nothing. She sighed, remaining motionless as he leaned in for a kiss. Jeremy's open mouth kissed her cheek. He stopped, pulled away, and sighed

"Nothing? Still?"

Destiny closed her eyes and nodded. "And it sucks, Jeremy. I really like you, and I have a great time with you—and your touch feels comforting. It's just that, when it comes to physical intimacy, the spark I need just isn't there. I'm sorry. I want it to be, but it isn't. It's not fair."

Jeremy shifted to face Destiny. She clenched her trembling fists as tears glassed her eyes. He cupped her free hand in both of his and said, "It sucks, sure, but it's who you are. We've discussed this."

She shook her head. "It's not fair to you. I'm not leading you on. I swear it. Shit. I like you. I'm attracted to you. It's just...not fair of me to continue promising that the spark might happen. It might, or it might not. You're a great boyfriend. I love being your girlfriend. Heck, I even like your family, and that hasn't happened before. Well, not in a long time."

"And they like you, and that's a rarity." Jeremy squeezed her hand. He shifted and wrapped her in his arms. Her perfume was clean and herbaceous. "I know I've told you I'm willing to wait, and there's a reason for that. Well, two. My dad taught me that consent is essential. But more importantly, I love you, Destiny."

A trembling smile graced her lips. She snorted as tears leaked. Destiny reclined her head so she could see his face. "I love you too, Jeremy. I really do."

And they cuddled until the clock struck midnight.

* * *

While Destiny and Jeremy dined at The Uncorked Bottle, Samantha Hain glared into her walk-in closet. She wore only a towel wrapped around her hair, and the few white and orange furs Sandy Paws left behind as she rubbed her human's freshly shaved legs. Martin would arrive in twenty-seven minutes. His mastery of calculating travel time amazed Sam on other occasions, but her opinion of his skills differed on this evening. The Craven Horn started as a gastropub, but Mezixis and Tinixia, the succubi owners, transformed the Horn into a fine dining restaurant that became Butcher's Bend's first Michelin Star restaurant.

Elegant with understated sexiness. Sam searched through her wall of dresses; she decided on a black off-the shoulder wiggle dress with a portrait neckline. Sam slipped into her black lingerie, including a garter belt and thigh highs. Raising the dress' back zipper required contortions and dance moves Sam did not know she had. She slipped on a pair of red stilettos and touched up her Victory Red lipstick. She brushed her hair, grabbed her purse, and waited for her date's arrival.

Formerly a Scars & Roebuck department store, Mezixis and Tinixia transformed the windowless, concrete building into a beautiful and elegant dining destination. Ivy draped over the red brick wall leading to the outside courtyard, where faerie lights hung suspended on invisible wires, illuminating those dining on the varnished oak and wrought iron furniture. Massive windows, framed by wrought iron-bordered stained glass tiles, brightened the dreary exterior. Inside, the chocolate leather booths and chair upholstery glowed in the candlelight's warmth.

When Carmilla and Sam stepped from the car, a maitre d' escorted them through the dining room, up the spiraling glass staircase, and into the upper dining room reserved for Veil Crossers and their guests. The maitre d' brought them to their table and pulled out their chairs. White linen cloths with infernal runes embroidered along the edges and golden, three-pronged candelabra adorned the tables. The faint smells of lemon and lavender filled the chamber, and Sam wished she had brought a jacket.

The Craven Horn's sommelier brought a Sanguinovese bottle to the table. He removed the cork and presented it to Carmilla. She examined it and nodded. He poured two glasses, bowed, and departed. The bottle remained on the table. Carmilla sipped and smiled.

Sam picked up her glass and said, "That was quick. He didn't even offer you a wine list."

"I called ahead, dear one," Carmilla said. "The Mailberg 1082 is a special treat I allow myself once a decade. It pairs nicely with three courses on tonight's special tasting menu. It may not be to your liking, but I ask that you try it. If you dislike it, I will order you a wine or a bourbon or whatever you desire."

"Once a decade?" The wine smelled earthy and spicy. *It is our last night before she returns to Austria. And aside from Zoom, I won't see her for a while.* Sam raised her eyebrow. "Something special planned that I don't know about?"

The wine tasted sweeter, smoother, and more mellow than Sam expected. She drained half her glass. Carmilla giggled. That was a rare sound, and Sam smiled.

"There is. I have an offer I wish to place before you."

Sam's heart stopped and then sped up. *An offer? We've only been back together since Christmas. I just bought my house. Is she asking me to move in? Oh, Destiny will have a field day with U-Hauling jokes.*

"What are you thinking, 'Milla?"

Camilla sipped her wine. The server brought the first course, a lamb tartare with a room temperature cockatrice egg. Sam's right foot bounced under the table. Carmilla spooned lamb and egg onto a toast point. Sam followed suit.

"Well, I was thinking, since you have a personal magical working room in your home, that perhaps we could—and forgive me, dear one, for I have read treatises on magical theory but do not recall the proper term—draw a magical circle that could be used for teleportation in the dungeon."

Sam blinked. She smiled and trembled. "The dungeon? Are you sure you'll be okay with that?"

Carmilla slid her unshoed foot up Sam's stocking clad leg and smiled as Sam sucked in a quick breath. "Now that Elisa rests in the family crypt, thanks to your diligent efforts, the dungeon is unused for anything beyond storage. And as I no longer have need of hiding my diary, that room could be converted into a magician's working chamber. My family's collection of alchemical equipment, grimoires, and treatises on esoteric theory—though likely outdated compared to what wizarding orders possess—are already there. That would simplify our travel, no?"

Sam's heart increased its speed as Carmilla's foot teased Sam's inner thigh, pushing her dress higher. Sam bit her lip and focused on her breath. Carmilla repeated Sam's name three times before Sam snapped to attention and said, "Yeah, yeah, it would. Sorry." She brushed her hair behind her ear. "Sorry, I got a bit distracted."

Carmilla licked her lips. "Oh? And what, my dear one, could distract you from our conversation?"

Carmilla removed her foot from Sam's leg. Sam whimpered and narrowed her eyes. "First, there's how gorgeous you are, naturally and supernaturally. Second, we could talk about the fact that the lace bodice of your dress, while tasteful and elegant, informs me you are not wearing a bra. And then there's the way you tease with your foot. And you know all of this distracts me."

Sam crossed her arms over her chest and cocked her head in victory. Carmilla folded her fingers over each other and smiled. She leaned forward and purred.

"If we are to speak of distractions, then let me describe how distracting it is that you chose a dress that allows me to see naught but the faintest outline of every delicious and tempting curve of your body. Shall I not mention how the neckline of your dress, while tasteful, reveals the curvature of your lovely shoulders. And while I glance at your milky skin, dear one, should I not mention how naughty and indecent it is of you to saunter through public spaces with your neck exposed that all might see your veins and arteries pulsing and pumping your life-giving—and life-saving—nectar. Is that not how your books describe it?"

Sam felt warmth build below her waist. Camilla knew what she was doing. She knew how that vocal tone affected Sam. Her chest heaved. Sam covered her neck with her hands as if she were covering exposed breasts. She paused. That looked silly. Sam blushed, moved her hands from her neck, and twirled her brown hair around her fingers. Carmilla smiled.

When she processed her lover's words, Sam asked, "And how many of my books have you read?"

Carmilla sipped the wine as the server brought plates of spiced lamb shank atop a bed of Egyptian treasure trove hummus. Carmilla held her little finger aloft as she sliced into the rare lamb while Sam scooped the hummus on the pita triangles. After Carmilla swallowed, she said, "Only four. The three you hide in your nightstand drawer, and *Romanian Knights.*"

Romanian Knights? I was still closeted—and in high

school—when I read that book...for the first time. Did she see the pages I dog-eared? No, she bought her own copies. Did she dog-ear any pages? Is that how she always knows what I like?

"'Milla, darling, you don't need to snoop my smut. We actually communicate, and sex has always been great.'"

Carmilla sighed. She nodded and said, "It was partially for that reason, yes; however, I also needed to silence a raging voice in my mind. I may possess the body of a woman your age, but I am nearly ten times your age. That you saw me as a person and not a monster was apparent from our initial meeting at The Four Winds; nevertheless, your willingness and comfort in robbing the crypt, as the fledglings say, concerned me. The cliched and euphemistic writing aside, these works helped comfort me."

Carmilla...insecure about...me? She always seemed confident on that front. I mean, beyond that whole nearly two centuries of being gaslit into believing she killed her last girlfriend and was responsible for her sister's death.

Sam reached across the table and held Carmilla's hand. She smiled. "If I'm being honest, until you told me your age, both Destiny and I assumed you were named for an ancestor. It didn't really hit what I was getting myself into until Countess Bathory grilled me in Bad Waltersdorf. And by that point, I was in love, so it didn't matter. Didn't matter then. Doesn't matter now. Heck, maybe getting older has changed things, but you don't feel as cold while sleeping as you used to. I know I've matured, and everything that happened in December helped me put things in perspective."

"December was beneficial for both of our perspectives."

They held hands until the server brought the dessert course of blood orange and dark chocolate souffle topped with a spiced rum sauce. They concluded their meal with personalize variants of The Craven Horn's signature cocktail, Seduction. The clock struck midnight, and Martin arrived. Martin raised the screen between the front and back seats, affording the lovers privacy as they cuddled, kissed, and fondled each other. They arrived at Sam's home. Martin stepped from the car, opened Sam's door, and extended his hand.

Carmilla raised her left hand and wrapped her right arm around Sam's waist. "I will escort her, Martin. Don't wait up."

Both of you need to drink water. If you recall, Miss Hain, I left the Countess' nutrient-infused water in your refrigerator.

Martin sent both Sam and Carmilla that text every five minutes until Sam responded. Sandy Paws sprawled atop both their laps, receiving pets from both women. When Sam rose to fulfill Martin's request, Sandy hopped from Carmilla's lap and curled up in Sam's seat. Carmilla chuckled and scratched behind Sandy's ears.

"Excuse me, Miss Paws, but Mommy was sitting there," Sam said as she handed Carmilla a glass of water. Sandy yawned in response.

Carmilla smiled and drained her glass. She shifted her posture and stroked her lap. "There are other places you could sit, should you desire."

"If my Countess so desires."

Sam slid onto Carmilla's lap, draping her legs over the green and black buffalo check sofa's oversized plush armrest. Carmilla supported Sam's back with a single open palm and guided Sam's lips toward her own with the fingertips of her other hand. She smelled Sam's natural scent of spiced honey and licked her lips. Sam's heart pumped faster. The vampire teased her lover with a series of gentle pecks that grazed Sam's lips. Sam wrapped her arms around Carmilla's neck and ran her fingers through the vampire's hair. Carmilla purred.

They tasted faint traces of wine and each other's signature cocktails as they kissed. Sam brushed her tongue against Carmilla's fangs. Carmilla's hand cupped the back of Sam's neck, and she deepened their kiss. Carmilla trailed hungry kisses, her fangs nipping at Sam's skin, from her lover's lips to her shoulder. Sam's breathing came in staccato bursts. Carmilla's right hand kneaded Sam's breasts. Sam held Carmilla's head against her shoulder, biting her lip and moaning, as the vampire kissed and sucked on her shoulder.

Carmilla's hungry eyes met Sam's as the latter panted. The back of Carmilla's fingers brushed Sam's cheeks. Sam kissed her fingers and said, "This dress is making doing anything fucking difficult."

Carmilla breathed onto Sam's neck, causing a shiver to run along her spine. "Then I suggest we remove our impractical clothing."

They made their way to the master bedroom. Sandy's ear twitched, but she remained asleep on the sofa. Sam and Carmilla undressed each other, their lips kissing and hands groping each newly exposed section of skin.

Carmilla released her hair from its bun. As it fell to her waist, her body, although she no longer drew breath, responded with the rapid rising and falling of her chest. She bit her lip. Sam slid behind her, kissed her neck and shoulder, and fondled the vampire's breasts. Carmilla moaned. Sam pinched her nipple; Carmilla squeaked.

"I love it when you make that sound, 'Milla." Sam giggled.

"You also love it when I do this."

Carmilla reclined her head on Sam's chest. Her tongue traced Sam's lips. Sam blinked. Carmilla slipped behind her and wrapped her arms around Sam's belly. She held her close, feeling her heart beat and her breaths rise and fall. Sam smiled and sighed. Carmilla was right; she loved this.

Sam took Carmilla's hand and led her to the bed. Their lips met, and Carmilla slid her tongue between Sam's lips. Carmilla's nose twitched; she smelled Sam's musky arousal. She growled. Sam slid onto her bed and lay on her back. Carmilla crawled between her legs. Sam's breasts heaved. Knowing Sam's distaste for having her feet touched, Carmilla trailed kisses from Sam's ankle to her inner thigh.

Carmilla blew a gentle breath along the length of Sam's labia. Sam gasped. Carmilla slid her arms under and around Sam's thighs. She slid her tongue up Sam's labia and circled her clit. Sam gasped; her his rose. Carmilla smiled, licked her lips, and kissed her way up Sam's stomach. Her tongue circled Sam's aroused nipples. Carmilla kissed Sam's neck, sucking and nibbling it. Sam moaned.

"You are wet."

Carmilla purred into Sam's ear. She slid two fingers inside of Sam and moved them in wavelike motions. Sam's hips rocked. She clutched the sheets. Carmilla teased Sam's mouth with rough but flitting kisses. And then she stopped.

Sam whimpered. "Why'd you..."

Her voice trailed as her eyes followed Carmilla's gaze. Poking up from the floor and making eye contact with Carmilla was Sandy Paws. Sam grumbled and threw her head into the pillow. Carmilla laughed.

"Borders change. Cultures change. But cats do not change."

She chuckled again and reached out and stroked Sandy. The

cat purred in triumph. Carmilla licked the fingers she had inside Sam. She lay beside her and wrapped her arms around Sam. She kissed Sam's cheek. Sam chuckled, rolled her eyes, and pulled the sheet over them. Sandy hopped onto the bed and curled up on the pillow above Sam's head.

Chapter 4

A golf ball sized shard of the streetlight's glass globe crunched and crumbled beneath the sole of my boot. Destiny was right about wearing combat boots out here. The thick, ash and slate storm clouds loomed overhead, cooling the March day and threatening rain. The crossroads of Highway 178 and County Road 2713 wasn't much to look at. Highway 178 was a standard pothole-laden, four-lane highway with litter scattered along the shoulder and in the side ditch. Twenty-Seven Thirteen was a two-lane gravel and dirt road; parts of it were paved at one point, but the county voted against funds for upkeep.

A breeze lazed through the air, carrying the smells of diesel and motor oil. The regular traffic on the highway whizzed by, but the single dual-cab farm truck on the farm road rumbled and sputtered as it slouched along. Most of the noise came from the workers setting up a carnival of some sort in the open field on the other side of the highway. The tatters and rust I could see from about a quarter of a mile away suggested this was a fly-by-night operation that probably had a ride called the Death Rattle. I heard the death rattle enough in Bannagh and when the Order of the Dragon attacked 'Milla's castle.

"I'm not seeing anything, Sam. Sam? Sam!"

A hand grabbed my arm. I shook my head to clear the

thoughts. Destiny's blue eyes shone with concern through her oversized pink sunglasses that looked like the Nintendo character Kirby with his mouth open. I shook my head again.

"Me either. I don't know why I thought there would be something here."

I kneeled in the dirt and grass beside the groove of some tire. A butt print sat less than three inches from the groove. Two sets of footprints moving in strange patterns. One had treads like combat or work boots. The other left flat imprints like a cowboy boot. Probably the fight.

"It's not a terrible idea," Destiny said. Her fingers sifted through the dirt and grass. She stood, arched her back, and groaned. "This isn't a situation I know anything about. You don't think it really is *him*, do you?"

I ran my fingers through my hair and sighed. "It doesn't sound like him. I know there are all those stories about Robert Johnson meeting him at the crossroads, and he all but confirmed to you the Charlie Daniels song happened. But a fist fight? That's not something he would do. For all that he is, Nick Scratch presents himself to us normal humans as a posh metrosexual. I mean, his nails are more manicured than a high femme. Speaking of, I'm due for a mani-pedi."

Destiny giggled, looked at her own nails, and sighed. "Yeah, me too. And no, he's not what I would have expected based on the stories that get circulated. I mean, though, he gets bad PR from Christianity. He *is* the devil and all, but he's not a *bad* guy. He's dramatic."

That was one way to describe Samael, the First of the Fallen, as he presented himself in the guise of Nick Scratch, owner and bartender at the pocket dimensional speakeasy he named The Four Winds. He was also a devoted, loving husband to Lilith.

They made a cute couple. He also had a devastating array of infernal puns that he claims to have learned from his father.

I walked to the edge of the footprints farthest from the truck tire grooves. I kneeled and searched. Old Tom's Hill had a broken faerie ring, which made a nice "search here" marker. That diary entry Lady O'Cuinn read to me that revealed a burial place for a chest where Liam O'Cuinn buried his contract with Zozo. No such luck here. At least I wouldn't have a demon beat the shit out of me tonight. What's this?

My fingers brushed a clump of loose dirt aside and found a half-buried straw figure, maybe two inches tall and wearing a black cloth robe, with its face on backwards. Splotches of yellow powder, no larger than a dime, dotted the ground in the area. I shook my head. Dark magic.

"Hey, Des, come have a look. I think I found something."

She examined the figure. She flattened her lips in that way all the Grimm women did when frustrated. "Looks like a poppet, but the head's wrong."

I nodded and pointed at the ground. "Yeah, and sulfur residue surrounded it. I don't know what it means, but I know two things. Nick Scratch isn't involved in this, but a sorcerer of some sort is. That makes things easier."

Destiny yawned and patted her stomach. "Kind of. And I know something too. I'm hungry. You want to grab lunch?"

We drove to the Porker Smorkersboard south of Fiddler's Ford on Brody Farm Road. The best barbecue places are always just outside a small town on an old dirt road with no streetlights. The Porker was one of those places with oil drum grills and smokers bigger than the dining area. Before entering, you smelled the hickory, pecan, and apple wood chips used to smoke the pork shoulders, pork ribs, and sausage and to enhance the flavors of the meats on the grill.

We smelled the smoke from a mile away. The parking lot, which was little more than a rope-fenced gravel lot, was packed, but we snagged the last spot. During business hours, they kept the main door open, and so we entered through the ripped screen door. Wood chips and dropped pecans littered the tile floor. Vinyl tablecloths in black and garnet gingham checkerboard and emblazoned with a cartoon gamecock suggested the owners were USC fans.

We ordered our food and found a small table in the corner. Not having to sit at the long picnic tables was a relief. Destiny sipped her Cherry Coke, and I checked my phone. Nothing.

"She's safe, Sam," Destiny said. "Martin is by her side, and so are several members of her clan. She's in a private jet and not the cargo hold of a random ship."

I sighed and nodded. Carmilla traveled in style unlike Dracula who hid who he was when he traveled—and who just hid when he traveled. "Yeah, I know. I know. It's just—even though she didn't stay with me while she was here—I enjoyed being this close to her. I got used to being with her daily. And now my bed is going to feel huge."

Destiny nodded and kept her tone flat. "Vampires are great for keeping the bed cool."

I shook my head and sipped my water. A sigh escaped my lips as I remembered our nights together. I licked my lips.

"The nights were anything but *cool*. I notice her body temperature when I wake up, but it doesn't jolt me awake. I don't know. Maybe I've just matured enough for that to no longer be an issue."

The server, a teenager with brown pigtails and green eyes who wore a flannel shirt that matched the tablecloths, brought our food. Destiny sliced the two sausage links on her Porka-palooza Platter, drizzled the cane vinegar barbecue sauce on the pulled pork, and frowned at the French's yellow mustard. She hated most American mustards. My Pokey Pig Sandwich should've been a knife-and-forker, but I was determined to fit that massive pulled pork, bacon, homemade pickle, and grilled pineapple sandwich into my mouth.

Her mouth full of macaroni and cheese, Destiny asked, "Have you tasted the Countess' personal wine blend yet?"

I looked at Destiny, searching her face to discern her meaning. 'Milla doesn't have her own wine blend. Yes, vineyards grew on her ancestral lands, but she didn't have her own...Oh! I blushed and then rolled my eyes. I opened my mouth to state that I have not consumed my girlfriend's blood, but then the conversation at the table beside us drew our attention.

"Darren, just give it a rest. Craig Wellington is a good man. And he just lost his grandfather. So you hush."

Our eyes slid sideways to see the speaker, a scrawny, middle-aged white woman with a misshapen lion and cross tattoo on her right arm and assorted curlers in her salt-and-pepper brown bob. She jabbed her plastic spork at Darren's chest. Darren looked as chubby as my dad was, but, based on the ginger tufts poking out of his Atlanta Braves cap, he had more hair. He also had a scrawny mustache and wore a white tank top. Their three kids, two girls and a boy, dined with them.

"Come on, Marlene," he said, slamming his fist onto the table. "Don't tell me not to laugh at that dumbass going around telling everyone he got his ass beat by the Devil at the crossroads south of town and how he's about to lose both his and his granddaddy's souls. I may only have gone to high school, but even I know that ain't possible. It's funny."

Destiny leaned closer and lowered her voice. "He's going around town telling everyone? That's not good."

I sighed. "If he doesn't stop talking, we'll have the S-T's to deal with. I'd rather not have their interference."

Destiny sipped her soda and nodded. She shrugged. "At least he's pretty much at rock bottom. I mean, his wife left with their kid. He's got a dead end job. And people make fun of him. It'll probably still suck, but how much more can they do?"

The S-T's, or Stith Thompsons, weren't the most ruthless and vicious of the Watchers, at least regarding physical violence; they preferred to ruin reputations and careers. In Germany and Austria, the Grimms protected the secret with efficient kills—often as far removed as three degrees of association. The Duilearga in Ireland had an almost crusader zeal for keeping the Veil secret. And word on the street was that the Yanagita recruited from yakuza ranks. Regardless of the nation, Veil Watcher involvement complicated matters.

* * *

By sunset, the Darque Starfall Travelers Carnival opened its rope gate to thrill seekers at sunset. The neon lights imparted an ethereal glow to the booths, tents, and rides. A chilly breeze pushed fliers, napkins, and random papers about the carnival grounds. Adults and children laughed, screamed, cheered, and cried as they partook of the amusements. Goats, lambs, Shetland ponies, and other petting zoo animals stomped and bleated. Their scents blended with that of stale beer spilled on the benches, the earthy richness of cigarettes, and the oil-fried scents of carnival food.

The man in black, John of Helmstadt, strode through the

Boulevard of Games. His purple and gold scholar's robe billowed as he walked; the bells sewn into the seams twinkled. His eyes shifted from side to side as he observed children tossing rings, teenagers in love hurling baseballs, and adults firing toy rifles. A few won prizes, but most lost. A young, curly-haired boy carrying a stuffed bear twice his size raced across John's path. The boy's foot caught on an exposed board; he fell, scraped his knee, and cried as mud coated his new bear.

John of Helmstadt smirked. Schadenfreude. He approached the boy and raised the bear from the mud. The glassy button eyes remained empty and lifeless. He straightened the purple and gold polka-dot bow tie and then waved his hand over the bear. John's eyes shimmered with silver and amethyst flecks. And the mud disappeared. The boy stared slack-jawed at the performance. John handed the boy his bear, winked, and continued walking.

"Whoa. He's a wizard," the boy said. John of Helmstadt smiled.

Thirty-five years ago, that arrogant wizard and his cocky apprentice returned me to this world, freeing me from my unjust torture in the Malebolge. A dark chuckle growled from his lips. *All to prove that their theories were more than arrogant suppositions and youthful fantasy. And yet, they did what I could not. Through my tinctures and potions, I provided medicine whereby entire cities escaped the plague and a thousand desperate maladies eased. I, Johann of Helmstadt, was then naught but Faust and a man. And now, what am I but a spirit in a borrowed shell, wandering in a world no longer his own, consuming spirits lest the strength magic has placed in these bones wane.*

Johann of Helmstadt, Johann Faust, turned right before the rusty Tilt-a-Whirl with its chipped paint and flickering neon sign. He paused. Adults and children crowded into the blue rope-bounded line so the attending carny, a tall and lanky man with uneven shades of cerulean added to his short hair and both arms and his neck covered in tattoos acquired in prison, can take their ride tickets and direct them to their whirling seats set upon the spinning frame. Delighted squeals and laughter filled the air. A grown man vomited as he exited the ride. Faust shook his head and resumed his journey.

How the world has changed in the six centuries since I walked it last. A festival such as this would occur on a saint's feast day or a day of liturgical significance. Yet the workers here bear more in common with the unwashed roaming travelers from the east with their jangly and gaudy silk clothing, love for cheap beer, vulgar diversions, and deceptive fortune tellers. It surprises me that the local constabulary has as minimal a presence here as it does. From the moment I joined their ranks while I contend with this little matter, I have witnessed all manner of debauched criminality. Does the king of this land have no power? Shame. Perhaps I will take this land, my own heaven of this hellscape, as my own when my business is complete.

Faust stopped outside the House of Seven Devils. The faded black plywood exterior of the carnival's scare house featured six recesses with a central door. A gargoyle wearing a red devil mask loomed in each recess, and the door itself was a giant devil face with its mouth open. A young woman, her hair dyed purple and her lips painted black, rolled her eyes as teenagers ran screaming. Faust chuckled.

Some things have not changed. Humans still find themselves fascinated by Hell, from morality plays to Dante's poem to diversions such as this house of "horrors." Warnings of damnation entertain the masses too stupid to grasp the truth behind the myth. What was that you said, you old liar, about being confounded by ten thousand new hells daily simply by being denied the presence of an uncaring god? Ha! Hell is circumscribed in one self place, and you dragged me there, old "friend."

Faust made his way to the darkened edge of the carnival. There, a purple, red, silver, and gold striped tent stood. The sign above the door flap read "The Miraculous Magic and Astrological Alchemy of Doctor Faust, Warlock Supreme." Faust winced as his cheek burned. He entered the tent and passed through the makeshift parlor, where glass bottles contained herbs, tinctures, and swirling liquids. Behind the circular table with a crystal ball at its center, he passed through a black silk curtain to his dressing and sleeping area. He hung his robe on the plastic coat rack provided and changed into his costume, a generic red and black velvet "Renaissance Man" costume the carnival provided, slipped into his coat and the pointy black wizard hat adorned with glittering golden stars and silver moons.

Faust opened the small yew chest where he kept his jewelry. He donned the ornate silver pendant with a fist-sized penta-gram. He slid the gold bracelet from which thirteen hanging bells tinkled. And then he held the silver ring adorned with a ruby dragon biting its tail. Wisps of black smoke swirled inside the gemstone.

Now, I, who was once named demigod of Heidelberg, am reduced to being a conjurer of cheap tricks who tells fortunes of the basest sort for the groundlings of an ungrateful age. Here I wait, traveling with this carnival of sorts, until word arrives of the last target. The magician's apprentice, after thirty-three years of silence, demanded I repay the debt I owe for my freedom. A strange request of five souls collected in one ring. None of these souls seem particularly important or powerful, all simple humans leading simple lives. However, a debt owed must be repaid lest they undo the magic that gives me more than one bare hour to live.

He slipped the ring onto his finger. The bells on his clothing chimed their song as Faust exited his tent and into the open air of the carnival. The starless night was dark but filled with promise. Each carnival attendee carried potentialities with them that Faust could exploit and, if needed, steal. Faust mused on what his new life had become as he recited the barker's script given him.

Dozens passed his tent, giving Faust little more attention than a glance. Insignificant people living their insignificant lives. After an hour of barking, the crowds thinned. A handful of carnival attractions dimmed their lights. Shadows length-ened, stretching its tendrils over the remaining attractions.

A woman in her mid-twenties broke from her group of friends as they entered the House of Seven Devils. Dark roots crept toward the hair tie that held her ponytail in place. She wore a black hoodie with the garnet logo of the University of South Carolina emblazoned on the left breast and a pair of black Nike shorts. Her phone screen illuminated part of her face as she sent a text and then wandered toward Faust' tent.

As she approached, Faust finished his lines and said, "And you, fair maiden, what troubles your soul that you approach Doctor Faust, worker of miracles, for divination and succor?"

The young woman blinked, looked around, and pointed at her collarbone. "Me?"

"Aye, fair maiden. The carnival offers naught but my humble tent for the soul who ventures to this edge."

She massaged the back of her olive neck and shrugged. "I mean, I guess I could use a bit of guidance."

"Then, prithee, come."

She followed Faust into his tent. He snapped his fingers. Candles sprang to light, and tendrils of incense coiled around the girl as she approached the divinatory table. Faust produced an ornate wooden box, opened it, and unwrapped a stained deck of ancient tarot cards, many of which had singed edges. He shuffled the cards face down and then face up. He shuffled face down once more, his eyes glittering in the candlelight and locking with the young woman's.

"Games of chance," he said. "Matters of fate. There is little difference, and the tools of both are identical. What troubles your soul?"

She sighed. "I don't have much money to pay. Sorry."

Faust smiled. "I can work with what you have to offer in compensation. What troubles your soul?"

The young woman exhaled. Her muscles tensed. She lowered her gaze. "I want to know if my parents will ever accept me for who I am."

Faust nodded. He shuffled the cards three more times and then directed the young woman to cut the cards. From beneath the cut, the fortune teller drew seven cards and placed them face down on the table. As his hands touched the side of the first card, he paused to make eye contact.

"Are you prepared to learn the truth?"

She nodded, and Faust turned over the first card. The card appeared to be inverted, and it depicted two upside-down wolves howling at a circular moon covering the sun in a starless sky.

"The inverted Moon. Interesting. Do not look so dismayed; this card suggests that you have an easy path to walk where little change shall occur. Beside the moon, we have the

Emperor, the Seven of Coins, and the Knight of Wands, all reversed. Fascinating. You have no authority to demand the changes you seek; impulse and impatience guide you, but you have neither desire nor readiness for the struggle that will be necessary to achieve your goal."

He paused. The young woman nodded and swallowed hard. Her trembling index finger pointed at the remaining cards. "Do they offer something helpful?"

Faust nodded and flipped the next card. The woman's heart sank as he revealed another inverted card. This one depicted a young man riding a white horse with six vertical staffs. Faust shook his head.

"I see no victory for you, if you continue the path you have been walking. Your lack of courage bodes ill for your desires. And now, the inverted High Priestess chastises you for refusing to listen to your soul's voice, your intuition. This is the problem you have, young maiden. You know what you must do. Your soul has spoken to your heart. And yet, your mind refuses to act. Unless you change, you will not gain resolution. And finally,—"

"No, please. I'll pay for the reading, but I—there's too much negativity. I don't want to know what it says."

She reached into her backpack to find her wallet. Faust slid a cloudy quartz across the table. The young woman paused. Faces appeared in the swirling clouds within the crystal, contorting in agony; as soon as she recognized features, the face disappeared. Faust fidgeted with an abacus. A faint glow filled the crystal and reflected in the young woman's eyes.

"What's this glowy crystal?"

Faust continued his calculations without looking at the young woman. "A diviner's crystal. It helps me see exactly what you can offer in payment."

She nodded. Her eyes focused on the crystal. A face appeared and mouthed, "Help," before the swirls of smoke encircled and shredded it. The young woman recoiled, but then she leaned closer. The outline of another face formed. Features clarified amidst the swirling smoke tendrils. The young woman touched the warm crystal. A golden glow flashed in her eyes. She gasped, and a smoke tendril snaked from her open mouth and into the crystal. Her body collapsed, lifeless, and then transformed into ash.

Faust collected the crystal and saw the young girl's face swirling within it. "I do apologize, fair maiden, but I must maintain this unnatural body lest I be dragged again to Hell."

* * *

Time meant little in the circles of Hell. Those damned therein remained for eternity beneath the darkened sky, illuminated only by volcanic eruptions, bursts of flame fueled by the eternally regenerating bodies of certain sinners, and infernal storms. Sleep, dreams, and rest never came for the damned, and so time became meaningless, a circle of suffering repeating itself until the universe ceased to exist.

In the Fourth Circle of Hell, those who earned damnation for overspending spent their eternity brawling with those who earned damnation for hoarding wealth and resources while those around them suffered. At the center of this eternal battlefield, stood a golden tower with onyx window frames and entrance doors. Rumors persisted among the damned, false though they were, that whichever side won the brawl would possess the tower and its wealth. Irony and hope proved cruel in Hell. The tower contained the Office of the Infernal Exchequer and Accountant, Orguluth.

Orguluth sat behind his counting desk on the tower's highest floor. He was a corpulent fiend, whose egg-shaped head attached directly to his shoulders. His golden eyes gleamed with cruel light as he weighed and counted each soul who entered Samael's domain. He wore loose robes spun from golden thread and trimmed with crushed onyx. Once weighed and counted, he transmuted the soul into a coin and slipped the coin into one of the nine slots on his desk; from there, the soul traveled to the appropriate circle of punishment, where it would suffer for eternity. He glanced at the melee outside his window and smiled.

His office door slammed against the wall. He growled and turned his attention to the sound and saw a guardian fiend, its black fur covered in red and black scale armor, dragging a human soul by a molten collar. The human soul, a young woman whose dark roots crept toward the ends of her hair and whose stained and tattered University of South Carolina sweater fell from her body, writhed and wept as the fiend jerked the chain.

Orguluth sized them up. His shrill voice echoed through the circle as he said, "What is the meaning of this interruption? Why do you bring this soul back to my counting house?"

The guardian fiend growled. "Forgive the disturbance, Lord Orguluth, but there appears to be a mistake with the assignment of this soul."

"I do not make mistakes. My work is precise. This soul bears the taint of corrupt magic. Those whose magics pervert divine law are sent to the fourth malebolge on the Eighth Circle. Is that not correct?"

The young woman screamed as the molten collar burned her soul. The guardian fiend nodded. "That is correct, Lord Exchequer; however, when Drogmannon the Lord of Fraud examined this human, he found the malefic taint to be applied against her. Thus, he commanded me to return her to you for reexamination."

Orguluth gnashed his rotten, yellowed fangs and growled. "Bring the soul closer."

The guardian fiend yanked the chain attached to the molten collar, and the young girl's soul stumbled forward. Orguluth produced an eye loupe from a drawer on his desk and set it on his left eye. He appraised the trembling, weeping girl. She begged to be set free.

She winced as Orguluth's shrill voice warbled in her ear. "Tell me, little goatling, what experience you have with magic, astrology, witchery that corrupts the divine order?"

She shook her head. Her voice trembled as she said in her southern drawl, "None. I mean, I checked my horoscope once in a while, but that was it. Well, there was that fortune teller I visited at a carnival right before I woke up here, but that was it. I swear. I'm a good Christian girl. I don't belong here."

Orguluth and the guardian fiend laughed. "I cannot count the number of *good Christians* whose souls have earned a place here. I would suggest speaking the truth of your damnation."

As the young girl opened her mouth, trumpets thundered through the Fourth Circle. The young girl cowered as best she could against her chains. White light filled the Infernal Exchequer's counting house; the fiends recoiled and shielded their eyes. The light dimmed, and a brown-skinned figure with curly black hair and Semitic features, who wore a white cloak and a golden breastplate, emerged. He brandished a flaming sword.

Orguluth gnashed his teeth. He bowed without taking his glaring eyes off the new visitor. "Michael, Archangel and Protector, what brings you here?"

The Archangel pointed to the soul of the young girl. His voice sounded of rushing waters. "In your possession, Infernal Exchequer, is a soul who belongs to the Most High God. Per the Golgothan Accords, her soul has been purchased. Heaven is her reward."

Tears flowed from the young girl's eyes as she looked upon the angel. "I knew it. Praise Jesus! Oh, thank you."

Michael nodded. "It is so." He narrowed his eyes and returned his gaze to the glaring, fang-gnashing Orguluth. "Per the terms of the treaty, her soul is to be extradited immediately. Release her and hand her over."

Orguluth waved a dismissive hand. The guardian fiend produced a bone-white key and unlocked the collar. He removed it from the young girl's neck, and she ran to Michael. He wrapped his free arm around her and said, "Consider yourselves fortunate that you have the opportunity to perform your own inquest, as Father has yet to inform my older brother of this error. Samael will not be pleased when he learns of this."

Michael and the young girl vanished in a ball of divine light. When the darkness returned, Orguluth growled and flipped his counting desk over. He kicked the desk and screeched at the guardian fiend, "Fine I will conduct the inquest."

* * *

It was a busy night at the Four Winds Bar, the transdimensional speakeasy owned and operated by the Devil himself under the persona of Nick Scratch. The golden candelabra that stood atop the black oak tables had a fresh polish, adding to the allure of their blue flames. Werewolves with black, mottled gray, and tan fur contended with a sleuth of red-furred werebears in a drinking contest. Pitchers of rich amber and coffee beers sat atop their booth's edge. The air glittered around the table where the Faerie Court of Spring sipped wine and engaged in riddle games. In the northwest corner, a massive serpent with crystalline scales on its body, horns on its head, and an opalescent gem shimmering on its forehead lapped its sparkling water.

From the stage on the southeastern corner, a beautiful, leather clad woman with skin the color of burned caramel and long onyx hair, belted "Highway to Hell" with a band of demons providing accompaniment. A dozen patrons, including a pale-skinned woman with braided white hair and an Elven woman in blue and gray robes, turned their chairs to listen, toe tap, and sing along. Nick Scratch leaned on the bar, smiling as his wife Lilith performed.

Scratch presented himself as a tall, handsome man with olive skin and slicked black hair. Three days' growth of stubble formed his beard. He wore a white button down with the sleeves rolled to the elbows beneath a black vest and trousers. Both had ruby pinstripes. Scratch polished the crystal drink ware while chatting with the kitsune who sat alone at the ruby-flecked black marble bar, drinking plum wine.

His angelic tenor voice assumed the accent of an aristocratic Londoner as he said, "No, Mikoto, you cannot sue an American video game development company over a kitsune character that bears a striking likeness to yourself. While I believe you certainly have a case, we exist in a world where bringing your case forward would bring the wrath of Watchers in both Japan and the United States. And while I would be safe, the bloodshed among your people would be greater than any desire."

The young fox spirit had lustrous amber fur and white tips on her nine tails nodded. She wore a white kimono decorated with pink cherry blossoms. "I know you to be correct, Lord Samael, but I wish it were not so."

Mikoto continued sipping her wine as the night went on. Half an hour passed, and the western door opened. Nick Scratch cleaned the bar and bellowed, "Welcome to the Four Winds Bar where all are welcome to sit, drink, and tell their tales. The first drink is always free, and the only rule is no magic in my bar. Oh, it's you."

Lilith, singing "Magic Man," continued her performance as an imp shuffled toward the bar. The brownish-green scales that covered its body protruded from the black-trimmed golden tunic that marked them as as belonging to the Office of the Infernal Exchequer and Accountant. The imp's wings sputtered. It lowered its head and made itself small and low.

The imp hopped onto a bar stool and slid a sealed vellum scroll across the bar. The imp's nasal voice produced words in a hesitant, halting pace. "Forgive the intrusion, Lord Samael, but His Excellency, Orguluth, Infernal Exchequer and Accountant, bade me hence with this message for you, our Great Lord."

The Lord of Hell flicked the wax seal with his thumb. The seal burst into white flame and vanished. Nick Scratch scowled as he read the note. Two elegant, black horns pushed through his forehead and curled upward. His skin reddened. A growl rumbled from his lips, and he crumbled the missive.

Nick Scratch glared at the imp. "Summon your master. Inform him he is to meet me in the fourth pit of the Malebolge immediately. Malthriir, watch the bar. I have urgent business to attend to."

Nick Scratch vanished in a flash of smoke and fire.

Samael, the First of the Fallen, appeared atop the Obsidian Stair that connected the Malebolge to his own throne deep within Cocytus. Wearing his obsidian crown and ruby-trimmed black silk robes of office, the Lord of Hell strode past the titans, chained for their rebellion, to the inner ring of Malebolge. With his ruby-tipped obsidian rod in hand, Samael walked through the concentric circles of ditches where those damned through fraud receive their punishments. The stale air reeked of noxious sulfur, boiling pitch, and burning flesh. Dragons roared as their flames scorched sinful souls. Long clawed demons, the Malebranche, ripped the flesh of those damned herein. As Samael passed, soul after soul cried for mercy, but the First of the Fallen turned away from their faces.

When Samael reached the fourth bolgia, a squat demon with a reptilian head, eyes at the base of its snout, three taloned fingers on its spindly arms, and tiny wings stood at attention. This fiend wore black-trimmed golden robes of office. The fiend bowed at the waist and held the position. Samael rolled his eyes and bared his fangs. After a dismissive wave of his hand, the fiend rose.

The Lord of Hell roared at the fiend, "Why do you hide behind a disguise? Think you not that I am unaware of all who exist in my domain?"

The fiend shifted his form into Orguluth's customary appearance. He bowed. Orguluth's shrill voice warbled as he said, "Forgive me, my Lord. Oh! Greetings, Great Lord Samael,

First of the Fallen. I, Orguluth, am unworthy to be in your presence. Thank you, O Great and Mighty Lord, for gracing your worthless servant thusly."

"Explain to me, Orguluth, how a soul is no longer suffering its damnation. For unless the divine laws have changed, once a soul is so judged as worthy of torment, that soul remains here for all eternity. And explain to me how a soul marked for my father's house found its way here instead?"

Orguluth cowered. He wrung his hands and avoided Samael's gaze. The fiend swallowed hard. "Well, my Great and Gracious Lord, I—well, it has, as of this time, not yet been ascertained how the soul escaped divine punishment; however, my Noble Lord, I, your ever humble servant, have identified which soul has escaped. And I believe the soul's escape and the appearance of a redeemed soul are connected."

Samael sighed and pinched the bridge of his nose. "And that soul's name is?"

Orguluth shuffled from one foot to another. "Johann Georg Faust, my Lord."

Samael turned his gaze upon the fourth bolgia. Here, all those who defrauded through corruption of divine law and power were punished. Astrologers, seers, fortune tellers, and sorcerers. Upon reaching the bolgia, fiends twisted their heads, so their eyes faced backwards. For eternity, they must walk in a straight line around the ditch; each time they step from line, one of the Malebranche rips into their flesh with flaming claws. The tears brought on by their pain blinds them, preventing them from guiding any behind them.

Samael's nose flared, and his red eyes blazed. "That arrogant charlatan? He denied our existence and my authority while treating with Mephisto. I suffer none to mock me, least of all arrogant mortal magicians who pretend to be gods such as Faust. How long has he been gone?"

Orguluth produced his ledger and scanned the pages. "According to my records, Sire, Faust was present for the last accounting—fifty years ago."

"And you have no idea what happened? No evidence? Nothing?"

Orguluth shook his head. "We searched with all diligence, my Lord, and we found nothing of meaning."

"But you found something?" Samael slammed the butt of his rod into the obsidian bridge, punctuating each syllable.

Orguluth fished something from his robe. He neither spoke nor made eye contact with the Lord of Hell as he handed Samael two minor items. Samael turned them over in his hand. The first was a two-inch figure of straw wearing a black robe, its face placed on the back of its head. The second object was a silver star with eight points that appeared to have fallen from a pendant.

"Interesting," Samael mused as he turned the star over between his fingers.

"These objects mean something to you, my Lord?"

The First of the Fallen nodded. "I do not know who assisted *Doctor* Faust in his escape, but I know who will fix it."

Chapter 5

"Have you kept up with the reviews for Countess Karnstein's show, Sam?"

Destiny didn't wait until I poured my morning coffee to start with the questions. 'Milla's opening reception was almost a week ago, and she returned to Austria yesterday. The exhibition would last for another two weeks before they changed to the next exhibition—a nature photographer. I promised myself I wouldn't look at any reviews while she was in town in case they shredded her. And then there was the Wellington case. I had no clue what we were up against beyond a magician.

I shook my head and poured coffee into my *I drink all this coffee, and yet I still can't function straight* mug. "Not yet. I take it you have?"

Destiny swiveled in her chair. She locked eyes with me and winked as she slid her glare-blocking glasses onto the bridge of her nose. A smirk tilted on her lips. I sighed. Destiny cleared her throat.

"Okay, so the reviews were positive, glowing even. Everyone praised Carmilla's technique, dexterity of stroke, and intelligent but emotional composition choices. They noted that, in line with her 'hokey vampire' persona, she has mastered techniques of previous centuries while keeping current on watercolor trends. There was only one negative I could find, and I found it in three reviews."

I whistled. "That's pretty good. Art critics can be vicious. So, what's the negative?"

Destiny giggled. "Are you sure you want to know, Sam?"

She drew out the word "are". Today wasn't Talk Like a Pirate Day, one of Destiny's favorite silly holidays. I shot her a sideways glance, and her grin intensified. "Go ahead. What's the one negative?"

She punctuated her words with laughter. "The only painting they neither liked nor understood was the, and I quote, 'plus-sized 1940s housewife turned pirate.'"

Destiny doubled over in laughter I knew could be heard on the sidewalk. Housewife turned pirate? That didn't make sense. 'Milla didn't paint anything like that.

"What are you talking about? 'Milla didn't have any pirate paintings in her exhibition."

When the giggle fit ended, Destiny cocked an eyebrow and said, "Really, Sam? Really? Did you not see the massive portrait of you, dressed for an investigation, with a rapier and a pistol? Did you not see that?"

"Yes, I saw that. She surprised me with that one. I mean, I posed for it over Christmas, but I didn't know she would slip that into her show. What does that...are you fucking kidding me? *Me?* What's wrong with that portrait?"

Destiny snickered. "Technically, nothing. They praised her technique and composition. They lauded her for being size-inclusive. The thing is, Captain Hain, they didn't see how it fit into the rest of her work."

It's not like I didn't worry about fitting into her world before. I mean, she's a vampire. I'm a mortal. She's rich, and I'm clawing my way into the middle class. Sure, I grew up with some money, but nothing that held a candle to her ancestral holdings. She's also ten times my age, and it can make relating to her challenging. I know she loves me, but that voice in the back of my head still lets me believe she might leave me for someone with whom she has more in common.

Destiny walked over and hugged me. Her eyes softened as she looked into my eyes. "Don't listen. I know what you're thinking. Carmilla loves you. The two of you are happy together. Whether some bougie art critic sees it in the painting or not, *you*, Samantha Blake Hain, are amazing. And you know Carmilla wouldn't be with you if you weren't as amazing as she and I know you are."

I smiled and blinked to keep from crying. I hugged Destiny. "Thank you, Des. How do you always know?"

"Growing up a Grimm, I've learned to recognize certain signs. Speaking of, don't forget you changed your therapy session from Thursday at two to Monday at one this coming week."

"Shit. I'm glad you remembered. I should have started therapy earlier, but we barely had money to survive."

Destiny sighed. "Yeah, I'll never get used to why Americans don't think healthcare is a human right. Anyway, any ideas on who or what beat the tar out of Craig Wellington at the crossroads?"

Before I could answer, the office door opened, and he walked in. Nick Scratch strode into our office wearing a black suit with red pinstripes, a red shirt, black tie, and his black wingtips had red soles. Dapper as always. His skin had a red tint. Was this an official visit? He rarely reddened his skin tone at the Four Winds. What in the, well, hell was going on?

"Miss Hain, Miss Grimm." He bowed as he spoke.

I nodded and asked, "Mister Scratch, to what do we owe this pleasure?"

"Yeah," Destiny said. "It's not the full moon, so this must be an important case you need handled. Let me ready the contract."

He snorted. "I am not here to take out a contract, Miss Grimm. I am, however, here to enforce one."

So it was time. I swallowed hard. For six years, the blank check I offered him in exchange for one hour with my mom each year on my birthday has loomed over my head. I've asked to repay him several times, but he has always brushed it off. Now here we are. Time to pay up.

"We both knew this day would come, eventually. So, Mister Scratch, let's go into my office, and we can discuss the matter. Coffee? Tea?"

He shook his head. "Neither, but thank you. Shall we?"

He followed me to my office, and Destiny locked the main door behind us. She grabbed her notepad and followed. We sat in the leather chairs I set up around a small wooden coffee table to discuss cases in a more laid back setting. His eyes surveyed the office and appraised the furniture. That made me more nervous than the implications of his visit. My heart pounded.

I exhaled and asked, "So, Mister Scratch, while I know we have old business to attend to, I do have one question—and I know what your answer is going to be—but I have to ask this. Did you beat the crap out of one Craig Wellington at the crossroads south of Fiddler's Ford right before the full moon?"

I sipped my coffee as he eyed me. My question surprised him. "Fisticuffs? Ha! I have not been involved in a physical altercation of any kind since The War, and had that pompous soldier not had Father's backing, I would have won. Nor have I ever visited a crossroads in this state."

"But," Destiny said, "you have been to a crossroads before, yes?"

He nodded. "The last time I met with a mortal at a crossroads was nearly a century ago. Eighty-eight years, to be precise."

"Who did you meet? What did you discuss?" Destiny continued her questions.

He smirked and winked. "That is confidential. Might I ask why, Miss Hain, you asked that specific question?"

I set my mug on one of the lesbian pride flag coasters. "My Full Moon Special this month believes that the 'man in black' who beat the crap out of him is you. Seems his grandfather tells the story of fighting this man at the same crossroads thirty years ago, and he always said it was the devil."

"Ah." He leaned back and spread his legs as he sat. "Well, thematically, we are at a crossroads, Miss Hain. You can choose to surrender your soul now or fulfill the terms of our contract."

"What do you require of me?"

Nick Scratch reached into the interior breast pocket of his blazer and produced a red silk handkerchief tied with a black cord. He placed it on the table and pointed. I untied the cord and saw the contents, a small straw doll like the one we found at the crossroads and an eight-pointed silver star. An Astrum Argentum pendant. I sighed.

"You are not tasking me with returning to that fucking order, are you?"

He shook his head. "I am not. These items were found in the fourth bolgia of the Malebolge. A soul condemned therein has gone *missing*."

Destiny and I shot each other a glance. She whistled. I swallowed hard and asked, "Missing? As in somehow escaped

Hell missing?"

"Astute as always, Miss Hain. The soul in question is that of one Doctor Johann Georg Faust. Your task is to find him and return him to Hell."

"He's real? I always thought he was only a morality tale type of legend." I said in hushed tones.

"I assure you he is, was, quite real. I'm surprised you did not ask your beloved Countess why she is in possession of his grimoire in the dungeon of her castle."

I exhaled. My hand trembled as I sipped my coffee. "I assumed all those books were theoretical treatises. So, Faust. What's with the Astrum Argentum pendant then?"

"My assumption is that one of that order facilitated his escape. The poppet suggests some form of soul transference. Traditional necromantic philosophy suggests they sent his soul into a corpse, thus re-quickening it; however such rites have never been performed on a soul that has been judged and sentenced. Well, not with any degree of what could generously be called success."

I nodded. Destiny clicked her tongue on the roof of her mouth. She said, "Sam, that little straw figure looks like the one we found at the crossroads."

"Yeah. The head is on backwards for some reason. I thought it was a novice mistake, but if there was an identical one in Hell, then maybe it means something."

Mister Scratch drummed his fingers on the chair's armrest. "Sympathetic magic. Yes, I know you know what this is, but perhaps it has been some time since you read your Dante, Miss Hain? The fourth bolgia of the Malebolge is where astrologers, sorcerers, and their ilk are punished. Among other facets of their punishment, their heads are twisted to face behind them.

And his exodus is not the most annoying and problematic part of this."

I blinked. "Do I want to know what is more problematic than a soul escaping your, for lack of a better word, clutches?"

Nick Scratch chuckled. His fangs poked through as he smiled. "He appears to be sending Hell souls, or at least one soul accounted for thus far, who are owned by my father. I am certain you understand the nightmare that causes."

I did. Well, I didn't *fully* understand the problem, but I recognized that souls bound for Heaven but winding up in Hell could cause massive problems in the universe. I nodded. "How is that possible?"

Nick Scratch growled. "At present, I do not know. I know the soul he sent has the taint of his malefic upon them, which I surmise has caused the mistake in placement. According to the Infernal Exchequer, my annoying brother Michael collected the soul in question and *generously* offered us a chance to rectify the matter before Father became involved. So, we are on a time crunch, Miss Hain."

I exhaled and ran my fingers through my hair. "I don't suppose you would be generous enough to advise me on how to collect his soul, would you?"

He smiled, revealing his fangs. "A simple soul binding spell should suffice. I'm certain your father has one in his grimoire."

Of course, *he* would have the spell I need in his grimoire. Given that I shot him in the knee while he tried to offer Frank Caldwell, a probationer of his own fucking esoteric order, as a sacrifice to that demonic entity Zozo, I'm not sure I could ask to learn something that specific. But if the spell was in his travel grimoire, which I confiscated, I should be able to learn it myself. I mean, I know the basics of occult theory, and I've performed a few spells in my day. Sure, none were that advanced, but I could decipher my father's notes. I didn't need training. And if I needed backup firepower, I still had my Walther.

I nodded. "Okay. We have a contract, and this is what you require of me. How much time will you grant me to complete this?"

Nick Scratch rested his chin in the crook between his thumb and index finger. "I will give you until St. John's Night of this year to complete this task. Should you fail, I will collect your soul on the thirtieth of October. Miss Hain, always a pleasure. I trust you will be successful."

Mister Scratch rose to his feet and nodded his head, tipping his nonexistent hat. He winked, and then a ball of blue flame and smoke surrounded him. When the smoke dissipated, he was gone, leaving the stench of sulfur behind. Destiny and I made eye contact, and I sank into the chair. Fuck.

* * *

One benefit of the Astrum Argentum's blue and silver ritual robes was the fact that they camouflaged the few dozen extra pounds Donal Hain carried. His daughter remarked that both the silver outer-robe and the blue inner-robe had more pockets than most of her mundane clothing. If only she respected the tradition and hierarchy of the Order. The hood of the sleeveless, open-front silver over-robe concealed his bald head. Over the last decade, he ceased wearing a toupee, choosing instead to shave the remainder of his red hair. His beard, however, showed the silvering that marked his age.

On the same Monday as Sam learned how she was to repay Nick Scratch, Donal limped as he exited the hired car that drove him from the Debrecen International Airport to the small 14th century keep, Nándor Castle, for his conclave. He winced; after two reconstructive surgeries on his right knee, the pain his daughter's bullet caused him remained. Neither magical nor mundane pain relief provided permanent relief. That compounded the hurt that her refusal to accept that he knew what was best for her caused him.

The official records classified Nándor Castle as abandoned in the 16th century. Much of the white paint adorning the weathered iron gray stone walls had fallen away; dirt and age darkened what remained. Parts of walls and towers had fallen over the centuries. Scavengers had taken many of the crumbled stones for their own purposes. Most of the red wooden tiles that formed the castle's roof remained, but holes opened several rooms to the elements and the sky. Rumors persisted of spectral and demonic activity; this kept most people away, and those who ventured into the castle to seek the truth rarely returned.

The Order of the Dragon encouraged these rumors, as this allowed them to use this castle as a commandery center of operations with minimal interference from others. Arch Magus Donal Hain entered the castle through the warped and broken double doors and descended the circular stairs to the dungeon. Stale, moldy air filled the hallway as Donal's Chelsea boots echoed on the stone floors. When he reached a rusted door guarded by armed soldiers wearing Order of the Dragon tabards over their Kevlar, Donal Hain produced both his Hermetic Order of the Astrum Argentum pendant and the insignia marking him as the Arch Magus. The soldiers nodded and opened the door.

Electric lights set into the wall sconces illuminated the square chamber beyond the door. A portrait of Vlad Tepes adorned the north wall. A circular table and six chairs of varnished oak sat in the room's center. Two men sat at the table. The first, Knight-Commander Paul Bertalan, had curly black hair, brown eyes, and dark skin. He kept three days of stubble on his chin. The other, General Florian Amanar, tied his long chestnut hair with a cobalt ribbon that matched his eyes. A slim goatee adorned the angular jawline on his olive face. Both wore the Order of the Dragon tabard over their suits. They stood and shook the Arch Magus' hand, and then he sat at the table.

Bertalan passed the Arch Magus a glass of Pálinka whiskey and, in his gravelly voice, said, "Pleasure to meet you in person, Arch Magus Hain. I trust your travels were smooth?"

Donal nodded. His Irish brogue was evident in his words. "They were, thank you. I see by the emptiness on this table that your efforts to retrieve my travel grimoire have failed."

General Amanar glared as Bertalan said, "They have. Our agent reports that not only was he unable to find the grimoire in your daughter's home, but the traitor's estate steward accompanied her when she returned home from her tryst."

General Amanar's bass voice thundered as he asked, "Tell me, Arch Magus, why you need this grimoire. Is it your only one?"

Donal Hain sipped the apricot liquor. It was sweeter than he preferred. "Do I need it? No. That said, I do not want my daughter to possess it, lest she make use of it against us."

Or, in her arrogance, she may attempt workings beyond her ability and knowledge that could hurt her. Or worse.

Amanar nodded, sipping from his own glass. "Are you genuinely concerned with that prospect?"

Donal shook his head. He sighed. "My daughter is resourceful. The events in Bannagh have revealed that. She is untrained and lacks the necessary focus of intent to perform many of the workings in my grimoire. However, that precludes neither her training in the arcane arts nor allying herself with a trained magician who could easily make sense of my notes. The destruction of our enemies in Chelm is complete, and it seems your plans to resurrect the Impaler nears completion."

Amanar and Bertalan nodded. Bertalan said, "Yes, and once our great leader returns, we can begin our great shared conquest. We will bring the East to heel, and your Order will enlighten the West. I must say, your forethought has been quite useful. Thirty-five years ago, you produced the perfect agent for our needs. However did you anticipate that?"

Donal Hain leaned back in his wooden chair. The Order of the Dragon did not share the Astrum Argentum's affinity for leather and velvet furniture. Practicality trumped comfort in their aesthetic choices. Different worlds, but when trying to bring about a better world, stranger allies have joined forces.

"A magician must always be open to the Will of the Universe, Knight-Commander. My late master, Magus *Ambulabo Ex Tenebris,* hypothesized a soul could be excised from Hell through the sacrifice of enough souls to feed either a stone or crystal to function as an artificial animating life force. Finding a suitable host body was the challenge. The Order mocked him, saying that his theory sounded like something from a child's game. Even tales from childhood present truths and lessons."

General Amanar leaned forward and stroked his jawline. "So that operation that provided us with our soul collector was an act of spite? You had no grand agenda?"

Donal smirked and chuckled. He tipped his glass to General Amanar. "In the circles I travel, being right is as great a victory as moral superiority. The grand agenda of any magician is power and enlightenment."

Knight-Commander Bertalan checked his phone. No notifications. He scratched his head and asked, "But why Faust? Surely there must be other souls—Aleister Crowley, for instance—who would have been more suitable than that medieval charlatan."

"Why Faust?" Donal Hain stroked his beard and relaxed his gaze. "I asked my master that same question. And he responded that he chose Faust for ironic reversal. Faust, as his legend accurately reports, sold his soul for knowledge and magical power while not believing in the physical reality of Hell. As such, choosing to steal his soul from perdition would be an ironic reversal of fate. One damned for his path to power freed by another along theirs. A heart attack claimed my master shortly after we completed the working, so he never got to enjoy proving the Order wrong. I enjoyed it greatly, however. How far along in your plan has Faust moved?"

General Amanar held a ring between his meaty index finger and thumb. "All but one. He has brought us the souls of William Seward, Amelia Holmwood, Jamie Harker-Mercaida, and Percival Van Helsing. The Morris heir is the only remaining soul needed so that our great lord may return at full power."

"Good. My apprentice is scouring the world to find us a suitable replacement for the sacrifice, as our benefactor in the Court of Autumn grows impatient, waiting for the war to begin. And where is Faust now? Has he found the location of this final soul, or has he returned to Helmstadt to gather souls and strength, given the temporality of his new body?"

Knight-Commander Bertalan scratched his nose. "It seems our good doctor has returned to his old tricks while we search for the location of the Morris heir. He's been traveling with a carnival that has pitched its tents south of Butcher's Bend, South Carolina."

"That places him in proximity to your daughter, Donal, does it not? And to your grimoire?" General Amanar leaned forward and pressed his fingers together. "Perhaps he could obtain your precious grimoire."

Donal Hain coughed and sputtered. "Unnecessary. I would advise Faust to avoid contact with Samantha. Can she match his magic? No. Could her firearm kill him? If our theories hold, yes, but she could not return his soul to Hell without first destroying his soul gem and binding his own soul to another object. It would then be a simple matter of providing him a new body to inhabit. That said, she has allies in Butcher's Bend, and together they could derail our work."

"Perhaps," Knight-Commander Bertalan said, "we could send an agent to assassinate your daughter. Then retrieving the grimoire would be easy."

"Do you not think that, after your last failure, that Samantha's allies—particularly the Karnstein-Bertholt vampires—have not increased security on her home? Your agent dropped his cell phone, issued to him by your Order. Given that clan's relationship to Vlad Dracula, I doubt negotiations will be possible."

Bertalan refilled his glass with the apricot liquor. He raised his left eyebrow and eyed Donal Hain's face with care. Hain was a barrister. Bertalan asked, "Is that your sole concern, Donal? I understand that our business has tested your already strained relationship with your daughter. Be honest. We understand that some part of you may desire to protect her."

Donal Hain tugged at his collar and snorted. General Amanar

leaned back and smirked. "Yes, Arch Magus. After all, you covered for her when she did not appear for the meeting with Count Bha'esi, chose another for the sacrifice to control Zozo, and fled the battlefield after she shot you, leaving your precious grimoire behind. Your magic could have turned the tide in our favor. Why did you not fight? Some might assume your loyalties and devotion to our shared cause is suspect. Is that the case?"

Arch Magus Donal Hain rose from his seat. He glared at the other men and, with the force and authority of both a barrister and a power magician, said, "Remember, gentlemen, that it was my magic, my focus, and the force of my will devoted to our shared cause that has thus far placed all but one soul in that signet ring. My magic and devotion have allowed us to obtain an extra-planar benefactor."

Donal walked to the door and, without turning to gaze upon his allies, added, "As any with knowledge of practical combat tactics would know, a tactical retreat to regroup is preferable to charging in when one falsely believes one has the advantage and thus failing horribly. Like that little squire you sent after Samantha in Austria."

He exited the chamber.

* * *

On the Saturday night after Donal Hain flew home to Dublin, Samantha Hain sat in the passenger seat of Destiny Grimm's Navarra Blue Audi A3. The late March night was cool and cloudy. Sam sipped her black coffee while Destiny ran into Don's Gas and Snacks to grab an orange vanilla Coca Cola and a bag of peanut butter M&Ms. Half an hour later, Destiny returned with plastic bags filled with Doritos, sour cream and onion Pringles, double stuffed Oreos, two Monster Energy Drinks, her soda, the M&Ms, and a microwaved burrito. A smiling sunflower wearing sunglasses charm dangled from her key chain. She handed Sam one of the energy drinks and started the car.

"Sugar to keep you awake; caffeine to make you social."

Sam narrowed her eyes and shook her head. She chuckled. "Trying to say something, Des?"

Destiny switched on her "War Songs" playlist. As "Bloody Tears" from *Simon's Quest* played, Destiny merged onto Highway 178 and then said, "You actually took a call from your dad today. That's never put you in a good mood. So, I'm trying to cheer you up with an evening of good, clean, family-friendly fun."

Family-friendly fun? Mini golf? I'd enjoy that. Given the snack haul, I'd almost say she planned for us to spend the night watching cartoons. But she was right about what talking to my father did to my mood.

Sam nodded and sipped the energy drink. "Fucking asshole demanded I return his grimoire. After trying to sacrifice Frank to that demon, whatever he got himself involved in with the Order of the Dragon, and after what those fuckers tried to do to both 'Milla and me in Austria, he acted like he could just order me around."

Destiny nodded as she bobbed her head to the music. "Hear me out. Give it back to him. I'm not done, Sam. Why do you need the book? We could scan the pages and have any information inside. Then, with the book gone, you wouldn't have thieves breaking in."

Why didn't I think of that? Shit. This is one of the many reasons I love Destiny. And yet, part of me feels I should keep this book from him. Mostly out of spite. But what if there's a clue that I haven't found? I'd give the book another look-over tomorrow. I was curious about Destiny's plan for tonight.

Sam tensed and closed her eyes. "I'm almost afraid to ask, but what do you have in mind?"

"You'll see." Her grin broadened. Her cell phone played the opening theme from *Yamada-kun and the 7 Witches*. She pressed the "hands free" button on the steering wheel.

"Hey, Jeremy. How was your day?"

"It was okay, babe. You on the road yet?"

She nodded. Her smile remained. "Yeah. Sam's in the car, so I'm going to sign off. Don't want you spilling the beans on the surprise. See you tomorrow?"

"You bet. And I can keep secrets. Sometimes. But yeah, I'm going to play some *Call of Duty* with Byron, Wade, Andrew, and Brian. Have fun! Love you."

"Love you too." She ended the call.

As "The Princess Striga" played, Sam laughed. "Y'all are cute together. Things seem to have picked up."

"Yeah. We had a talk, and I was ready to break up with him. Then he said he loved me, and you know I love him too. I have romantic feelings, and then we cuddled until after midnight. I told you all that, but we've been cuddling a lot more. And I don't know, maybe things are changing? I don't know. I love him, so yeah."

Sam placed her hand on Destiny's shoulder. "I'm happy for you, and I support your decision either way. And I won't even use your romance as inspiration for fanfiction."

The pair laughed. They continued chatting and laughing as they drove down the dark southern highway. They neared the crossroads where Craig Wellington fought a man Sam now believed to be connected to the emergence of Doctor Faust. Maybe he was the magician who freed Faust. Unlike the fantasy novels she and Destiny read, many ranking magicians in the Astrum Argentum also worked out extensively. Donal Hain was not one of them.

She shared Craig's concern, because she owed Nick Scratch that favor, and he called it in. Return Faust to Hell. And she needed magic beyond her training and experience. She had no time to train. Her father said she needed years to reach a level of mastery, and she had until the summer solstice. Or she would spend eternity in Hell. Sam sighed.

The carnival's neon lights illuminated the darkness. They pulled into the grass field that served as the parking lot. Destiny turned and, with a smile that rivaled a Gotham City supervillain's, said, "Your Destiny brings you to the carnival."

Sam shook her head and smiled.

A thick crowd milled about the Darque Starfall Travelers Carnival on this cool, cloudy March night. Conversations, laughter, and barking filled the air. As they moved through the Boulevard of Games, Sam was thankful she wore her orange cardigan over her sleeveless blue swing dress. Destiny bounced, wearing her Pikachu hoodie and skinny jeans. Sam debated if the constant movement resulted from sugar intake or Destiny's natural energetic personality. Perhaps it was both.

After failing to win any prizes by tossing ping-pong balls into fishbowls, flipping rings onto milk cartons, or whacking mechanical moles, the Wylde West Rootin' Tootin' Shootin' Galleria called to Destiny. The carny working that booth wore an oversized blue ten-gallon hat, a blue western shirt with red trim and fringe, and a silver-trimmed blue star on his chest. The young man, whose gangly body suggested a teenager, had a haggard face that looked far older. His costume, which resembled a cross between a vintage Hollywood cowboy and a Dallas Cowboys mascot, did not suit him.

Sam traded her tickets for what resembled a Daisy Red Ryder painted in patriotic stripes. After two practice rounds, her third attempt knocked over a single bullseye on the middle tier. This earned her a plastic "Deputy" star. Destiny traded tickets, examined the rifle, thought for a second, and then fired three shots. Three moving armadillos on the far row fell in rapid succession. She waved away the prize and traded tickets for another round. The more wooden armadillos fell. This time, she accepted her prize, a chestnut teddy bear the size of a German shepherd with a white belly and muzzle.

Satisfied with her performance, they left the shooting gallery. Sam said, "That's amazing. How'd you do that? These games are always rigged."

Destiny hugged her bear and nodded. "Sure are. KSK training. The gun felt heavier than it should have, so I checked. The barrel was slightly thicker on the right side, so I knew to compensate. That is how I won *Panzerschwein* here."

Sam blinked. "You named the teddy bear *Panzerschwein*? I've known you since college. How does this surprise me?"

"Don't you make fun of my son's name. He's a beary good boy. Later tonight, I'm going to buy him *lederhosen* to match my *dirndl*. And don't you—ooh! Funnel cake."

The Tilt-a-Whirl upset Sam's stomach, but Destiny whistled while devouring her funnel cake. After she cleaned up and fixed her makeup, they continued their nocturnal adventure. With a giant corn dog in one hand and *Panzerschwein* in the other, Destiny led Sam through the carnival. The young carny and several attendees glared as they exited the House of Seven

Devils in laughter. They knew Dante's vision of Hell was far closer to fact than this classic *Loony Toons*-inspired horror show.

Sam and Destiny walked around the edge of the carnival and noticed a large crowd gathered outside a purple, red, silver, and gold striped tent. From the gasps and cheers of the crowd, the reek of burned sulfur, and the cheesy banter, they surmised this to be a sideshow magician. Sam rolled her eyes, but Destiny hooked her arm around Sam's elbow and dragged her into the throng in time to see the magician pull a bat from his cheap-looking Renaissance fair costume hat, snap his fingers to summon a cloud of pink smoke around the animal, and transform it into a dove. The crowd applauded, but Sam focused on the sign above the tent's flap, "The Miraculous Magic and Astrological Alchemy of Doctor Faust, Warlock Supreme."

She nudged Destiny's shoulder and gestured with her chin. "Look at the name. Got to be a coincidence."

"Duh. At least he's entertaining. He's oddly cute too, but in a dirty, Geralt of Rivia way. Also, he looks like you'd need a dozen shots after you even kiss him."

Sam feigned nausea. "He's got the dirty and diseased look down, but the 'Warlock Supreme' title? So tacky. Come on, let's go."

Destiny turned her right ear toward him and closed her eyes. "His fake accent isn't a terrible Bavarian. Almost sounds natural."

While they whispered, the crowd around Doctor Faust thinned. And then Faust said, "Perhaps, young ladies—yes, you two with the giant bear—perhaps I could answer a question regarding your futures? The cards and the stars know all, and they reveal secrets of love, family, career, and fate to me. Why not step into my tent and allow Faust, your humble servant, to pull aside the veil of mystery?"

Sam rolled her eyes, turned toward Faust, and waved her hand. "Thanks, but if I need life advice, I have a bartender I can go to. And he has a controlled climate."

"Oh, come on, Sam," Destiny said. "This'll be fun." She leaned close to her friend. "Either we have a good laugh later or we learn something that helps."

"You don't really think that he's real, do you?"

"No." Destiny winked and trotted toward the tent. She smiled at Faust and said, "My friend's a bit shy, but we'd love a tarot reading."

Sam sighed and shook her head. And then she joined Destiny at the tent. Faust lifted the entrance flap, bowed and extended his arm in welcome, and followed the women inside. He snapped his fingers, illuminating the candles. Destiny gasped and flitted about the racks of potions whose liquid contents swirled and sparkled in their glass vials. Sam, gazing upon the gaudy decor, bit her tongue as laughter threatened to erupt. Faust moved behind the table and produced the box containing the tarot cards.

"Well," he said. "I am Doctor Johann Georg Faust, alchemist, astrologer, miracle worker, and warlock supreme. With whom do I have the pleasure of spending a few moments this evening, and which of you will learn their fate first?"

Sam rolled her eyes at his recitation of Wikipedia facts. Destiny raised her free hand and hopped in front of the table. "I'll go first. I fear not the decree of fate, for I am Destiny."

Sam rolled her eyes again. Faust shuffled the cards and said, "Well then, Destiny, who fears no fate, focus upon the question you desire answered and cut the cards where you feel is correct."

Destiny cut the cards. Sam heard her mother's admonition about rolling her eyes out of their sockets. She bared her teeth. This was ridiculous. Faust arranged the seven cards in the form of a horizontal cross. At least he chose the Saint George's Cross spread instead of the basic Celtic Cross that every drunken, hemp-wearing hippie white girl did for free at college parties. He flipped over the first card, an inverted knight in a golden tabard and holding a lance riding a red horse.

"You lack patience," he said. "But you also lack the courage to take the path you know you must walk." *Oh, I can't imagine how you guessed Destiny lacks patience. Whatever could have enabled such a penetrating insight.* Faust continued by flipping the second card. "Ah, I see a balance of giving in this situation. Please do not hesitate to continue giving of your wealth, be it coin or knowledge or skill, but be willing to accept such gifts in return."

Destiny turned her head and said, "That sounds more like you, Sam."

Sam shook her head. Faust continued the reading. He praised Destiny for her vision and forethought, encouraging her to think bigger. She nodded when he asked if her endeavor began poorly. He noted that although she has achieved much, she felt constrained and shackled by her current path. Destiny lowered her gaze and swallowed. She hugged *Panzerschwein.*

Faust flipped the last card, the inverted Ace of Wands, and said, "If you continue along your current path, you will have no growth."

"Yeah, I figured that." Destiny's voice was soft and quiet.

Sam placed her hand on Destiny's back, and Destiny offered

a weak smile. "Come on, Des. Let's go."

Faust turned his gaze to Sam and asked, "Do you not wish to know your answer, Samantha?"

Oh look, he extrapolated my full name from Destiny's sarcasm. Sam shook her head. "No thanks, Dumblesnore. I'm good."

Sam turned to leave, but Destiny held back. Sam opened her mouth to speak, but Destiny cut her off. "Come on, Sam. We're here. Yours has to be better."

Sam narrowed her eyes. She sighed and softened them. "Only if you let me treat you to something fun and light afterward, like ice cream and *Mario Kart.*"

Destiny nodded and smiled. Sam hugged her and then she walked to the table. Sam's face screamed annoyance and unbelief. Faust smiled and shuffled the cards. Sam cut them near the bottom of the deck. Faust lay out the spread and then flipped the first card. Its inverted image depicted a family beneath a rainbow of ten golden chalices.

Faust lowered his head. "I am sorry. You did not come from a happy family. An only child, ignored by one parent and abandoned by the other."

Sam clenched her teeth. Destiny slid beside her and placed a hand on Sam's back. Faust observed her response as he flipped the second and third cards. "The Two of Wands. I see success and neutrality. You have plans, plans you need to make, tasks you need to accomplish, but you have taken no action. That will not serve your purposes. And the inverted Nine of Wands tells me you have been careless. With all the energies swirling around you, acting without forethought could lead to trouble."

Faust turned over the next card. Death, wearing black armor, trampled adults, children, and clergy as he rode on his horse. Sam held her breath. "Something must come to an end.

Perhaps an attitude, a relationship, or a cherished ideal. That which holds you back must fall away. And here we have the miserly, change-fearing Four of Pentacles and the combative, short-tempered Page of Swords. Aren't we resistant to change, to aid, to advice without any good reason?"

As Faust touched the final card, Sam turned and said, "That's great. I've had enough. Come on, Des. I don't need a stranger to insult me simply because I didn't want a fucking Tarot reading."

She stormed out of the tent. Destiny narrowed her eyes and pursed her lips. Arguing with Sam when she was in this mood would only end in a shouting match. As the tent flap swung closed behind them, Faust flipped the last card, a tower struck by lightning. He smirked and said, "The stars still move, time runs, the clock will strike."

Chapter 6

My shower started running. My eyes shot open, and I sat up in bed. Traces of light crept through my curtains. I grabbed the bat I kept under my bed. The balcony door was still locked. I heard footsteps. My heart raced. Where was Sandy Paws? Was she okay? I inhaled and held the breath. Calm down. Think. Be rational. The Order of the Dragon wouldn't try again so soon. Would they? The Astrum Argentum maybe? I tensed my body and then released my breath.

I slipped on my bathrobe and crept into the hall. The footsteps came from the master bathroom. They stopped, and I heard the plunk the toilet lid made when raised. The key to my working room and altar were still in my bedroom, so why was the thief in my bathroom? My breathing quickened and became shallow. I winced, closed my eyes, and shook my head. I'll get them with their pants down. I won't freeze like last time.

My feet inched toward the bathroom door. A yawn escaped my lips; I slammed a hand over my mouth. Shit. Did they hear it? I tensed every muscle in my body and reached for the doorknob. You can do this, Samantha. This fucker is still on your toilet, so they can't react to a surprise attack. On the count of three. My arms trembled. One. I took a deep breath. Two.

My heart thundered. Three. I burst through the door.

A woman's scream startled me. The bat thumped as it hit the floor, and I saw Destiny fucking Grimm seated naked on my toilet. My chest heaved. I panted and braced against the sink. Sandy Paws trotted in and licked my toes.

When I regained my composure, I asked, "Destiny, what the fuck are you doing?"

She spread her legs and looked down. Then she locked eyes with me. "Pooping. And then I'm going to take a quick shower. Don't worry, I'll save you most of the hot water."

I ran my fingers through my tangled hair. "It's too early in the morning for this."

She rolled her eyes. "It's almost ten. We have brunch at one. And thanks for the impromptu sleepover last night."

I nodded and smiled. "Those readings were something else. I don't know why we don't do these sleepovers more often. It's like the good old days in college."

Destiny smiled. "We should. I mean, we always *could* do these, but now that we're both in better places financially and all that, we should do these once a month. Just without the baseball bat."

I shrugged. "Sorry about that; my brain doesn't function first thing in the morning."

"I know," she said. Sandy Paws jumped onto her lap. Destiny shook her head and stroked Sandy's fur. "I've already fed the baby, and there's fresh coffee in your press. That pod machine is stupid and unnecessary. You drink way too much coffee to not know that. Just add hot—not boiling—water. Get your brain in gear, and I'll be done by then."

I left the bathroom and made my way to the kitchen. Sandy Paws followed. True to her word, Destiny prepped my coffee, and I saw she also took out the trash and started the dishwasher. She even set out my *I work hard so my cat can have a better life* mug, my medications, and a glass of water. Having Destiny sleep over felt like college. We met in Dr. Paulson's Intro to Psychology class when I arrived early and this cute, bubbly blonde who sat in front of me spun around and asked if I wanted to grab free pizza at the Anime Club's meeting. I'd never watched a single episode of any anime. Destiny spent the next ten minutes explaining the plots of her favorite anime, which didn't make much sense to me, but I thought she was cute, so I agreed.

I was still closeted at the time and terrified to talk to girls, a fact that hasn't changed much over the years; Destiny became my wing woman. Her charm and natural authenticity made me seem like I was so much more interesting than I was, especially when people couldn't learn certain truths that we both knew. Her knowing about the Veil helped. And I could talk to Des about anything. She was the first person I came out to, and when I came out to Mom, she asked if Des and I were a couple. I knew she had no interest, but we became inseparable. She really is my best friend.

Destiny finished her shower and dressed before I drained the French press. She wore a cream blouse with a Peter Pan collar embroidered with birds and flowers and a robin egg blue suspender skirt. We chatted as I finished my coffee. Sandy Paws moved between us, demanding and receiving pets from us both. I set my mug and French press in the sink and went to shower. I laid my yellow fit and flare dress with a white Peter Pan collar on my unmade bed. Then I set my hair in a bun, dressed, and Destiny and I headed out.

This March Sunday was colder than a sleeping vampire.

That meant everyone was inside City Star Grill's red brick building, so we got to sit outside. A hostess had already seated Laura Kensington and Kamama Thomas at one of the circular wrought iron latticework tables when we arrived. The bottles of prosecco and peach nectar on the table signaled today was bottomless bellini day. I'd prefer a brunch with bottomless Old Fashioneds, but Bellinis were better than mimosas. Laura's plum pant suit and lavender button down made her eyes pop, and Kamama's Cherokee features shone in the copper pencil dress she wore over her olive skin. We hugged and sat.

After Destiny and I made our Bellinis, Laura tapped her spoon on her champagne flute and said, "Now that we have all arrived, the March Meeting of Girls Only Brunch can commence."

Girls Only Brunch was our tradition once we realized how busy our lives became. On the last Sunday of each month, the four of us gathered at City Star Grill for brunch. This was our time. No one else, not even partners, could join. Sure, we brunched as a group with our significant others on other Sundays—just not on *this* Sunday.

"So, Kamama," I asked between sips, "how's the bookstore coming along?"

Kamama thought for a moment. Then she scrunched her face, shrugged, and exhaled. "I'm tired of filling out and filing paperwork. I'm glad I have friends like you and Laura to can help me navigate all the legal necessities. But, barring any other global meltdown, The Reading Raven Bookstore and Cafe will open its doors to the public on November 1st. And we should be able to have a special opening event for your birthday, Sam."

"That's about a month ahead of your estimate. Awesome."

I was happy for her, but I couldn't tell her I might not be there.

I mean, everyone here knew about the Veil and everything else for various reasons. That's one reason we met and bonded. All I had to do was trap the soul of a powerful magician who escaped from Hell and return it to Nick. Nothing I couldn't handle. Easy. And then party with my friends here and then spend time with Mom at the Four Winds.

Destiny asked, "You got a menu for the cafe yet?"

Kamama nodded and sipped her drink. "Anders and I have a tentative menu. We're going to have four sandwiches with three bread options, two seasonal salads, three seasonal desserts, and a New York cheesecake. And thanks to Laura, I've got local artists contributing to the decor with pieces they get to sell."

"When friends and neighbors help each other, the community gets stronger," Laura said. "Always said that creators have to help each other, because it's both hard to get your name out there and scary to try it alone. But when we do, everyone benefits. Speaking of benefiting from the connectedness of the arts, Sam, how'd it feel to be the subject of a painting?"

Destiny snorted and whistled "Wellerman." I shook my head and sighed. "I wasn't surprised-surprised. She painted me from our second date, the first time we dated, which was at the Zed opening reception here. That surprised me. I posed for this one, but I didn't expect to see it in her exhibition. Or get the reaction it got."

Our server brought our food. As the runny yolk sank into the fluffy biscuit City Star used in their eggs benedict, I thought how ironically perfect—no, maybe unsettlingly perfect—that review was. Out of place. Didn't belong. Who makes a deal with the devil and gives him a blank check? Couldn't develop a normal unhealthy coping mechanism like bourbon or shopping, could I?

Laura cut her croque madame in half and dragged a fork filled with hash browns through the oozing mornay sauce. "Yeah, the critics didn't get it. And with you right there, I'm surprised they didn't. But I liked how the piece looked out of place at first glance. But when you really examined Carmilla's work, you saw she put all her technique and passion into depicting you on canvas. I thought it unified the collection in a smart, subtle way. But the critics loved her work; that's what's important, and you are the reason she agreed to display her talents for mortal eyes."

Destiny drizzled hot honey over her chicken and waffles. Her face remained devoid of emotion as she said, "Plus, we all want to hear about the adventures of the dashing pirate, Captain Samantha Hain, scourge of the Patriarchal Seas and freer of the oppressed and endangered, but when a pretty woman appears on deck, disaster strikes our heroic Captain Hain silent."

She smiled as she chewed. Laura and Kamama laughed. I rolled my eyes and chuckled. "I'm sure when you take a break from your night-long cuddle sessions with Jeremy, you'll write those tales for us."

Destiny stuck her tongue out at me and stabbed one of my home fries with her fork. As she devoured the "potato tax," Kamama leaned forward and smirked. "Night-long cuddle sessions? Destiny Ilsa Grimm, is there something you're not telling us?"

"Nope. I might have had something to tell you today, but Sam and I had a slumber party after that creepy fortune teller at the carnival gave us disturbing tarot readings. Great funnel cake and corn dogs, though."

My father called during brunch; I dropped my phone into

my purse. Brunch continued for four more bottles of prosecco. We cut Destiny off during our fourth bottle when her German accent grew thick and she sang love songs to her potatoes. She sipped her sparkling water with a mock pout on her face, occasionally mumbling something about the lack of proper beer at City Star. After paying and tipping our server, everyone hugged. It might be one of our last group hugs, but only I—and perhaps Destiny—realized that.

As we drove back to my house, Destiny said, "And you know I'll watch both Sandy Paws and your house while you're getting some R&R in Austria. Also, I'm going to spirit the 'you-know-what' from your working room to my safe while you're gone. Just in case."

"R&R?"

She smiled. "Research and relaxation."

I laughed. "Time to fuck up my sleep schedule."

"Literally."

Destiny snorted and guffawed the rest of the way home.

* * *

Fiddler's Ford Southern Baptist Church stopped Sunday night services three years ago when the Department of Motor Vehicles ordered a deputy to take away Mrs. Hattie Davis' driver's license because of blindness. At that point, Reverend Ezekiel "Zeke" Daniels realized the aging population of his congregation meant adapting the service schedule to the needs and abilities of their aging congregation. Besides canceling Sunday night services, Wednesday night services only happened between April and September. Reverend Daniels also purchased a twelve-passenger van that he and Aaron Walker, the choir director, used to transport elderly parishioners.

The church itself was a small tuning fork-shaped wooden building dressed in chipping white paint. A small steeple rose over the sanctuary's double doors where the deacons offered burnt offerings of Camel before and after the services. Cathedral windows lined the walls. The church's burgundy van and Reverend Gordon's white Chevrolet Malibu sat in the gravel parking lot that connected the church to the parsonage.

Reverend Zeke Daniels was on the younger side of Southern Baptist ministers in this part of South Carolina. A married man with two sons, Daniels was in his mid-thirties, had dad's body earned from second helpings of fried chicken and a farmer's tan from years of yard work and construction. His brown hair started thinning when his first son, Joshua, started driving last year. His chocolate eyes radiated kindness and love. He sat in his office behind the sanctuary and prepared his sermon for Wednesday night's service. Engrossed in his work, he did not hear Craig Wellington arrive until he stepped into the sanctuary.

Craig's boots echoed as he stepped onto the varnished pine floor in the sanctuary. He walked along the central aisle between the two rows of sixteen varnished pine pews with their burgundy cushions and slid into the second from the altar at the front. He sighed as he sat on the threadbare spot where his grandmother sat during her sixty-two years as a member. The garnet *Baptist Hymnal* and a black copy of the King James version of the Bible sat in the pocket-like shelf affixed to the back of the first pew.

"Service isn't until Wednesday, Craig," Reverend Daniels said in his Appalachian tenor. "Did you need something?"

Craig ran his hand over his bald head. He stood and shook

the pastor's hand. "I just needed a safe place to sit and think, Zeke. Things have been, well, rough lately."

Craig sat, and Reverend Daniels sat beside him. "Amy hasn't come home yet?"

Craig shook his head. "And everyone thinks I'm crazy for knowing what I know. You and every other preacher we've had has told us that we're fighting a war against the devil. We sing about being Christian soldiers. But when I say that I got the shi—sorry—the poop beaten out of me by the devil and that he threatened to take my soul and my grandpa's. Can he do that? Can he rip grandpa's soul from Heaven and drag it to Hell?"

Reverend Daniels exhaled hard. He placed a supportive hand on Craig's shoulder. "You've been going through a dark valley lately, and no one blames you for being upset and afraid. I don't know what to say about your fighting the devil in the flesh, but I know for a fact that if a soul is in Heaven, the devil can't take it to Hell. And if you've accepted Jesus Christ as your personal savior, he can't take your soul either. Whoever told you he could lied to you. A lie straight out of Hell."

Craig nodded. "I was hoping you'd say that. If you don't mind, I'd like to just sit and think. Maybe pray."

Reverend Daniels nodded. He rose and left Craig to his thoughts in the unlit sanctuary. His mind drifted to the evening when Amy's parents drove away with Amy and Justin. Craig begged her to stay, but she said she could not stay with someone whose reckless behavior threatened their family. The sound of a Jack Daniels bottle shattering as it hit the wall echoed and reverberated through his mind. The knob on the front door clicked and turned. Craig turned. No one was there.

Craig scooted over as if for one person and stared at the cushion. That was his grandmother's seat. Her funeral was standing room only. They placed her pine casket with its burgundy velvet cushions atop the church altar. Everyone sang "I Need Thee Every Hour," and tears fell from Craig's eyes as he remembered his grandfather breaking down on the line "I need thee every hour, in joy or pain." Indistinct whispers lurched from the back pew. Craig turned. No one was there.

Both funerals ended with "Just As I Am." Grandma Wellington always said, "If that's good enough for Billy Graham, it's good enough for me." Craig stared at the altar, a simple pine table with the words "In Remembrance of Me" burned into the side facing the pews and with a purple velvet table runner draped over it. A piano played softly. Craig's gaze shot to the church's upright piano. No one was there. Reverend Daniels must have put music on in his office. Craig sighed and tears rolled down his cheeks.

Craig leaned forward and folded his hands. His elbows rested on the first pew. "Hey, God, it's me, Craig. I've been talking to you a lot, because I don't have anyone else to talk to these days. They all think I'm crazy, but you know I'm not. Right? Anyway, I wanted to thank you for the nice weather we've been having, and I thank you for welcoming Grandpa into Heaven. I hope he's enjoying himself in his robe and crown, singing your praises and holding Grandma's hand. I know he was anxious to see her again."

Soft footsteps sounded behind Craig. He brushed them off. His heart beat faster, and he bit his lip to try and slow his breathing. His hands trembled.

"And I'm sorry I didn't believe Grandpa's story. I know he didn't mean us no trouble, but it's not fair, God. It's not fair that the devil can come after us. Isn't that why you sent Jesus to the cross? So we would be safe from the devil? Why is he attacking our family? It's not fair. I want my wife and son back, God. I want my life back."

The footsteps grew louder. Craig continued praying. Tears fell fast, choking the words as they emerged from his mouth. The feet, encased in black boots, belonged to Doctor Faust, who, dressed again in black, walked into the church. He made his way to the pew behind Craig and sat directly behind the praying man. The grin of a lone, hungry wolf curled over his lips as he spread his arms on the back of the pew and listened.

"Please, God, I ask you to protect me from the devil who stalks me everywhere. Send your angels to shield me so he can't harm me. I saw him at the Taco Bell on Cherokee. You know, the one that used to be a Pizza Hut? Yeah, and he followed me to work. He didn't do nothing. He just stood there, staring. When I asked people if they saw him, everyone said no. Why is this happening? Please, God, keep me safe.

"And finally, God, thank you. I know you can do all these things, but thank you for sending that one angel who promised to help me. Give her the knowledge and the power to send the devil and all of his evil back to Hell. I ask this in Jesus' most holy and powerful name. Amen."

Faust leaned forward and whispered into Craig's ear. "A noble prayer, Craig Wellington of Fiddler's Ford, but it will avail you not. Your weak, uncaring little godling can do naught to protect you or anyone else. Where was he in my hour of darkness when I called out to him? He turned his back and darkened the sun that I might brood in darkness, alone, forgotten, and unloved. And now he sits upon his golden throne where his saints hurl worship and praise upon him. Is that a god? Or is that a megalomaniacal narcissist?"

Craig sat upright and sucked air into his lungs. He held his breath. His heart stormed and thundered in his chest. Every muscle tensed; he clenched his fists. He slowly turned his gaze to his left and swallowed. Faust' face, adorned with a mocking grin, loomed one Bible page's thickness from Craig's nose. Faust placed a finger over Craig's lips.

"Silence. I'm not here to take your soul. Well, not here, but I will have it. Consuming it gives me life and revenge. Hope your grandfather enjoys what bit of Heaven he can get, because it won't last forever. Your grandfather should have known the old stories and their admonitions. Let him who holds the devil hold him well, for he will not be caught a second time. See you soon."

Faust disappeared in fire and sulfur. Craig exhaled and panted. His eyes scanned the sanctuary floor. Ash and burn marks scarred the cushion and the floor.

* * *

Half an hour before noon on Monday morning, Sam drove to Sal's Pies and Pastas, but her plans did not include eating. Sal and Donna had served Italian–American favorites and traditional Sicilian dishes here since 1957. Three years ago, they remodeled the interior to resemble a 1990s Pizza Hut and began offering a book club for adults. Sam beat the lunch rush and asked the hostess, a young ginger named Emily, if Donna Fuera was available for a consultation. Emily asked Sam to wait at the bar; the Donna was supervising the kitchen.

Sam sat on one of the black cushioned barstools. The rich earthy and meaty scent of Donna's ragu alla Bolognese filled the air and mixed with the lingering joyful homeyness of fresh bread; herbaceous basil and toasting pine nuts cut through the earthy scents. From the vintage jukebox's speakers, Sammy Davis, Junior, sang about the birth of the blues. The bartender, a slender but muscular black man who pitched for James Roanoke State until he graduate last year, walked over and set a white napkin before Sam.

"Hi, Miss Hain, what'll it be?"

Sam smiled. "Morning, Darrel. I think I'll just have a Heaven's Door on the rocks."

Darrel nodded. "Keeping it simple? No need for a whiskey as sour as your mood?"

Sam laughed at what had become an inside joke. "Why, Darrel? Is my father here?"

"No, ma'am. And lately, you've been in a pretty good mood. Dining in too?"

Sam shook her head. "Not today. I'm waiting to see the Donna."

Darrel poured Sam's drink and continued his duties while she waited. Diners filed in and started eating. After a few minutes, Emily returned and told Sam that Donna Fuera was available. Sam finished her drink, left Darrel a tip, and walked to the back.

Donna Fuera's consultation parlor sat next to the restaurant's main office. Lavender and jasmine incense masked the bold, spicy smoke from Donna's cigarette. Two white candles dripped wax onto the mahogany desk. Donna Fuera was two years Sal's junior and looked to be in her mid-forties; a silver shock of hair on the right side of her head mixed with the thick, black curls that cascaded down her back. She rolled a Mercury dime from finger to finger. She smiled as Sam approached, hugged her, and kissed her cheeks.

As Sam sat in the mahogany chair opposite Donna Fuera's throne, Donna, in her Sicilian accent that she refused to abandon, said, "Samantha, it's good to see you. How are you these days?"

"I'm well, Donna, and I hope I find you well. Oh, I have something for you."

Sam took a tin from her purse and handed it to Donna. The tin was about the size of a deck of playing cards. Donna opened the tin, saw the rich caramel and oak colored leaves, inhaled their aroma, and smiled. She nodded, closed the tin, and set it on her desk.

"Irish Flake, a nice tobacco. Thank you. Now, what can I help you with? Trouble in love? Is your asshole father still disturbing you?"

Sam laughed. She shook her head. "Love is wonderful. I'm traveling to Austria after I speak to you. And my asshole father is still an asshole and still my father. I came because I need help with a case that has me stumped. I was hoping for clarity."

"And what shadow obscures your path, my dear?"

Sam exhaled. "My Full Moon Special came to me after, well, losing a fistfight against a man in black he believes to be the devil. This guy apparently marked him with some curse or something and said that he'd give my client another try in one month. Should my client lose again, this man in black will take his soul to Hell. Now, I've talked to Nick Scratch, and he, as I'm sure you can guess, denied demeaning himself to fisticuffs. Oh, and he called in his contract and wants me to capture and return an escaped soul to Hell. Oh, when I examined the crossroads where my client fought this man in black, I found this little straw doll, and Nick found an identical doll in the circle of Hell where this guy was being punished. I guess they're the same, but that seems too easy. That, and I don't know what to do for either."

Sam handed Donna the straw doll. The strega examined it, nodding, as she listened to Sam. She smelled the sulfur residue. She focused her gaze on the reversed head. When Sam finished, Donna Fuera said, "I concur that this man in black is unlikely to be the devil. Physical violence in such an undignified manner is beneath him. However, the position of the face and the sulfurous residue suggest an infernal connection."

Sam nodded. "Yeah, I guessed that much. My gut tells me the two people are the same person, but that little voice in my head says that's too easy. Things can't be that easy. Like I said, Donna, I just want clarity."

Donna Fuera nodded. "Then give me a moment, child."

The strega took a deep drag of her cigarette and blew the thick smoke onto the doll. She gazed into the doll's face and chanted in Sicilian. She fell silent, and her eyes rolled up.

"I see the man of this doll. He is pale and dressed in black, lean and hungry. Deep sunken eyes burn with hatred and hunger for revenge. A soul mismatched to its body, ancient with new, always looking over its shoulder as if pursued. I see a dragon behind and a dragon before, and he makes the choice which one will destroy him. At the edge of life and death, he walks, devouring to satiate a hunger unending. That is who you seek."

When Donna Fuera's emerald eyes returned, her trance ended. Sam nodded. "I don't suppose you have a name for me?"

Donna's face and voice remained devoid of emotion. "You had your answer before you entered my parlor, Samantha. You know what you must do."

Sam nodded and thanked Donna Fuera for her help. After her conversation with Donna Fuera, Sam drove to Riddle of You

Psychiatric Services on Acacia Avenue in the Veiled Heights. This blush pink Victorian served as the office space for six therapists who specialized in mental health issues afflicting Non-Human Mythics and humans familiar with the Veil and its impacts on society. Both Maria Johnson and Rayna Rosenthorn recommended them after Sam returned from Austria when she admitted that her recurring dreams and flashbacks to Old Tom's Hill had gotten worse.

Sam entered the foyer where Perry Flynn sat at the antique mirrorless vanity that served as their desk. As the door chime sounded, Perry slid their head to the side of their charcoal Dell monitor. They smiled and said, "Hello, Miss Hain. Here for your noon with Doctor Khouri? You're...one minute early."

"Sorry about that, Perry," Sam said with a smile. "I had a work-related meeting. Guess it ran long."

Perry laughed. "You're one of the few people I know who sees one minute early as being late. Go up the stairs, have a seat in the library, and I'll let her know you're here."

She nodded and walked to the end of the foyer, where spiral stairs ascended to the second floor. She walked into the library and sat in one of the mocha leather chairs in the corner. Bookshelves lined the interior walls, and landscape paintings by local artists hung from the exterior wall with its two large windows. Shortly after she sat, the door on the wall opposite her chair opened and Doctor Marwa Khouri, an Egyptian woman in a plum pant suit, entered the library.

"Sam, are you ready?"

"Yes, Doctor." Sam followed Doctor Khouri into her office.

Doctor Khouri's office was a large, square room with tan carpet, two plum velvet-cushioned armchairs and a matching sofa; all the furniture had golden tassels and trim. On the floor opposite the sofa was a large plum cushion. Doctor Khouri walked toward the floor cushion and shifted to her natural form of a large black furred sphinx with gold feathers on her wings. She curled on the cushion, and Sam sat on the sofa.

Doctor Khouri's golden eyes met Sam's brown eyes, and she said, "Sam, how has your week been?"

Sam exhaled. "It's been a week, Doc. 'Milla's back in Austria, and we've discussed my attachment style and how I get lonely and grumpy after being with her for a while. Still isn't the right time to U-Haul over there. Work is going well overall. I'm still dealing with dreams and flashbacks, and now I've got the stress of knowing what Nick Scratch wants from that blank check I gave him years ago."

Doctor Khouri purred and nodded as Sam spoke. "I see. And how do you feel about knowing what he expects of you?"

Sam slipped out of her shoes and drew her knees to her chest. She rubbed her temples, exhaled, and ran her fingers through her hair. "Sorry, I'm terrified. I don't think I can do what he wants, and now I'm kicking myself for being so impulsive and emotional."

"And what about being impulsive and emotional upsets you so much?"

Sam fidgeted with her sleeve. "All of it, and I know—I know—that's not a helpful answer. Okay, I impulsively quit college and struggled for years. Then I impulsively offered a blank check to spend an hour a year with mom. Sure, that led to meeting 'Milla, and that's been really great. I almost blew that by being impulsive and following her sister's ghost instead of playing things by the books. I guess it's realizing I've gotten lucky more times than not when I was impulsive, and now it feels like the universe is forcing me to face the consequences of all my impulsive actions at once. And it doesn't help that things have been going well, and I'm terrified of losing everything and everyone in my life."

Doctor Khouri sat up. "I see. And what do you think you can do?"

Sam shrugged. "I don't have many choices. I can figure out how to return a soul to hell, or I can roll over and give up. There's nothing else."

Doctor Khouri narrowed her eyes. "I meant what can you do about your impulsiveness, since by your own admission, it is causing you trouble?"

"Oh, yeah, that," Sam said. "I know I need to work on that like I've been working on my stubbornness. I know I have to recognize when I'm being impulsive, pause, and think things through. It's just that until Nick's bill came due, everything's turned out okay."

Sam's conversation with Doctor Khouri continued for another half hour. When her session ended, Sam confirmed her appointment for next week with Perry and then left. As she sat in the car, Sam texted Destiny, and then she drove home.

* * *

Sandy Paws sat in Sam's cobalt Samsonite suitcase as Sam rummaged through her closet for clothing. Destiny sprawled on Sam's bed and scratched Sandy on her eyebrows, earning both purrs and kisses. Sam needed clothes for her tour nights in Austria. She needed stylish but comfortable clothing for research trips during the day and more daring and flirty ensembles for her evenings.

As Sam narrowed her selections, Destiny said, "Don't forget

your flannel pajamas. Austrian castles are drafty and cold this time of year, even without a sexy but cold snoring vampire next to you."

Sam spun around, holding a blue and green plaid midi skirt and blue blazer. "What do you think? Would this plus a cream blouse for research trips give off cute but serious grad student vibes? Also, 'Milla doesn't snore, and she hasn't been as cold lately."

Destiny rolled onto her back, her head leaning over the side of the bed. Sandy Paws climbed onto Destiny's chest and purred. Destiny scratched the cat's cheeks, and Sandy drooled on Destiny's chin; she giggled. "You'll look like a vampire teacher's pet. So, have you two been swapping fluids other than the normal ones?"

With Sandy distracted, Sam folded the clothing and placed them in her suitcase. She smiled as Sandy flicked her rough tongue over Destiny's nose. "That's one down. And what do you mean? What fluids would we be swapping that other couples don't... oh! Blood drinking has only been one way. Why does that matter?"

"First, it means you like it raw, you freak." Destiny laughed for five minutes as Sam rolled her eyes. When she calmed, Destiny said, "Second, were you starting down the path to becoming a vampire, theory holds that you cease to notice little things like cold temperatures and subtle flavors. Also, I was going to tell you to start that paperwork now, because Germany and Austria have five times as many forms for vampiric siring as the States do."

"Why isn't it more streamlined over there? I can't believe anywhere has more paperwork than here."

Sandy Paws moved to the suitcase, and Destiny scrambled

to stop her, pulling the cat into a cuddle. Sandy narrowed her eyes and growled in annoyance, but her growl became purrs as Destiny kissed her and scratched under her chin with both hands.

"The process is simpler, and the online portal is clean and straightforward, on the mortal side anyway. The vampire side, well, *that's* where all the paperwork comes from. Certain forms can only be filed during certain phases of the moon; others can only be filed in certain seasons, and the final form can only be filed on Vlad Dracula's coronation day. And the order you file matters for social politeness. It's a pain in the ass."

Sam exhaled. It was good no one was planning on Sam becoming Carmilla's progeny. They had never discussed it. Would that make things awkward? Some vampires turned their lovers, but the ones Sam knew who did that ended any romantic relationship shortly after. Did Carmilla want to turn Sam? They could be together forever that way. Did Sam want to be turned? She wanted Carmilla in her life, but immortality would be another matter. Right? Sam had no answer.

"Of course, it wouldn't get weird if you did, since you've only got daddy issues. But if you vamped out, would you call her 'Mommy?'"

Sam glared as Destiny rolled with laughter. When Sam finished packing, she closed the suitcase and asked, "What makes you think I have daddy issues?"

Destiny sat up and crossed her legs. "Well, have you met your father?"

Sam nodded. Her parents divorced when she was six because of her father's repeated infidelities. Despite having access to numerous teleportation circles and travel portals, Sam saw her father occasionally until her thirteenth birthday. He had nothing to do with her, would neither answer her calls nor respond to her emails, until her mother died by suicide when Sam was twenty. Once he reentered her life, his domineering nature and patriarchal attitude, when set against his daughter's independent and stubborn nature, ensured he and Sam would clash often. And they did.

Her packing finished, Sam grabbed the bird-on-a-string that Sandy Paws loved. They played until Sandy grew bored. Sam smiled as her cat hopped into Sam's reading chair and fell asleep. Sam texted Martin, and when he replied, she hugged Destiny.

"I'll only be gone for four days. Just keep things going smoothly and send me pictures of Sandy. Okay?"

Destiny laughed. "I know the drill, but you do realize that you're traveling through a teleportation circle, right? You can come home whenever you need to. But you go have a lovely *research* trip while staying at your girlfriend's castle. I'll guard the castle here and keep the princess safe."

They hugged again, and Destiny helped Sam carry her suitcase and duffel bag to her magical working room. She lit the altar candles and the pillar candles at the four cardinal points. Standing at the center of her circle, she performed the basic banishing and opening rites Magus Fingal, and her father, taught her. Sam then performed the door opening ritual she used to enter the Four Winds, changing the destination name to Castle Karnstein.

A small silver light point shone on the wall opposite Sam. She repeated the incantation once more, and the light point moved, tracing the outline of a door. When the light point completed the tracing, the pillar candles ceased burning. A click sounded. Sam snuffed the altar candles, grabbed her bags, and opened the manifested door. She stepped through the swirling galaxy vortex.

Sam emerged in a gray stone room within the dungeon of Castle Karnstein. She blinked. Were those LED torches protruding from the wall sconces? Carmilla's diary no longer rested on the mahogany desk against the wall where she once kept it chained. Pens, a notebook, and a Dell Inspiron laptop sat atop the ancient wooden structure. The shelves containing ancient grimoires and arcane treatises had been dusted and organized. Martin, dressed in a midnight blue suit with gold pinstripes, stood in the door frame, holding a silver serving tray that carried a glass of water.

Sam smiled. "No, coffee, Martin? Don't you know how to greet a lady?"

Martin bowed. "You may have your coffee later, Miss Hain. First, you will hydrate."

"You sound like Destiny. Always worried I'm not drinking enough—don't give me that look. Fine, Martin."

Sam took the water glass and drank. Martin smiled. "Miss Grimm contacted me and asked that I ensure you hydrate properly. As you know, magical workings can drain the reserves of even the most trained occultists, and you are not one of them. In addition, I have noted that neither you nor the Countess demonstrates attentiveness to basic nutritional needs."

Fuck, he's right. Martin could end Batman by convincing Bruce Wayne to get therapy. He continued, "Take the glass and trot off to the drawing room. It has been well cleaned since your last rendezvous. I shall bring your bags to the Countess' bed chamber, prepare your coffee, and provide you with whatever assistance I can before dinner this evening."

Sam blushed, brushed her hair behind her ear, and made her way up two flights of spiral staircases to the drawing room. Medieval tapestries, Carmilla's watercolors, and a photograph of Carmilla and Sam sitting beneath a Christmas tree adorned the mahogany walls. Sam smiled as she walked past the burgundy velvet sofa. She and Carmilla made quite the mess on the sofa and on the bearskin rug in the days following Christmas. Sam licked her lips. She sat in one of the two velvet cushioned chairs flanking the fireplace.

After a few minutes, Martin entered with a serving tray containing a mug of hot black coffee, a crystal glass filled with blood wine, and a crystal snifter of blood orange brandy. Sam moaned as she sipped her coffee. Martin swirled his brandy and said, "According to your messages, Miss Hain, you need to research information on Johann Faust for both your current case and also for Samael's contract. You are aware he is dead, aren't you?"

Sam sighed. "Was dead, apparently. Look, Martin, I won't pretend I actually understand the arcane theory involved, but someone in the fucking Astrum Argentum helped bust him out of Hell. Seems his soul has been shoved into a new body, and he's trying to collect some poor man's soul. I know it doesn't make any sense, and I'm wondering if, after the events in Bannagh, if the Order of the Dragon isn't somehow involved. I just can't connect the dots there."

Martin nodded. He sipped the brandy and sighed. "I do not know much regarding Faust's life, and I can say without sarcasm this time that my memory on this has faded. He was an astrologer, an alchemist, and a charlatan; though he possessed quite the education. Faust was a guest here some six—no, five—centuries ago, long before the Countess was born, at least by mortal reckoning. Count Adolf, the Countess' father was quite taken by his tricks and promises, but we learned Faust was quite taken by the Countess. He was branded, thrown out, and ordered never to return. I doubt that will assist you."

Sam thought while sipping her coffee. She shook her head and shrugged. "I don't know what I'm looking for, Martin. All I had to go on was something Nick Scratch mentioned about Faust' grimoire being in the dungeon here. I had hoped maybe that might offer some clues."

Martin drained his snifter. He sighed. "His grimoire is in the dungeon; yes, right beside, I believe the mortal tradition is to say, 'He-Who-Must-Not-Be-Named's grimoire. After all, he studied at Samael's school. While you may peruse that tome as well, I would not mention doing so to the Countess."

Sam's eyes widened. She nodded. "I've seen how enraged she gets when someone just mentions Dracula's name. When I learned what he put her through." She paused and exhaled. "I won't mention his name unless absolutely necessary. And that, Martin, is a promise."

As Sam and Martin chatted, Destiny returned to her townhouse with Donal Hain's travel grimoire tucked into her Bulbasaur backpack. She switched on her electric kettle and grabbed her chipped dusty rose mug with a black silhouette of Kiki and Jiji flying on a broom. She steeped a Companion Cube infuser filled with toasted pecan Earl Gray tea. She stirred wildflower honey into her tea and grabbed a bag of spicy mustard pretzels from her R2D2 cookie jar. Carrying the pretzel bag in her mouth, she took her tea and the grimoire up the carpeted stairs to her library.

Destiny lined the walls of her library with tall maple bookcases to coordinate with the maple floorboards and the lavender sofa and mint velvet reading chair and ottoman. History, fiction, American graphic novels, folklore studies, manga series, biographies, and a collection of tawdry romances filled her shelves; she arranged them by alphabetically by subject, and action figures, anime statues, and other trinkets marked division points between genres. She set her mug on an octagonal side table where she kept a glass vase of marigolds. She bought the vase from a glass blower when she and Sam went to Mythical & Medieval Fest in Myrtle Beach while in college.

She curled up in her plush reading chair with the grimoire and pretzel bag on her lap. She sipped the tea and opened the grimoire. The first few dozen pages contained the Arch Magus' notes on standard protection, evocation, summoning, and teleportation workings. She shook her head. Like many a grimoire, the pages contained outlines and notes but lacked detailed instructions on how to perform the rites. Did Sam remember enough from her brief and tumultuous training to successfully perform these workings? Pretzels crunched as she snacked while reading.

A yawn escaped her lips. She rolled her neck and blinked several times. Destiny exhaled. She thought about restructuring her three Blue/White decks before the *Magic: the Gathering* tournament next week. The prize was a five-hundred-dollar gift card for Mason's Gaming Castle. She shook her head and refocused. Something important had to be in this book; that was why both Donal Hain and the Order of the Dragon kept trying to get it back.

She treated the grimoire like it was her second semester physics textbook. She lost her place several times and returned to earlier sections. She grumbled in frustration and shook her head. She yawned before draining what remained of her tea.

She riffled the pages, feeling the rough, uneven edges. And then a folded piece of paper slipped onto her lap. This paper was pure white with a smoother texture than the grimoire's pages. The outline of an opened wax seal remained. Destiny unfolded the paper and read the note.

As you are aware, our shared Great Work cannot proceed until after the resurrection of His Nocturnal Majesty, Vlad Dracula, King of the Vampires of Christendom. Per our wizards from the Dumont–de Rais clan, empowering the ring requires the souls of four mortals drawn from the lines of those responsible for his regicide.

Your task now is to persuade this entity Zozo to collect the souls for us by offering a sacrifice worthy of such a task.

Florian Amanar, General in the Most Holy Order of the Dragon

Destiny's eyes shot wide, and she whistled. "Shit. I've got to tell Sam about this."

Chapter 7

A feminine yawn sounded. I searched for its source, and Martin checked his phone. He rose from his chair and took hold of the silver serving tray holding Carmilla's evening breakfast.

"That is only my alarm, Miss Hain. The Countess has awakened."

I grinned and grabbed the tray. "Allow me."

The elder vampire cocked an eyebrow but nodded in acquiescence. He pointed to the wineglass and said, "As you desire. Before you engage in any strenuous activity, be certain she drinks the fortified Sanguinovese. Otherwise, she will be no different from you in the morning when you do not have coffee. I will serve the first meal in three hours. Unless the Countess says otherwise, I will serve the two of you in the drawing room."

I smiled. "Got it."

I held my breath as I ascended the stairs. I waited tables in high school and during my freshman year of college, but a tray full of cheap glasses and bulk white plates and an actual silver tray with a crystal glass were different. Also, I never had to carry trays up narrow spiral stairs in an Austrian castle. First time for everything.

Carmilla whined as I entered her bedroom. The burgundy

curtains on her mahogany canopy bed were still drawn. I bit my lip to stop from giggling as she pleaded with "Martin" for five more minutes. Without a word, I set the tray on the nightstand and warmed the glass in my hands. Carmilla sighed.

"Fine, Martin, I will get up. At least Samantha will be here sometime this evening." She threw open the curtain and blinked. Her already pale skin took on an additional pallor when she awoke from the death-sleep. She was still beautiful as her long black hair flailed about her body. Carmilla leaned forward and squinted, focusing. A smile curved over her face, and she licked her lips. She said, "You are not Martin."

"No," I said as I slid onto the bed beside her. She wrapped her arms around me, and our lips met in a gentle kiss. "But you are my Countess. Oh, Martin said drink your breakfast."

'Milla pouted as I handed her the glass. A wicked smile flashed on her lips. She ran a single finger along my leg and up my torso. I drew a sharp breath into my lungs. She leaned close; her breath was cold. The hair on my neck shivered and stood. "You know, my dear one, the best breakfast is a warmed, fresh breakfast."

I exhaled. She knew what I liked. A pre-dinner romp with a little blood drinking for added orgasmic impact sounded amazing. Carmilla trailed kisses up and down my neck. My head fell back, and I whimpered as her fangs grazed my skin. I wrapped my arm around her head and stroked her hair. 'Milla purred and guided my lips back to hers. They felt like ice, and her tongue shot frigid darts through mine as their tips touched. Deepening the kiss, I pushed her onto her back.

I trailed kisses down her chin, along her jawline, and up to her ear. She whimpered. I said, "That sounds lovely, and that can certainly be provided for you; however, my orders are for you to drink this glass before we engage in any strenuous activity. So, drink up."

Carmilla rolled on her side and cocked an eyebrow. "I am Countess Carmilla Karnstein, Matriarch of the Karnstein-Bertholt clan of vampires, firstborn and heir of the line of Ziegwulf the Bloody-Handed of Thracia and, annoyingly, rightful ruler of all vampires in Europe and the Levant. I am ten times your age, Samantha Blake Hain, and you speak to me as my equal?"

"Yes, I do." I booped her nose like I did Sandy Paws when she acted cute.

"And I love that about you." She smiled and sat up, extending her arms. "Fine, I will drink my breakfast from this glass. However, I, Countess Carmilla Karnstein, do formally request a second course after you have been properly warmed."

Carmilla drained the glass and then, after an hour of pleasure, drank from me. We chatted while she bathed, dressed, and descended to the drawing room. The crisp, sweetness of pine burning in the fireplace filled the room. Martin left two serving trays on the side tables; each had a silver cloche, a bottle of fortified sparkling water, and a single glass of wine. He prepared braised beef tips in a red wine demiglace, potato puree, and roasted asparagus tips wrapped in bacon.

Halfway through dinner, Carmilla asked, "I have you for four nights, but are your four days to be spent in research on this special case of yours for this month?"

I shook my head. "No, but yes. Okay, it started with Nick Scratch calling in that blank check I gave him the night we met, but then all evidence points to the supernatural trouble my Full Moon Special got himself into is the same guy. So, I've got two weeks to learn how to trap Faust' soul and bring it back to Hell.

Well, I guess I'll deliver it to the Four Winds."

I shrugged. Carmilla sipped her wine. "Have you given thought to further arcane training? There are other orders of magicians besides your father's." She tensed and exhaled. Her expression darkened. "And I would even be fine were you to study at Samael's university."

The Scholomance, a magical university in the Carpathian mountains where Nick Scratch trained ten students, but only nine graduated. While I would learn the most powerful, and the darkest, magical rites there, rumors circulated that the final exam was tough as hell. But I knew that wasn't her worry. *He* studied there.

I reached out and held her hand. I squeezed it and said, "Hey, I'm not going to connect our future to your memories of him. And I'm not joining an esoteric order. I'll figure this out. With you and Destiny at my side, I can handle anything."

The morning came earlier than I expected, even if I woke at noon and left our shared bed closer to two in the afternoon. Martin brought my coffee and breakfast—lunch?—to the dungeon where I sat with the Karnstein family's assembled collection of grimoires and esoteric tomes. Cold, dry air filled the dungeon. It was still a dungeon, after all. Modern lighting, a laptop, and internet access made the drudgery of Google-based translations more bearable.

After translating the first twenty pages of Faust' grimoire, I realized he was an arrogant fuck-wit. For starters, he named himself the "demigod of Heidelberg," which is laughable. He was that guy whose email was "sexxxysugardaddy69" or something similar. The kind of guy who commented on a lesbian's Instagram that he could give her "the good dick." Gross. He interspersed his astrological charts, alchemical formulae, and ritual notes with diary entries about the dozens of women he bedded, the nobles he deceived out of small fortunes, and the towns he cursed. According to one entry, he rained flaming stars upon Wolframs-Eschenbach while satisfying three peasant girls. That was an eye-roller.

I skipped past the end of a story when I realized Faust was wand-waving about having bested a team of three Inquisitors in a witch trial. It was like listening to my fucking father brag about, well, anything. I ran my fingers through my hair and yawned. This felt like studying for finals. After doing a few neck rolls, I stood, stretched, and paced the chamber. Faust' grimoire had nothing useful. Nothing. I couldn't make sense of his notes, and his arrogant stories only made me hate him. What was I hoping to learn from his grimoire? I don't know.

Carrying a tray with a mug of coffee, a glass of water, and a bowl filled with berries, Martin appeared in the doorway. He set the tray on the desk and said, "I see you have reached the stage of research where you pull at your hair in the hopes that your answer has magically inscribed itself upon your skin. Take a break, Miss Hain."

His gaze moved from me to the chair. I sighed, nodded, and sat. Strawberries, blueberries, and cherries filled the bowl. I popped a blueberry into my mouth. It burst at my tooth's slightest touch. I looked up at Martin. "How'd you know?"

He sat on the desk's edge and chuckled. "In the centuries I have served this family, many students have resided within these walls. When an examination looms, frustration becomes common, and basic physical needs often become forgotten. Thus, I brought you refreshments."

And my examination was in a life-or-damnation format. I offered Martin a weak but honest smile. I hope he read it as tired. "Thank you."

He nodded. "Your expression screams that you have found nothing. I hope I am misreading you."

I sipped the coffee. Hot, black, strong. Martin made damned good coffee. I sighed, and my shoulders relaxed. "I don't know what I was hoping to find. A weakness, maybe. That one thing that I can use to win. I've only found two things. Proof that Faust is an arrogant shit like my father, and indecipherable arcane notes."

Martin pointed to the water glass, and I sipped. He smiled gently. "Arrogance reveals more character than humility. Perhaps you have found what you need, but you do not recognize what you have found. The past often repeats in the present, informing us of how to respond, but do not let searching the past shackle and blind you. And trust your instincts."

I nodded. I came without a plan. Well, I planned to research by day and relax with 'Milla by night. But what information did I need? The extent of his powers? Faust' own words are so grandiose that I can't separate fact from bullshit. Why was he brought back from Hell? His grimoire from the sixteenth century wouldn't have that information. How was I supposed to fight and defeat a wizard who managed to escape Hell? Why was the Astrum Argentum involved? Maybe I should call my father.

No. That wasn't happening. Not after everything he's done. Not after he tried to sacrifice Frank to that fucking demon. I exhaled and nodded. "I'll try, Martin. Thank you."

He stood and bowed. "I will return in two hours to check on you, Miss Hain. Work hard, but take care of yourself."

He departed.

* * *

The next morning arrived earlier than desired. After half an hour of protests and whines, Martin coaxed Sam out of bed. A long journey to Innsbruck lay ahead of them, as Carmila had arranged for Sam to access the historical collections at the University and State Library of Tyrol. Martin supplied coffee and breakfast, and he gave Sam silence to sit, sip, and slouch awake. The sun rose before they left Castle Karnstein. Sam flew into and out of Innsbruck when she visited during December; she smiled, realizing she would no longer need to make that flight. Sam yawned.

Sam finished her coffee and sighed. She ran her fingers through her hair. What did she hope to find? Internet searches uncovered a dozen differing and often contradictory life histories. The only things they agreed on was that Johann Faust was an educated but greedy grifter and con artist; Sam surmised he had to have sold his soul to earn his specific place in Hell, because all historical accounts she found through Google labeled Faust a charlatan and a fraud. A few suggested Faust did not believe in Hell's existence. Death and damnation may have changed that.

The University and State Library of Tyrol was a reddish-brown roofed, two story building of white stone with a brown stone entrance. Martin stayed by Sam's side as she ascended the stairs to the room holding their late medieval and early renaissance collections. As she searched the catalog, Martin aided in translating the unfamiliar words, but he deferred to Sam's judgment in selecting texts to examine.

Their collection had little to offer her unfocused search, but she selected a fifteenth century treatise on diabolism and magic. Perhaps learning what rituals Faust might have used to summon Mephistopheles would offer Sam insight into something. She was uncertain what. Sam sighed as she scanned the Latin text, doodling in her notebook but finding nothing meaningful. Martin sat at the table next to her, reading in silence.

Halfway through the treatise, she found the author diverged from his moralization on why communing and working with fiends was no different from praying to saints; he listed the sinful delights a bound succubus might provide. *Consent never really was a concern of these fucking magicians, was it?* Sam's phone buzzed. Destiny sent her a picture of a note, along with a request to call her. Sam magnified the note and read. She snapped her pen. Martin's ear twitched. He turned and cocked an inquisitive eyebrow.

Sam rose and whispered to Martin that she had to take a business call. He nodded and returned to his book as she exited the reading room. When Destiny answered her call, Sam asked, "What the fuck in the nine circles of Hell is that?"

"A note. I found it in your father's grimoire the day you portalled out. I'd have texted you then, but I figured you'd enjoy a night or two of supernatural pleasures."

Destiny laughed. Sam closed her eyes, shook her head, and sighed. She smiled. "You aren't wrong, Des. My research has hit nothing but dead ends. This gives us a piece of the larger puzzle at least."

Destiny nodded. "Yeah, but it's not a good piece. I mean, your dad is in *deep*. Seems like he knows the big plan, that Great Work, whatever it is."

Sam sighed and massaged her temples. "Fuck. Now we know what he was doing in Bannagh and why he was offering Frank as a sacrifice. But why do they need Dracula back?"

"I don't know, Sam. But if demons and human sacrifices are involved, it can't be good. Didn't realize this neophyte was so important to your dad. You may want to warn your girlfriend about this."

Sam nodded. "I'll tell Martin. 'Milla knows the Order is moving toward his resurrection, and she's concerned. Given their troubled history, I'm impressed with how well she's holding together. Wonder how close they are? Did you find anything else of interest?"

"I kind of stopped there. Let me grab the book." Destiny walked to her library and plopped into her reading chair. She grabbed the leather grimoire and thumbed through it. "Seems pretty standard, Sam. Banishings, protections, teleportation stuff, a few bindings. He's got notes on the Order's major ceremonies and rites. I see a few attack spells and curses. Goetic conjuration notes. I don't know, Sam. Looks like there's nothing here."

Sam paced as she talked. "Keep looking. There has to be something."

"Alright." Destiny kept scanning the pages. "I don't know, Sam. I think the only important thing is the note about—wait! Oh fuck, this is...wow. That's so sickening. I don't know if I should tell you, send you pics, or just say, 'Wait until you get home.'"

"Just tell me what it is. I'll read the details when I get home."

Destiny took a deep breath. Her heart sped up. "Okay, Sam. Well, there's an involved ritual covering how to prepare a body to receive a soul brought back from death."

Sam's heart sank. She swallowed hard. Sweat formed on her forehead and hands. "Does this ritual involve small figurines by any chance?"

Destiny tugged at the collar of her t-shirt and said, "Among *other* things involved in the ritual, yeah. Well, at least we know who smuggled Faust out of Hell. That's good, right?"

Sam closed her eyes. Of course, Donal Hain was responsible. But why? What was his goal? What was this "Great Work" the note mentioned? Why did they need Zozo specifically? A single tear formed in her eyes; she wiped it away.

"Yeah," she said. "That's a lead, at least. Thanks, Des. I'll talk to you later."

Sam returned to the reading room, closed the manuscript, and returned it to the librarian. She thanked him, and she and Martin departed. Martin started the car and drove away. He said, "Your face is troubled, Miss Hain. Is all not well at the office?"

Sam sat in silence for a moment; her eyes were closed. She sighed and opened them. "Martin, I know you remember when you told that police detective I was 'Milla's fiancee. Go ahead and laugh, you smug asshole. Anyway, let's say that were the case. I just learned there's no way in hell my father would get a wedding invite."

He glanced at her through the rear-view mirror. "I see. What did he say to you this time?"

Sam shook her head. "Nothing. That was Destiny on the phone. She sent me a picture of a note she found in his travel grimoire. It seems he's been involved with helping the Order of the Dragon resurrect *him*. And that's step one of some big work."

"I see. That would put a damper on the festivities of such a day, yes."

Sam leaned forward and placed a hand on the front seat.

"Martin, if it's not out of line, can I ask why 'Milla isn't the, I guess, Queen of the Vampires of Europe and the Levant? I know she's the heir to the line of the firstborn of the three brothers, so why isn't she on the throne?"

Martin nodded. Now he remained silent. Sam sank into her seat. "It is our tradition to keep such knowledge from those who are not a part of our community, shall we say; however, as you are the Countess' champion, I suppose I could divulge some of the information."

As they departed Innsbruck, Sam said, "Don't cause yourself any trouble, Martin. I can dig—"

"And cause more trouble for us both than you intend. I know your investigative skills, Miss Hain, and I know your stubbornness. I will provide you with the gist of the matter. Should it become necessary, we will tell you more. Vlad Dracula is older than your mortal history attests. I would surmise he is eight centuries older that the most conservative estimate of his age. In a time of great crisis for our kind, his charisma and strength allowed him to unite us behind a successful campaign against our troubles. King Reinhardt, the Countess' grandfather, accepted death after passing his crown to Vlad Tepes as a reward for what he did for our kind. And many of the clans remain loyal to him to this day."

Sam nodded. "And 'Milla hasn't taken the crown because many clans believe she was involved in his murder?"

Martin nodded. "She lacks the desire for the throne, but yes, the other clans' belief in her guilt keeps her from challenging for the throne."

The final two days of Sam's Austrian trip did, in fact, fuck up her sleep schedule; she slept through the day, waking a mere hour before sunset. When he presented her first round of coffee, Martin checked her pulse and body temperature. He offered a sly smirk and a response of "merely a precaution" when she inquired about his motive. She rolled her eyes and laughed.

That Carmilla wore nothing but her lace-trimmed burgundy dressing gown when she had no reason to dress surprised Sam, but dining in dressing gowns, Sam's being blue satin with orange trim and belting, felt both relaxing and decadent. On her last night, Martin poured Sam and Carmilla glasses from one of the last two remaining bottles of a 1722 Morgarten Sanguinovese as an after-supper treat. He served them in the drawing room, bowed, and departed. Age had mellowed the crisp tartness of the blueberry and oak notes, providing a smooth and pleasant drinking experience, even for a human unaccustomed to blood wine.

As they snuggled on the burgundy velvet sofa and sipped the wine, Carmilla said, "I am sorry that your visit has proven less fruitful for your case than you had hoped it would, but having you here has been enjoyable. I will miss you, my dear one."

Sam nodded. She leaned in and kissed Carmilla's neck. "I keep telling myself I'm only a teleportation spell away, so it's not like we're that far anymore. But I think I can say for both of us, I'm going to miss sleeping next to you. And I'm ecstatic that I don't freak when I wake up first. The death-sleep doesn't bother me anymore."

Carmilla gave Sam a gentle kiss, tasting the pistachio-crusted lamb and wine they had for supper. She pulled away and smiled. "I concur. And knowing that our sleep schedules can align makes me hopeful."

Sam rested her head on her lover's shoulder, and Carmilla wrapped an arm around her. Sam sipped the wine and smiled.

A contented sigh escaped her lips. "This is amazing wine. And it was cute how flustered you got when Martin suggested it. Were you worried a wine this old would taste like vinegar?"

Carmilla smirked. "You seem to enjoy the taste of other things as old as this wine."

Sam's face scrunched in confusion. "Wait? What have I been tasting that's like three hundred years old?"

Carmilla kissed Sam's forehead and whispered, "Me."

Sam shot upright. Her eyes widened, and her mouth gaped. She turned and faced Carmilla, her eyes darting between the wine remaining in her glass and her lover's smiling eyes. Carmilla lifted Sam's jaw with a gentle touch and kissed her once more. Sam returned and deepened the kiss, closing her eyes. Her blood quickened as it moved through her veins.

When they broke the kiss, Sam raised a finger and said, "Hold up. You mean this wine is from the year you were born, and you mentioned something about there only being two bottles left. You meant left-left, like in the world, right?"

The vampire nodded. She opened her mouth, paused, and closed it. She blushed. "Yes, and tonight, we drink one of those bottles. The last, well, family tradition decrees it be saved for luck, but we shall not worry about that tonight."

Carmilla hoped Sam would not probe for details. The Karnstein family reserved one bottle for a child's wedding night. The couple drank the bottle before consummating the marriage. Carmilla's romantic history has been less than successful. Her first love died from poisoning; one of Dracula's agents poisoned her to frame Carmilla and, seemingly, secure Dracula's dominance over European vampires before he planned to extend his empire to the rest of the world. She smiled at his failure and at the memory of watching him die. She isolated herself until one night six years ago when, at The Four Winds, she overheard Sam offer Samael a blank check for a favor. Carmilla approached the brash young woman, and both a friendship and a brief romance began. Now, they had a second chance, and Carmilla wanted to make the most of it.

Sam drained her glass and nodded. "I feel like I've tasted this before, but I've only had blood wine when I'm with you." She shrugged and snuggled into Carmilla's arms again. "It's delicious. And I do love old things. Old fashion, old movies, old books, and old women."

Sam smiled. When Carmilla's face stiffened into the same face Destiny made when she needed to remain polite and not utter a devastating retort, Sam guffawed and snorted. Carmilla rolled her eyes and shook her head. She smiled and sighed.

"Samantha Blake Hain, sometimes, you are fortunate you are so adorable."

Sam smirked and booped Carmilla's nose. "And you adore me."

Carmilla opened her mouth to speak, but Sam threw her arms around Carmilla and claimed her lips in a deep, sensual kiss before any sound could escape. Carmilla's breath was warm and spiced, and touching her pale skin felt like returning home after a long trip. Sam sighed. She ran her hands through Carmilla's hair; the vampire purred and nibbled Sam's lower lip. Sam's cheeks flushed, and she broke the kiss.

Panting, her eyes locked with Carmilla's. The vampire smiled and set her glass on the side table. Sam bit her lower lip and did the same. Carmilla's dressing gown slid open, revealing the delicate curve of her neck and proud but gentle curves of her collarbone. Sam's eyes followed every visible curve on Carmilla's body. Her cheeks and the inner curves of her breasts were pink.

"See something you like, my dear one?" Carmilla's voice dropped an octave.

Sam's heartbeat and breath stopped for a moment. Warmth spread through her body. She nodded. Carmilla shifted forward, gripping the sofa's armrest with one hand and touching Sam's bare shin with the other. She blew a gentle breath on Sam's neck. Sam's shoulders relaxed.

"You're skin's flushed. It's different."

Carmilla brushed her fangs against Sam's neck. The hair stood tall, and Sam gasped. Carmilla chuckled. "I have been drinking young blood lately."

Did that have an effect on a vampire's skin tone? Sam came harder when Carmilla drank her blood during sex, so it made sense. Carmilla trailed kisses from the base of Sam's neck, along her collar, down the center of her chest, and over to her breast. Sam whimpered. Sam's back arched as Carmilla sucked her nipple; her arms slid around Carmilla's back, holding her close. Carmilla's rose and violet perfume sauntered into Sam's nostrils. Her breathing quickened.

"Yes. Please."

Sam begged as heat spread through her body. Carmilla's nails trailed up Sam's leg. Warmth built between her legs. Sam's heart pounded. The vampire's tongue traced the outline of Sam's rosewood areola and flicked over the nipple. Sam slid one hand down and groped Carmilla's ass while her other hand massaged and scratched the vampire's scalp. A deep, hungry purr escaped Carmilla's lips.

She leaned forward and captured Sam's lips with her own. Carmilla parted them with her tongue. Sam moaned. *She could stop right now and just hold me, and I'd be happy.* The vampire's hand kneaded Sam's inner thigh. She spread her legs. Carmilla's nose twitched. She trailed kisses down the center of Sam's body, pausing briefly to untie her belt. Sam raised her hips as Carmilla's lips and hand converged. Carmilla's middle finger slid between Sam's inner labia and over her clitoris. Without breaking eye contact, Carmilla smirked and licked her finger.

Sam gasped as Carmilla slid her middle finger inside of her. Her hips bucked in rhythm to the wavelike motion of Carmilla's slender finger. The vampire watched, licking her lips, as her lover's head fell back. Sam moaned. Sweat beaded on her forehead. She pushed short, hot breaths from her lungs. Sam's hands dug into the sofa's cushions.

"Wait. Wait. Wait." Sam begged as she forced herself to calm. "The sofa. Martin cleaned. Not messy."

Carmilla chuckled. She slid her finger from between Sam's legs; Sam whimpered. "Then, shall we retire to our bed for the night?"

Carmilla helped Sam up from the sofa; the vampire's red eyes scanned Sam's body as her robe fell open. She smiled. Sam crossed her arms over her chest and said, "My eyes are up here, 'Milla."

The vampire closed the gap between herself and her lover, wrapped one arm around Sam's waist, cupped her chin with her hand, and said, "I have intimate knowledge of your anatomy, my dear one."

She planted a quick kiss on Sam's lips, biting her lower lip as she pulled away. They raced from the drawing room to the spiral staircase, stopping every fifteen feet to kiss and grope each other against the wall. Halfway up the stairs, Sam kissed Carmilla, pushing her against the cold stone wall. The vampire gasped; drinking blood and arousal allowed her to feel cold more acutely than usual. She smiled as Sam's robe fell to the stair. Sam dropped to her knees and groped Carmilla's ass with both hands.

"Here?" Carmilla asked. Her voice became husky with need.

Sam winked. She kissed Carmilla's navel and trailed gentle kisses down her lover's core. A thick tuft of pubic hair tickled Sam's nose as she inhaled Carmilla's aroused musk. Slow licks teased Carmilla's labia. The vampire purred, her back arching against the stone wall. She never allowed another to pleasure her first; perhaps that would change. Sam licked her index finger and slipped it inside Carmilla's wet vagina. As she beckoned with her finger, she smiled, loving the way Carmilla's moans plummeted an octave and then ascended to an uncontrolled warbling high. Carmilla's hands pawed at the stone. Sweat beaded on her forehead. Her body flushed as blood rocketed through her veins.

Confident, poised, reserved, and dominant described Carmilla's public persona, but here, in the unlit stairwell of her castle, she thrashed in pleasure. Sam sucked Carmilla's clitoris while her finger undulated. Carmilla's hips rocked, thrusting against Sam's face. Her hands gripped Sam's hair. Carmilla moaned, whimpered, and begged. Heat spread through her body; sweat dripped down Carmilla's face. Pressure built; Carmilla's body trembled. Electric bursts shot through her nerves. Their intensity grew stronger, faster. Carmilla's screams soared higher.

Recalling its former need to draw breath, staccato gasps punctuated Carmilla's moans, cries, and screams. Shorter and faster they came, bursting from her crimson lips. Almost there. Sam moaned, sucked Carmilla's clitoris taut, and flicked her tongue across it. Carmilla's juices slicked Sam's chin. Her eyes rolled back, and a high screech burst from her lips, plunging into a guttural moan as waves of pleasure pulsed through her body. Carmilla's legs trembled. She thrust her hips forward, burying Sam's nose in her crotch. Gasps and ecstatic cries replaced her moaning as climax after climax exploded.

When the pleasure subsided enough she could think, Carmilla looked down at Sam's smiling, glistening face. Sam licked her lips. Carmilla kneeled and brushed Sam's hair from her face and kissed her. Her body re-centered, slowing the reflexive breathing. A lover's kiss on a castle stairwell, a scene from chivalrous romances, felt unrealistic before this night. Carmilla's red eyes met Sam's brown eyes. They said nothing, but their smiles sang in harmony.

A moment, a lifetime, an eternity passed. In a flash, Carmilla scooped Sam into her arms. Sam blinked and said, "Sometimes I forget how strong you are."

Carmilla smiled. "Let us finish this night in our bed."

* * *

Destiny Grimm sat at her desk and paid the bills. The sweet scent of caramel apples wafted from the miniature Master Chief helmet she repurposed as a wax burner. Her blue blocker glasses slid to the bridge of her nose as she sipped her tea. She glanced at her screen's clock; Sam was two hours late. Destiny giggled, remembering Sam spent the last four days fucking up her sleep schedule. Her ears perked when she heard Sam's voice outside the office door.

Sam spun into the office with her phone pressed between her ear and her shoulder and a large White Wolf Roasters coffee cup in her left hand. From behind her oversized sunglasses, she waved to Destiny and set her coffee on the spare coaster at the corner of Destiny's desk. She nodded into her phone and said, "Okay, Craig, I'm at the office. Let me put you on speaker so Destiny can hear too."

She set the phone on Destiny's desk and sat in the client's chair. She pressed the speaker button on the screen and said, "Okay, now say that again."

Craig's warbled voice crackled through the phone's speaker. "Have you found a solution? Please. I can't take this any longer, Miss Hain. Hi, Miss Grimm. As I told your boss, the devil's showing up everywhere I go. I got fired twice since this started, because I can't focus. I see him all the time. He's like just across the street or outside a window. I can't sleep. I can't eat. Please. And now he's showing up at church! I mean, he's the devil. How can he walk into the house of God without bursting into flame?"

Destiny tilted her head and clicked her tongue against her teeth. "He's showing up at church? That's odd. What's that story?"

Static crackled. Craig panted. "Sorry, let me pull off the road. Anyway, I was sitting in the Baptist church when no one but Reverend Daniels was there. He was in his office but came to talk with me a bit. He left me alone, and I started praying. Empty churches are scary, and you could hear footsteps or hoof steps everywhere. Well, someone sat behind me, and then he spoke. It was him. He mocked God, threatened to take my soul and grandpa's soul. Said taking souls gave him life. Please, if I ain't safe at church, I can't be safe anywhere."

"I know you're scared, Craig," Sam said. "And I know this has fucked over your life, but I hope you take comfort knowing that this man you keep seeing isn't the devil. He's a man."

"He's the devil." Craig's voice trembled. "He cursed me, and he vanished in fire. Can a man do that?"

"A magician, a wizard, or a witch could," Sam said. Her father could do both those things, but she did not say that. "Powerful ones can be terrifying."

"A wizard can't take souls. And they're just agents of the devil whose illusions lead us away from the path of righteousness."

Destiny and Sam synchronized eye rolls. Sam shook her head. Her father took a soul; technically he took one from Hell and placed it into another body. And Nick Scratch would be offended hearing that Faust was his agent.

"Look, Craig," Sam said. "I promise you, this guy isn't the devil. Trust me."

Craig sighed and grumbled. "Well, if he isn't the devil, why did he say, 'He who holds the devil had better hold him tight. He cannot hope to catch him again?' Huh?"

"I'll get back to you, Craig, but I've got a plan."

A thought crossed Destiny's mind as Sam ended the call. She frantically searched the internet, cursing in German as she ran into one dead-end after another. Sam sipped her coffee.

"What's up, Des?"

Destiny raised a finger. "I know that line about holding the devil. I've heard it in *Hannibal*, I think, but I know it's from somewhere—ah! There it is. Goethe's *Faust*, Part One. *Den Teufel halte, wer ihn hält! Er wird ihn nicht so bald zum zweiten Male fangen.* Faust said that. He's not being subtle."

Sam exhaled as she ran her fingers through her hair. "Doesn't matter, because we're basically waiting until his next showdown with Craig. Where would we even look?"

"Did you find anything of interest in Austria that wasn't a vampire?"

Destiny met Sam's glare with a sweet but knowing smile. A growling chuckle escaped Sam's pursed lips as she shook her head. She massaged her temples and said, "Not really. Faust has always been an arrogant prick. Martin referred to him as a charlatan who pretended to have knowledge and power to get money and pussy. Same reasons I do this glamorous work."

"Reckless and stubborn are the words I'd use, but sure, glamorous work is fine." Destiny sipped her tea. Sam blew her a raspberry, and Destiny winked in response. "Look, recklessness and probably grief got you into this mess. Sure, it attracted Carmilla's attention, but you signed that contract with Nick Scratch. So now we're going to get you out of this hellhole with German resourcefulness."

"You mean stubbornness." Sam smirked.

Destiny stuck out her tongue and pouted. "Whatever. From what you've found out, the historical Faust sounds like a carny. You don't think that walking STD we saw at the carnival?"

Sam waved the question away. "Too much of a coincidence, Des. There's no way the real Faust would hang around a dirty, rundown carnival."

Destiny shot Sam a disbelieving look and said, "It would provide brilliant cover for his little jaunts to torment Craig, and we don't have a better lead to pursue. Let's go play some ring toss and help a wizard tell his own fortune."

Sam shook her head. "I don't know. I don't think this case will be that easy. Did you find anything else in Donal's grimoire?"

Destiny shrugged. "I found the spell Nick mentioned. I also found a pocket on the back cover where he keeps one of your school photos from back when you had pigtails and extra-chubby cheeks. You were so cute and innocent."

Sam rolled her eyes. "Did you bring it? You mentioned the ritual used to return a soul from Hell. I want to see it."

Destiny tensed and blinked. "Are you sure, Sam? It's not pretty."

"It can't be that bad. Just let me see."

Destiny exhaled and nodded. She handed Sam the leather-bound book and swallowed hard, tensing her muscles. Sam flipped to the back and looked at the small photograph of her from first grade, where her pigtails cascaded over her frilly pink dress. The neon laser background looked "cool" then, but she cringed upon seeing it now. On the back, she wrote *I love you, daddy.* She glared and scoffed. She thumbed through the pages, her mouth moving as she read silently. When she found the soul retrieval ritual, her index finger scanned the page as she read. And then her eyes bolted wide.

Sam's face paled. Cold sweat formed on her forehead. She exhaled and nodded. Her hand trembled as she closed the book and dropped it into her purse. "I see. Well, let's get to the carnival."

The Darque Starfall Travelers Carnival was silent on this Tuesday afternoon in early April. Children were still in school, and their parents were still trudging through the workday. College students and retirees milled about the filthy carnival grounds for pleasure, for laughs, and for nostalgia. Sam and Destiny, a corn dog in one hand and blue raspberry cotton candy in the other, traipsed through the litter-strewn grass. The stalls, games, and attractions appeared dirtier; the broken signs appeared sharper, and lights flickered their forlorn dances during the day. And the stench of overflowing toilets, rotten wood, bottom-of-the-well whiskey, and old urine perfumed the crisp air.

They passed the House of Seven Devils and made their way to the edge of carnival where they remembered Faust' tent standing. An empty patch of dirt, littered with corn dog sticks, needles, popcorn bags, paper cups, and gum wrappers greeted them. They searched the area and found several foot trails, the tent's outline and spike holes, and a gold ring with a princess cut sapphire. A grizzled older carny, his neck, arms, and torso covered in fading tattoos, noticed them and walked over.

He asked in a nasal drawl, "Hey, ma'ams, you lose something?"

Sam scanned the man and shrugged. "Where's the fortune teller? I thought his tent was here."

"You cops?"

"Not anymore." Destiny's German accent emerged as her voice trailed to a whisper. Sam squeezed her hand and offered a comforting smile.

"You sound like you're from the same place as him." The carny pointed at Destiny. He squinted his seaweed green eyes and scratched his neck, causing his stringy gray hair. "Yeah, was here. Just up and left a couple days ago. Good riddance to him."

Destiny asked, "Didn't like him? He seemed okay if not a walking red flag. Do you know where he went?"

The carny shook his head. "Said something about meeting a man at a churchyard or something. And didn't really get to know him. Kept to himself and wouldn't camp with the rest of the family. Makes sense, I guess."

"What do you mean?" When Destiny grew inquisitive, Sam stepped back. She smiled.

"We picked him up on the road outside Spartanburg. He convinced Mister Starfall and Mister Darque he had skill with fortunetelling and illusion. They hired him on, but none of us really got on with him. Strange man. Cocky bastard, always talking about his degrees and shit. Talked funny, like he was quoting literature or something. We thought it was part of his act, but he did at camp when it was just us. He gave me the creeps, and I've been doing this for fifty years. That ain't easy to do."

* * *

As the sun set, Sam and Destiny sat in the front seat of Sam's Subaru, which was parked beneath a streetlight opposite a large ranch style home whose exterior resembled a log cabin. They cracked the windows to let the cool evening air circulate. A Nikon D7500 DSLR camera and two pairs of binoculars sat on the dashboard. Sam sipped her Dr. Pepper, and Destiny dipped her fried chicken tender into her curried ranch sauce. Stakeouts called for fried chicken tenders from Foxie's Hen House.

The house sat one block from the corner of Nobbs and Vimes. Both were quiet streets. Cars entered the Ankmoor Park subdivision through the gate on Vimes, which had been stuck in the open position since Valentine's Day. The little white gatehouse by the entrance to this upper middle class neighborhood had been unattended since Stephen Gonsalves died from colon cancer in November. Regular police patrols kept most crime at bay.

They sat and observed the house as part of one of their regular cases. Charlene Meyers' friends and coworkers fed her rumors that her husband, Randal, was unfaithful. She dismissed them until she received an email from a woman named Randi Matherne, who not only claimed to be Charlene's husband's mistress but also to be pregnant with his child. Her husband, of course, denied the claim, and so Charlene hired Sam to investigate.

Sam leaned forward and squinted as the sky darkened. Nothing unusual. "So, Des, you think we'll find something tonight?"

"It's probable," Destiny said, her mouth full of French fries. She swallowed and sipped her Orange Fanta. "Based on my careful analysis of Facebook posts, two hours after Randi Matherne posts a video of kids with nasal voices singing the Oscar Mayer song, Randal Meyers posts about going for an evening drive to clear his head. Thus, based upon the timing of seemingly unrelated posts that together create a series of dick jokes, tonight's the night."

Destiny laughed. Sam chuckled and shook her head. "If anyone else suggested that connection for that reason, I would've told them to grow up, but not you, Des. The weirder your hunch, the more likely it is to be true."

Destiny smiled. They returned to a comfortable and focused silence, interrupted only by the sounds of eating, as they ate and observed. Sam's mind drifted.

I should never have taken on so many cases. Maybe I shouldn't have taken on any supernatural ones, but then I wouldn't be in this line of work. I was doing a study abroad in Ireland, and Flann MacMagnus, that stupid leprechaun with a gambling problem, approached me and begged for help. It was such a rush, even if it earned me the ire of Michael fucking Cormack and the Bardic College of Seamus Duilearga. My shoulder still hurts when it's cold, but that bullet didn't kill me. I failed that class, but it was the start of my new career.

Sam sighed and lowered her eyes. *That was the start of Mom going downhill. I didn't notice. How did I not notice sadness, loneliness, fear, and worry dog pile her? I didn't want to notice; that's the short of it. She saw me through my licensure period and my first couple of years as a P. I. I was so thankful Destiny came to work with me before Mom ended her life.*

Sam exhaled and checked her phone. No messages. Carmilla knew she was on a stakeout. Still, a text or a suggestive photograph, which would be Carmilla's first, would have been appreciated. Sam sighed. Destiny offered a look of concern, but Sam shook her head.

Mom's death led to meeting Carmilla. I was upset, couldn't sleep thanks to Donal calling me at three in the morning, and lonely. I walked into the Four Winds, fully intending to make a logical deal just to see Mom again, but then I offered the fucking devil a blank check. To his credit, he asked me three times if I was certain. We signed the contract; he left me alone, and then she approached me. I fell harder and faster than I wanted to admit. Then I broke it off, but we remained friends. Everyone knew we'd get back together, and I haven't been happier.

And now here we are. Everything comes to a head with these overlapping nature of the Wellington case and my recklessness at the Four Winds. I don't know if I can handle this. I don't have a choice. At least the S-T's haven't gotten involved. I don't need the government breathing down my neck when I've already got Hell itself looming over me.

Destiny shook Sam's arm, snapping her from her thoughts. She pointed to an SUV pulling into the driveway. "Sam, look, it's showtime."

The SUV, a dark Ford Explorer, stopped midway along the drive. It was too dark to make out the color, but it appeared to be either a dark green or a dark blue. Sam readied the camera, extending the lens, and snapped three photographs of the vehicle's license plate. She held her breath and waited. A balding white man in his upper thirties stepped out of the vehicle. Sam snapped another photograph. She started her Forrester and inched forward, one hand on the wheel and the other on the camera. A pregnant Randi Matherne greeted him with a kiss, and Sam captured her final photograph of the night.

Destiny's thumbs tapped furiously at her phone screen. She pulled her left hand away and tapped a final time with her index finger. "And license plate info request sent. This case is in the bag, boss."

Sam smiled and drove away. "We'll get copies made and send them to Charlene. 'Milla's probably asleep, so I'll read for a bit and then turn in early. What about you? Raid night still on?"

Destiny shook her head. She slurped air through her straw; she was out of Fanta. "Ylianara can't make it. I'm not tanking Briarstone Keep without my best cleric. I'm going to play some *Hollow Knight* 2 while browsing YouTube videos."

As they left Ankmoor Park, Sam said, "I know I always tell you this, but I couldn't have done anything today without you."

Destiny snorted and waved her hand. "Of course you could. You have before. I know you've got a lot on your mind, so if I can take some pressure off, I will. You're my best friend. If you didn't suck at night driving, I'd hug you."

I don't suck at night driving. Sam pretended to pout for a moment. "You've got such good instincts, and I know it's not just your training. You're such a natural. If you want to get more involved with the Full Moon Specials, I'd probably squee like you do when a new *Pokemon* game is announced."

Destiny nodded and turned her gaze to the window. A bodybuilder walked his chihuahua beneath the flickering street lights. Destiny sighed.

"I can't, Sam. I'll help with interviews or evidence gathering, but I can't do more. The last time I was in the field, I did everything right. I followed all the rules, observed all the protocols. I chased him from the discotheque where he transformed. We fought. He was strong, fast, fought through instinct. I broke his legs. As he lay there, whimpering like a scared dog, I put a silver bullet between his eyes. They never told me werewolves transformed back when they died. The fear on his face, frozen. He was five, maybe six, years younger than me. I followed orders, and I killed a kid. I can't, Sam. I can't. I'm sorry."

Sam nodded. She knew not to push Destiny on this matter. Melissa Etheridge's "Come to my Window" played over the speakers. They drove home in silence.

Chapter 8

Thursdays were quiet days around the office, unless it was a full moon that day. Since today wasn't a full moon, I enjoyed a peaceful morning sitting at my desk, organizing the documents for Charlene Meyers, and sipping black coffee. Joan Jett and the Blackhearts drowned out the construction sounds from the street behind me. We were well into the black again this month. Activating a teleportation beacon in Castle Karnstein effectively removed the "long distance" from my long distance relationship. I glanced down at my mug and smiled; I was living my best Hayes Code violating life.

One glance at my father's traveling grimoire proved enough to dissuade me from arrogant happiness. It wasn't what he did, that was horrible enough, or who he was, but it was what loomed in the next few months. My confrontation with Doctor Johann Faust, whom my father helped escape Hell. I had to drag him back there, or I would take his place. Nick Scratch loved his irony. I made the deal. Now, the consequences of my actions breathed hot, dry, and hungry air on the back of my neck.

Destiny entered, holding a stack of envelopes in her hands. "Mail's here, Sam," she said. "We got the usual assortment of bills, junk, and a new mall Chinese place opened down the

street. They deliver, and they gave us coupons. We'll have t
check them out. Oh! Here's a letter from your father."

She handed me the envelope from Hain & Corrigan, Barris-
ters. The envelope was light, so it was likely just a letter. My
heart pummeled my ribs as I held it. I shook my head and tossed
it in the trash. "There. It's been filed."

Destiny shook her head and sighed. "Look, Sam. I know you
two have a strained relationship on a good day, but he took the
time to write you a letter. There's no harm in reading it."

I growled and returned to my work. "You're welcome to dig
it out and read the trash he spews."

Destiny glared. She grabbed Donal's letter from the trash and
returned to her desk, muttering about me being as stubborn as
an Irish mule. She meant well, but after the events in Bannagh,
it wasn't happening. I was ready to give Donal a chance after
I returned from Faerie, but then I saw him on Old Tom's Hill,
trying to sacrifice Frank to that demon as part of some work he
was doing alongside the Order of the Dragon. And then what I
read in his grimoire, what he did so he could pull a soul from
Hell, no fucking way. Mom wouldn't be happy.

Mom. I clenched my jaw and sighed. I got myself into this
shit hole because I didn't want to accept that she died. That she
died the way she did. I put my elbow on my desk and rested my
chin on my hand. I exhaled. Mom hated what I did. As much
as she enjoyed both the one hour reprieve each year and the
additional time we spent together, she worried my recklessness
would get me killed or damned. Like her.

I kicked my desk and then winced. My breaths came faster.
I rolled and stretched my neck before grabbing my mug. It
was empty. I walked into our main office and poured myself
another cup. Destiny sat at her desk, paying the bills that came

in. I smiled. This was the first time in our business history we could pay our bills as soon as we got them. Donal's note lay on the corner of her desk.

I walked over and asked, "Was I right? Nothing in the note?"

She clicked send on our water bill, spun her chair to face me, and said, "You need to read it. This isn't about sentiment or warm fuzzies and giving your dad a chance. This is about information regarding open cases and current events. Don't think like a daughter. Think like an investigator."

"Fine."

I sighed and snatched Donal's letter with my free hand. I glared at it and stormed into my office. The door slammed behind me. A sip of coffee calmed me enough to look at the letter. Handwritten. The fucking asshole hand wrote a letter. Why? His handwriting was terrible. Couldn't he have just dictated his bullshit to his secretary? I'm sure she would love to type this for him. I growled as I started reading.

To my daughter, Samantha,

My flight from Debrecen has given me time to both think and write out my thoughts. And so I pen to you this letter that I hope reaches you in safety and security. Look, you and I have a strained relationship. Some might even argue that our relationship might be likened to a house without a sturdy foundation. And my actions over the past decade have in no small way contributed to the current state of deterioration our relationship exhibits.

Before you ask, yes, I traveled to Debrecen to meet with allies of my order. Yes, they were members of the Order of the Dragon. I am not the one who negotiated the alliance; that was my predecessor, the late Arch Magus Manibus Divini Spiritus, who performed that action. When asked to return, I inherited his duties and relationship with that extra-governmental military order. That is of no importance, but you need to know the dilemma your actions have placed me in.

My actions have placed *you* in a dilemma? I'm not the one who poisoned two babies in order to bring a damned soul back from Hell. I'm not the one who tried to sacrifice Frank to Zozo. Fucking arrogant asshole. It's never your fault, is it, Donal? Always someone else to blame. It was mom's fault you fucked your secretary while she took care of grandma on her deathbed. You fucking disgust me.

That said, as your father, I want what is best for you. Currently, your actions have made it difficult, if not impossible, for me to protect you. The Order of the Dragon has declared you an enemy on par with the families of those who killed Vlad Dracula over a century ago. Had you not spurned either my advice or my invitation in Bannagh, you would be safe now. I will continue to do what I can to protect you, but you will need to take responsibility for your actions and be careful.

I sort of gathered they were after me when I was in Austria, dad. They sent an agent, albeit an idiot, to try and kill Carmilla and me. So was that agent really after your grimoire, Donal? Or was that the excuse to kill me? He might have succeeded; I froze. Memories of Bannagh—of the night I shot your fucking knee on Old Tom's Hill—flooded my mind.

My heart pounded. My breathing became shallow and rapid. Fuck, just remembering the flashback set me off. I growled, ran my fingers through my hair, and slammed my fist into the desk.

The best way you can protect yourself now from what they are planning is to return to your magical training.

Not going to happen, Donal.

I am not offering to train you. I do not have the patience to curtail your attitude, and I doubt you would submit and become my apprentice.

Right on both assertions, barrister. I can see why you get to try those high-profile cases.

There are, however, many noble and honorable men within the ranks of the Hermetic Order of the Astrum Argentum. You can trust them. They will train you well.

Oh, so you still want me to join your misogynistic, patriarchal boys' club? I'm going to have to pass on that like it's a kidney stone, Donal. In case you've forgotten in your old age, I was almost kicked out when I *did* listen to your advice because I told Magus Chesterfield to "fuck off with his shit-spewing fuck hole" after he said that a woman's place was kneeling beside a man and providing him with food. Still not sorry. Still not going back. Nice try.

If I have failed in persuading you of anything with my preceding words, then permit me to implore you to take the high road. I know you will not turn back from your present course, and even should you do so, it might be too little too late to protect you from the Order of the Dragon's wrath. Meditate, develop your focus, and, if you will do nothing else I ask, master the spells and rites in my traveling grimoire. If you can cast aside your childish anger and focus, these magical workings will provide you with the best chance you have of being safe.

"Fuck you, Donal."

I ripped the letter in half, crumpled it, and threw it in the trash. I hated you before, but when I read your ritual for retrieving a soul from Hell and saw it required killing two children with poison, you transmuted that hatred into disgust. You'll learn one day, Donal, bullets kill wizards and Dracula fanboys just easily as they kill normal people. I don't need you, and I don't need your help.

* * *

Sam sat at her desk in the corner of her magical working room. Steam rose from the coffee cup she set atop a wooden coaster. The LED lamp's soft glow illuminated the text in her father's traveling grimoire while casting minimal shadows against the room's curtains. She stared at the pages; her eyes unfocused, and the words blurred. Sam blinked, scratched the back of her neck, and grumbled. She flipped back to the beginning and started again. She slammed the side of her hand into her palm as she rested her elbow on the desk.

"Focus, Samantha, focus." She growled and sipped her coffee. Sandy Paws's plaintive meow traveled through the door. Sam turned and, with a sigh, said, "Not now, Sandy. Mommy needs to focus."

Sam turned back to the grimoire and exhaled. She massaged her temples and sighed in exasperation. Sam rose from her chair and walked to the bookcase containing her small collection of occult theory and practice books. She kept them for case research, never intending to practice, but here she was. She ran her finger across the spines of *Magick In Theory and in Practice, Practical Witchcraft, Ritual Magic,* Agrippa's *Three Books of Occult Philosophy, The Garden of Pomegranates,* and the complete alchemical writings of Paracelsus and rested her finger on a nondescript lavender notebook. Sam returned to the desk and opened the notebook to one of the few pages containing her handwriting.

Alright, Sam, think. Those notes have to be there. You've learned the basics, and you should be able to do this. You've mastered the

Basic Pentagram Banishing Ritual, the Angelic Elemental Calling Ritual, and that basic Mind Shielding Ritual. You can access the portal network, but you still need a teleportation beacon set up in a location to teleport there. Focus. Please.

What was that he always said at the end of my lessons? Here it is. "Your focus and intent determine your reality, for where your mind focuses its intention, your will brings about changes." I know I need to focus. That's always been my downfall in magic. Okay, so my issues with my father didn't help matters. I need to focus. Ugh! There's just so much going on. Fuck.

Sam grabbed an orange incense cone Rayna made for her. Having a witch on speed dial had benefits beyond friendship and Rayna's amazing bread baking skills. She flicked a match across the box's striker, and a flame hissed to life. She lit the incense and put out the match. As the smoke perfumed the room with scents of apple, cinnamon, clove, nutmeg, and blood orange, Sam closed her eyes, slowed her breathing, and sipped her coffee in silence. Meditation was a challenge, but she learned that with apple cider incense and coffee, clearing her mind became easier.

When only ash and empty mug remained, Sam's eyes opened, and she exhaled slowly. She opened the grimoire once more and flipped through its pages. Her lip curled, baring her teeth, in a scowl as she passed the ritual her father performed to retrieve Faust's soul from Hell. Sam's nose flared; her cheeks burned, and her fists clenched, seeing the instructions to inject scorpion venom into the hearts of living infants, infuse grain alcohol with sulfur and poisoned hearts, then create a potion combining the infant blood, the heart infusion, and yew tree sap. That potion was then distributed through the host body's circulatory system like a corrupted embalming. Seething, Sam ripped this ritual from the book.

Sam found the soul binding ritual Nick Scratch suggested she master. Her eyes shot wide, and she swallowed. Donal Hain provided a complete set of instructions, which meant he had not mastered the ritual. The ritual required a bell from the cemetery where Faust was buried, a book from the school he attended, and a candle burned in the church where he was consecrated. A trip to Germany loomed before her, and she hoped her internet research on the historical Faust proved accurate.

I should start with something simpler to get back into practice. I'm not ready for this.

Sam sighed. She thumbed the pages and cocked an eyebrow. Why was the ritual to summon a familiar last? That was one of the easiest rites in this book. Scanning the single page of notes, Sam nodded. Her altar was ready. She had purple, yellow, and white candles. What was personal incense? Did she need to make incense? Or would incense that represented her work? It was time to find out. She opened her supply closet and gathered the needed components. Sam closed the shades and turned off all lights in the room.

Sam arranged her standard altar tools in their appropriate stations. Her censor sat on the eastern edge, centered between the black and white taper altar candles. She centered her wand on the southern edge. A small silver chalice rose on the western edge. She placed a palm-sized silver disk with a raised pentagram on the northern side. Sam arranged the small gold, purple, and white chime candles in a triangle at the altar's center. Between the candles and the chalice, she rested her father's traveling grimoire. She angled her ritual dagger in the northwest of her altar, and she set a matchbox in the southwest.

She concluded her preparations by placing a cone of the apple cider incense Rayna made for her inside the censor.

Sam nodded and centered herself. A single breath escaped her lips. With a flick of her wrist, a match spat to life. Sam lit the black and white altar candles before snuffing the match. She took the black candle and lit the incense. Taking the dagger in hand, she knocked thrice on the altar with its pommel. The censor warmed her hands as she held it at eye level and circled her altar clockwise. She took the dagger and performed the Basic Pentagram Banishing Ritual, taking care to intone the divine and angelic names with proper vibration. An electric charge warmed the air as she finished. Sam stood at the circle's center, at the western edge of her altar, and felt the energy flows around her.

Alright, Sam, let's do this. Stay calm. Stay focused.

Sam opened her father's grimoire to his notes for summoning a familiar. She passed each of the colored chime candles through the incense smoke and then lit each with the black altar candle. A scratch tickled her throat. Sam swallowed; she blinked and paused as her breaths quickened. When calmed, she stared into the darkness and began the incantation.

"*Bestia voco, et bestia me vocat. Mea voluntate, per divinum nomen Tetragrammaton. Saltare ad crepitum cordis mei. Audite me veteres, et —*"

Dry, hacking coughs burst from her mouth. Sam winced and cursed. Her heart increased its pumping speed, and her breathing quickened. Sam pressed her palms against her temples. A low, rumbling growl vibrated as it passed through Sam's mouth. Another string of coughs escaped her lips. She assumed the lotus pose, focused on her breathing, and calmed herself.

Sam sighed as she stood and returned to her spot at the western edge of her altar. She took three deep breaths, grabbed her father's grimoire, and, in a louder and more forceful voice, said, "*Bestia voco, et bestia me vocat. Mea voluntate, per divinum nomen Tetragrammaton. Saltare ad crepitum cordis mei. Audite me veteres, et Spiritum manifesta. Fur vel pinna, vocem meam audi ad magica familiarium...*"

As she intoned the incantation's words, her eyes shifted toward the ceiling. Did she repeat the space cleansing and banishing before the second attempt? Should the words be spoken with a classical or ecclesiastical pronunciation? Was Sandy Paws her familiar? If not, would Sandy and her familiar get along? What if they hated each other? Realization hit her. And then she slammed her palm into her face.

Fuck! Damn it, Sam, you lost your focus again. This always happens. This is why your fucking father yelled at you when he tried training you. Do you remember that? Can't let him be right. Not on this. Not on anything. And especially not now. Focus, Sam. Come on. Focus!

Sam curled her fingers into claws as she mentally berated herself. Though the warm, comforting scent of blood orange apple cider filled the cool, dark room, only ash remained of the incense cone. She snuffed the chime candles with three pinches, removed the ash from the censor, and placed another cone inside it. She paced the room, counting her four-count breaths as she worked to calm herself. When her heart rate and breathing returned to normal, she pulled her hair into a ponytail, performed her space cleansing, and then began the ritual once more.

"*Bestia voco, et bestia me vocat. Mea voluntate, per divinum nomen Tetragrammaton. Saltare ad crepitum cordis mei. Audite me veteres, et Spiritum manifesta. Fur vel pinna, vocem meam audi ad magica familiarium. Creatura terrae, aeris, venti vel aquae, Veni ad me, matrona me. Ego pro te curabo et honorabo te."*

Sam stood in silence within the electrified air of her magical space. Vibrations in the air caused her skin to tingle; the hairs on her arms and the back of her neck stood and swayed. Silence filled the room. The purple candle flickered, trembled, and snuffed itself out. Sam eyed it curiously. She held her breath and leaned forward. The wick swayed and sparked. Sweat beaded on Sam's forehead. Staccato breaths slipped through her lips. The sparking stopped. And there was silence once more.

Nothing happened. No familiar spirit appeared. Why? She performed the ritual correctly. She knew that. Why did no spirit come to her aid? Sam gnashed her teeth and clenched her fists. Her nose flared. She breathed hot, hard, shallow breaths as tears welled in her eyes. Sam sniffled and bit her lip. She had succeeded without magic so far, and she needed no magical shortcut for this. Her father's notes were likely incorrect, as magicians had a habit of leaving falsehoods in their grimoires to confuse others. Sam grabbed her father's grimoire and hurled it at the corner of the room. It fell open as it hit the floor.

As Sam stormed from the room, she said, "Fuck it. I've got a gun. Bullets kill arrogant wizards too."

* * *

The next morning, a nondescript black Lincoln Town Car drove south from Fiddlers' Ford and pulled up to the crossroads of Highway 178 and Old Highway 76. Over the factory-issued speakers, Paul McCartney's "Band on the Run" faded into The Band's "The Night They Drove Old Dixie Down." Two men wearing navy suits and dark sunglasses sat in the front seat. A white man in his early thirties named Jeffery Smith drove. He kept his curly brown hair short. A few gray streaks had creeped into his hair over the past few years. Wrinkles formed on his forehead; a half-empty pack of Camel Blues sat in his shirt's breast pocket. Damon Washington, a tall black man with a gold earring in his left ear, sat in the passenger seat. His bald head revealed the autumnal foliage-hued undertones of his rich dark umber skin. He checked his phone every few minutes.

Workers spent the day dismantling and packing the Starfall Travelers Carnival as Smith parked. Smith and Johnson exited the Town Car and scanned the area. A cool breeze caused their blazers to flutter. Jeffery Smith squinted behind his generic sunglasses. Damon Washington squatted, running his fingers through the dirt and grass.

He looked up at Smith and asked, "You sure this is the spot? Seems like too open a place."

Smith nodded. "Briefing says it happened almost a month ago. Carnival wasn't set up then, so this place would've been deserted. Nothing live around here for fifteen or twenty miles."

"So tell me again, Jeff, what we're doing here?"

"Report says this is the scene where the fight took place. Well, where both of them took place, but we can't do anything about the one thirty years ago. Protocol dictates we survey the scene of the incident before we talk to anyone involved and any witnesses. And there was that barbecue place we saw, the Porker Smorkersboard, won't start serving until eleven."

Washington sighed and raised his arms. "Alright, what can we find here this long after the event?"

Jeffery Smith squatted by the light post and stroked his stubbled chin. He pointed to scorch marks with yellow powder at their edges. "See that, Damon? Sulfur powder at the edge of a burn. If the reports are accurate and not just somebody talking up a local legend, this suggests black magic is involved. We'll have to requisition either a cursebreaker or HexShield gear."

Jeffery Smith lit a cigarette. Damon Washington nodded and grabbed a stick of gum. Smith scanned the dirt and grass. He tapped the outline of a boot, stood, and placed his foot next to it. His foot was noticeably larger. Washington scrunched his face and cocked an eyebrow. He asked, "What the heck are you doing?"

Smith took a drag from his Camel, causing Washington to wrinkle his nose. Smith said, "Examining footprints. Two sets. Small. They're likely women's footprints."

"Are you saying that there's a woman involved in this? The report didn't mention any women."

Smith shook his head. "No, but yes. We're south of Butcher's Bend, so I'd wager Samantha Hain was here."

Damon scribbled notes in his pocket notebook. "She a podcaster? Paranormal investigator?"

"P. I. Damned good one, and she's licensed to handle NHM cases. If this is a legit Piercing, then I'd say that guy who's been talking this up." Smith skimmed his briefing notes, nodded, and said,"My guess is this Craig Wellington hired her to take care of the matter for him."

"So she's competition?"

Smith shook his head and laughed. "Only if we make her competition. I made that mistake when I was a rookie. Her M. O. is to keep everyone safe and alive—human and NHM—so don't go talking about how we keep the public in the dark. That'll turn her off, and she'll take it as a challenge to beat us. She knows this work better than you or I, and the community trusts her."

Washington surveyed the area. No vehicles traveled either of the roads that crossed where they stood. Something felt off about there being a carnival right here. He shrugged and shook his head. "So we going talk to her?"

"Maybe. First, we're getting lunch. Then we'll have a little chat with Mister Wellington. After that, we'll decide if Miss Hain can be of assistance."

Smith and Washington left the crossroads and drove to the Porker Smorkersboard for lunch. Small talk with other diners afforded them general information on Fiddlers' Ford and its history. The locals' words and tone suggested no one believed Craig Wellington's story. They made note of that. After lunch, they drove their black Town Car pulled into the driveway of a modest, tan, ranch-style home. The unkempt yard, blue tarp duct taped to the roof, and the plywood covering two of the three street-facing windows spoke volumes regarding the house's story. A blue F-150 rested near the ripped screen door.

As the car stopped, Damon asked, "So, who are we today?"

"Folklorists," Jeffery said. "We're from UNC's Department of American Studies, and we're researching a book on cross-roads folklore in the Appalachians, focusing on encounters with spirits."

Damon nodded. Jeffery handed Damon a UNC faculty identification card with his name and photograph, identifying him as an Associate Professor of Literature in the Department of American Studies. They exited the car and walked to the front door. Jeffery Smith knocked on the front door. After a few moments, a series of grunts and uneven footsteps informed them Craig would open the door. When he did, Smith and Washington saw a man with droopy eyes and a patchy, dirty blond beard. He swayed and bobbed as he stood there, and even through the screen door, they smelled his aura of beer and whiskey.

Craig leaned forward and squinted at them and said, "Yeah? Who are you?"

"Hi, Mister Wellington, is it?" Jeffery Smith said. "I'm Doctor Jeffery D. Smith, Professor of Folklore at UNC, and this is my friend and colleague, Dr. Damon Q. Washington, a Professor of Spatial Ethnography. We're sorry we didn't call first, but we were in the area, and local gossip suggested you could help us with a book we're working on."

Craig Wellington eyed the two men with suspicion. In his drunken state, his suspicion and thought process were made exaggeratedly clear. Every family within fifty miles of the Appalachians told stories of scholars coming in to collect their stories back in the day. None of the families ever saw profit. Some even believed these "scholars" were nothing more than government agents; anthropologists and folklorists were the worst for that. Craig cocked his head and scratched above his ear.

"I don't know." He slurred his words as he spoke. "I'm not much for college, and I don't know any good stories. So I think I'll decline."

Jeffery Smith nodded. "That's fair, Mister Wellington." He turned to Damon Washington, patted him on the shoulder, and started to walk away, saying, "See Damon, I told you we can't just trust local gossip. No one around here has any stories about meeting the devil at a crossroads. We'll need to head down to Georgia or Mississippi for that. Shame."

Damon Washington's jaw dropped, and his eyes widened as he watched Jeffery Smith walk away. His gaze shifted from his partner to Craig and back to his partner several times. Craig shrugged and offered an apologetic glance. He paused, and his gaze lifted skyward as he processed what the man said. He opened the screen door and stumbled forward.

"Hey, uh, hey, Professor, did you say something about the devil at the crossroads?"

Jeffery Smith smiled as he opened the car door. He stopped but did not turn around. Smith nodded and said, "Yes. We're researching legends, folktales, and stories where people met the devil at a crossroads. We heard you have a story—one that doesn't follow any of the expected narrative structures. If this is so, then we may have come across a new tale type, which would lead to a revision of the Aarne-Thompson-Uther Tale Type Index. A major find. And you could be a part of that."

"What do I get out of it?" Craig asked.

Damon Washington's eyes lit in realization. He nodded and said, "You get to be part of helping us better understand the stories we tell. We'll put your name in our book."

"Do I get any money for it? You see, my wife left me with our son, and I lost my job. And I've kind of got bills to pay, so I'd appreciate some help if you use my story."

Smith turned and smiled. "We can't give you any money—at least not up front, Mister Wellington. I can say that if you tell us your story and it suggests what we think it suggests, then you'll be safe in the long run. We can promise safety, but nothing up front."

The alcoholic reek from Craig's belch caused Damon Washington to wrinkle his nose. He massaged the back of his neck with one hand while fidgeting with something in his pocket with the other. He shrugged. "I don't know. I need the money, so I guess I'll say, 'No.'"

Damon Washington's breathing became shallow. His eyes narrowed, and his nostrils flared. Jeffery Smith scratched his neck, offered a dejected glance, and nodded. He walked back to Craig and held out a business card. "I understand, Mister Wellington. Thank you for your time. If you change your mind, you can call or email me. Damon, let's go."

Craig took the card and shoved it into his pocket. Jeffery Smith returned to the black car and sat in the driver's seat. Damon Washington took a single deep breath, shot Craig a stern look, and said in a forceful voice, "You call us. It's for the best.

Damon stalked to the car and sat in the passenger seat. Craig and Jeffery waved goodbye. As the black Lincoln backed away, Craig pulled the business card from his pocket. It looked legitimate, but he never knew any college professors who wore anything other than tweed blazers with mismatched socks. These men looked more like accountants or the FBI agents Craig saw on television. He shrugged and stumbled back into his house.

As the Lincoln Town Car drove away, Damon Washington asked, "Okay, why the hell did we leave? We could've flashed our badges and made him talk to us."

Jeffery Smith turned left onto Osbourne Road and nodded. "We needed to stay in character. Professors can't force people to talk to them. Made that mistake before. Badge flashing can make things worse. It's best to keep a low profile until we gather enough evidence to justify taking action. Besides, he was drunk off his ass. Let him sober up. He'll call. If not today, then soon. Either way, I'll introduce you to Miss Hain tomorrow."

* * *

While Smith and Washington began their investigation in Fiddlers' Ford, Destiny Grimm lounged in her townhouse's den. Sprawled across the plush Tiffany blue cushions in her Korilakkuma kigurumi, she writhed in pain, clutched her lower torso, and moaned. Bags of Kinder and Ritter chocolates and their empty wrappers lay strewn across the floor; steam from a mug filled with hot black tea and honey rose from her side table. Taking a day off for illness was a rarity, as her family taught that duty and sacrifice were their obligations, but on this heavy flow day, she made an exception.

She whimpered as she sat up and sipped her tea, inhaling its earthy scent and its warmth. Jeremy's ringtone played on her phone. She leaned over and grabbed it. Her voice emerged as a weak whimper when she said, "Hallo, babe. How are you?"

"Concerned," he said. "I called you at the office to see if you wanted to grab lunch today, but Sam answered, saying you were out sick. Since we started dating, I've seen you work through the flu and a case of step throat, so what's up?"

Destiny scrunched her face and then winced as an invisible assailant twisted the jagged knife into her intestines. "Oh, nothing really bad. It's just lady stuff."

Jeremy nodded. "Heavy day? Look, Des, you can say it's your period. I've got a mom and two sisters, so I've dealt with this before. I mean, when my sister Nicole got her first period the July before she started fifth grade, mom dragged me to school with her when she went to talk to her teacher about how to handle periods during the school day. Sure, I was twelve, and it was embarrassing then. I'm used to it now."

Destiny bit her smiling lip as her eyes welled. She blushed and said, "I'm sorry. I'm so used to American men being grossed out by even euphemisms for my menstrual cycle. You really are great. Thank you."

He shrugged. "It's part of life. Sure, blood is a little gross, but this will happen monthly for, well, decades. More importantly, do you need anything? Chocolate, schnitzel, or pretzels? If you need tampons or pads, would you please text me a picture of the box? I get the names confused sometimes."

Destiny thought for a moment. "Would you bring me two of those giant soft pretzels the Eleven-to-Seven convenience store sells? One garlic and Parmesan and one plain salted?"

"Sure. I'll swing by on my lunch break. Love you."

"Love you too."

Destiny sighed as she set the phone on the side table. The clock struck nine in the morning when Jeremy called. She looked at her Switch and her PS4 and thought about delving into her "To Be Finished" video game pile. Her eyes turned to her SNES Mini, and she thought about playing one of her comfort games from childhood. She winced, cried, and sipped her tea. With a sigh, she grabbed her custom Sailor Mars PS5 controller.

As she scrolled through the games, she mused, "Alright, what looks fun? No, that's too frustrating. If I play that one, I'll have to suffer online through a bunch of dudebros who can't even wipe their own asses, let alone clean an assault rifle. Superheroes are boring me. Oh! I could rip a few spines out, but I've already got enough blood around me. Alternative history Nazis? *Nein danke.*"

She growled in frustration and then whimpered. Destiny threw her controller onto a pillow at the far end of the sofa, reached over with her foot, and pulled her wireless Switch controller toward her. "Let's see what I've got here. Really? I haven't changed the cartridge since *Metroid: Dread* came out? Have I downloaded that many games onto the SD card? Yes, yes I have. Something cozy? I haven't checked on my island in a few months. Poop! I don't want to spend my day picking weeds and killing roaches. Don't feel like solving a mystery with Jenny McClue."

Her eyes smiled wide as she said, "A Metroidvania! That's what I need to get some dopamine into my brain and rage out of my body. So, which one? I don't know. Well, I did just start another playthrough of *Vigil*, so let's keep going there."

The game loaded, and Destiny controlled Leila as she leaped and climbed from platform to platform beneath the Maya Bridge. She opened a treasure chest and found a portrait of a noble woman. Destiny nodded and returned it to the painter, completing the quest and earning the cerulean ocarina. After returning to the Catacombs, Destiny guided Leila to the Ceremonial Stone Monument and played the cerulean ocarina, opening the portal to the Shadow Disaster.

Destiny's mind wandered as she guided Leila through the gray, skeleton-littered landscape with thunder raging in the background. The time neared for Craig Wellington's, and by extension, Sam's, confrontation with Doctor Faust at that lonely crossroads south of Fiddlers' Ford. Destiny cursed as Leila plummeted from a missed jump and died. Her stubborn Irish mule of a best friend intended to handle the matter on her own and, against the advice of Nick Scratch, without magic. She grunted as Leila fell to her death again. This battle was beyond Sam's skills, and Destiny did not possess the magical skills to help. After another falling death, Destiny hurled a string of German curses at the game and threw her controller onto the floor. She ate a Kinder Bueno and then called her father.

Working from his manor in Hanau, Werther Grimm sat in his office and read through the open case reports emailed to him. His once blond hair had silvered over the years, and stress, worry, and age had etched deep lines on his face. His phone rang. He shifted his gaze and smiled at its screen.

He switched on the phone's speaker and, in his German bass voice, said, "Destiny. Hallo, darling. How are you?"

"I'm cramping, and I'm bloated. And I'm moody. It's my period. And I'm out of Kinder eggs, Papa."

He nodded while scrolling. "I can ship you a dozen, but your cycle will be over."

"I can still eat them, but that's not why I called."

"I had hoped your call would be for more than candy. Is all well?"

Destiny whimpered as she shifted onto her back, allowing one leg to drop to the floor and the other to drape over her sofa's armrest. She reached her free hand over the armrest and, holding her breath, lifted the tea mug over the armrest and onto the sofa next to her. She sipped her tea and cried.

Her words flooded into the phone as she said, "Overall, things are fine. We're doing well business-wise, but then we got a special case this month. It was a weird one, Papa, and I don't mean that the guy was weird. He seemed like a redneck down on his luck, which was sad. I mean, his wife left him and took their kid as a result of his incident. I don't know how to say this, but he got into a literal fistfight with Doctor

Faust at a crossroads, but he thought Faust was the devil. Long story. Anyway, Faust beat the hell out of him and put a mark on his soul. Sam agreed to help him. Oh, and it seems that Sam's father kind of sort of broke Faust out of Hell, and now Nick Scratch demands Sam send him back. And she won't use magic, because, well, you know how stubborn she is. And I'm worried. And I don't know what to do. Beyond that, our cases are going fine. Jeremy and I are becoming more serious. He said he loved me! But I'm worried about Sam."

Werther Grimm exhaled and nodded, taking in his daughter's words and the emotional turmoil that caused her voice to tremble. "I am glad that some things are going well for you. While you calm yourself as best as you can, why do we not speak of pleasant things? You have mentioned this young man to me before, but you said that things are becoming serious?"

Destiny nodded and smiled, sipping her tea. "He's bringing me pretzels for lunch. Fine, Papa, I promise I will eat more today than chocolate and pretzels, even though those are wonderful period foods. I know you've sent agents to follow him for the first few weeks we dated. Jeremy didn't notice them, but they weren't subtle. But we had a talk a few weeks ago, and he said he loved me. I said I loved him. So we made things Facebook official, and he's a wonderful boyfriend. I'm happy."

Werther smiled and laughed. His eyes scanned a report from Stuttgart where a runner claimed to have seen a kobold attempt to shoot her with its darts. "That gladdens me, Destiny. And yes, I sent agents to learn all we could about this young man's character and family, but it also makes for a low stakes training exercise. You always call when you notice them. I would not be upset if you spoke to them directly and taught them how to better perform their duties."

Destiny rolled her eyes and lifted the mug. She raised her head but lost her grip on the mug. Tea spilled onto her pink D-Va hoodie as the mug crashed to the floor. "Shit!"

"Language, Destiny."

"Sorry, Papa." She blushed. "And I don't think they'd listen to me, just because I'm your daughter."

"You are also a former agent, Destiny. Have you kept up your training with firearms and martial arts?"

Destiny walked to her kitchen and grabbed a roll of paper towels. She wiped herself off and removed her hoodie, revealing the *InuYasha* spaghetti strap tank top she wore underneath. She activated the phone's speaker mode and raised her hands as if they were scales. "Sort of. I've taken up Krav Maga, but I don't shoot as much as I know you'd like. Sam and I are hitting the range tomorrow, but none of that will help with, you know, trapping a soul and bringing it to Hell."

"I had thought—hold a moment, darling." Someone knocked on his office door. An attractive, middle-aged woman with a blonde bob and hazel eyes who wore a lightweight beige trench over her blue dress. "Magda, come in. I'm talking with Destiny."

The woman smiled and walked toward Werther's desk. She leaned over and said, "Destiny? How are you, baby?"

Tears welled in Destiny's eyes. "Hi, Mama. I'm well enough, given it's my heavy day, but papa promised me Kinder eggs." How are you?"

"I'm well, darling. A bit wet from the drizzle outside the butcher's. How are things with your suitor? I saw on your Facebook that you changed your status. Are you not seeing him?"

Destiny rolled her eyes. "We're fine, Mama. We made our relationship Facebook official, which means we just publicly stated we are a couple. So, yes, things are well."

"Oh, I thought that feature was only for marriages and divorces. Well, perhaps your papa and I will invite the two of you here for Christmas this year to discuss your future and perhaps his views on grandchildren."

"Mama," Destiny grumbled.

Werther laughed and said, "Magda, we can all discuss this later. Destiny has a work-related query to discuss."

Magda Grimm bid her daughter farewell and kissed her husband before leaving the room. Destiny exhaled; her shoulders relaxed, and she said, "Thank you, Papa. I'm worried about Sam."

Werther stroked his chin with his index finger and thumb, nodding. "I could contact a friend in Washington, which would allow you to join the Stith Thompson Federal Agency Overseeing Non-Human Mythic Criminal Activity, but that would provide Samantha with little, if any, immediate assistance."

Destiny doubled over, wincing as the serrated knife twisted inside her. Sweat beaded on her forehead; her heart pounded, and her breathing sped up. Berlin nightlife, a silver bullet, and a werewolf younger than her flashed before her eyes. She returned to the sofa. Her voice trembled, and she shook her head. "No, papa. I can't. Not after my last case. I can't. I'm a researcher, not cut out to be a field agent."

Werther softened his expression, a fact Destiny gleaned from his softened voice. "My darling Destiny, you were young, and it was your first case. I know it offers no solace to remind you that you followed protocols without flaw. Unfortunately, as the night unfolded as it did, you learned the ugly truth of our work.

It is not glamorous and is often performed in the shadows to protect us from our own truth as well as the world from its actuality. If you will not join Samantha in the field, then your best chance at helping her is to convince her to return to her occult studies."

Destiny snorted. "Sam's as stubborn as her dad, Papa. They're both Irish mules. I mean, her own dad and Nick Scratch have both advised her to join a wizard order and actually study magic. She keeps saying that guns kill wizards just as easily as they kill normal humans. She's technically right, but something bothers me."

"And what might that be?"

She shrugged and blew a raspberry. "I don't know. I mean, you'll roll your eyes when I say that it feels like something from a video game or D&D. Sam's dad sacrificed kids—he poisoned them, Papa—to create a potion that he used to prepare a corpse to house Faust's soul. And there's something about a gem to collect souls to feed the body and keep it from rotting and falling apart. Nothing in the training I've had, in the books I've read in any official library, or in my conversations with ranking magicians in multiple esoteric orders suggests that *that* would work. But it did. I don't know."

Werther paused in thought. He smiled and nodded. "Our knowledge is far from perfect, my Destiny. All human knowledge is. I agree that what you have told me sounds like one of the games you have played since childhood, but you have empirical proof that such rituals work. My advice is to persuade Samantha to obtain formal magical training. If that fails, all you can do is be her friend."

Chapter 9

The following morning, a clear and cool Saturday in early April, Destiny and I drove to the Blue Ridge Bullet Range for target practice. Located beyond Butcher's Bend's western city limits, this small shooting range offered both indoor and outdoor ranges. Although we were semi-regulars, the range attendant checked our firearms and went over all safety rules and procedures. Destiny carried an H&K USP, and I had my trusty Walther P38. After paying for the "Zombie Apocalypse Training" mode, we grabbed their range bags and headed for the outdoor range.

The outdoor range had twelve lanes set into three berths of four. Each berth had a long wooden table where shooters could set their firearms and associated gear between firing bursts. Hay bales and grass covered the earthen berm that rose twenty feet behind the wooden backstops. Small patches of wild flowers grew amidst the grasses. We donned our protective goggles and noise-canceling headphones. Even though they were the only shooters on the range, the attendant pushed a button, causing signs to illuminate and speakers to declare the outdoor range was live. We walked to our chosen backstops and placed our targets on them before returning to other end of our respective lanes.

We each fired two magazines. I fired in rapid but uneven bursts while Destiny fired at a slower but steady rate. I signaled to the attendant, who declared the range live, and we went to inspect our targets. Of my sixteen rounds, I only hit the edge of the fucking target four times and scored two shots in kill zones. I uttered a lengthy string of curses. Destiny missed the target once out of her thirty rounds. She earned twenty kill shots and nine wounds.

The "Live Range" signals repeated, and the attendant brought us each a clean paper target. With the targets in place, the attendant left, and then we resumed shooting. After emptying one magazine, I glared at the untouched target and growled. My magazines were smaller than Destiny's, so I emptied two more in erratic bursts while Destiny remained even in her firing rate. Her results were similar to the previous round, except for two additional kill zone shots. I kicked the floor and grunted. Sure, I scored seven kill shots, but no other fucking shots hit the damned target.

When we drove away Forrester, I switched off the radio and drove in silence. My hands strangled the steering wheel. Destiny's eyes slid sideways. I clenched my jaw and glared at the road from behind my sunglasses as a jackass in a white Dodge Ram pulled out in front of me, slammed on his brakes, and turned at the next intersection. Destiny exhaled softly.

After a few moments of silence, Destiny asked, "What's wrong, Sam?"

I switched on my left turn signal and sighed. "Nothing. I'm fine."

Destiny let a heavy sigh pass through her lips. "Your jaw is clenched. The steering wheel is turning blue from that stranglehold you have on it. Oh, and you normally shoot better than that. So, what gives?"

"Not all of us have special forces weapons training. I'll do better next time."

Destiny's gaze dropped to her lap. "I'm sorry."

Sam sighed. She ground her teeth and shook her head as she turned onto Azalea Street. "I'm sorry, Des. That—I didn't mean that."

Her eyes remained closed, but Destiny nodded. "I know. So what's wrong?"

"Nothing. I'm just having a bad day. Can't afford one of those right now. I'll be fine."

Destiny nodded. "We're both worried about what's coming up, Sam. It's okay to be scared and upset. We'll get through it. Together, we always do."

I shook my head and sighed. "This time feels different, Des. I don't know how to explain—"

"That the consequences of your own actions are breathing down your neck like a hungry animal?"

"Let's grab lunch at Sphynx Cafe."

The Sphynx Cafe took over the old Pizza Hut on Allain Drive near Mockingbird Court. The new owners, Nicky and Nasia Moustakatos, painted the exterior a satin black adorned with bronze figures that depicted scenes from the various works of Hesiod. Though the restaurant had a formal, artistic exterior, the interior, with its blue and white tiled flooring and large tables with built-in lazy Susans for family-style dining, gave the place a warm, welcoming feel.

They seated us in a small, two-person booth in the corner closest to the kitchen door. Destiny stabbed a slice of chicken from her shawarma and gyro platter while my knife slid through the medium rare flesh on my lamb shank. As Destiny sipped her mint and honey tea, I said, "You know, I've been thinking about spending the next few days in Austria. There was an old grimoire in 'Milla's dungeon I may check out."

Destiny slipped a bite of hummus-laden pita bread into her mouth and said, "That's not the only thing you want to check out in her dungeon."

I narrowed my eyes and slid my fork beneath the saffron rice. I shook my head, opened my mouth to speak, and paused. A sigh escaped my lips. "That too. Might be my last time."

Destiny stopped her eyes from rolling. She offered me a sympathetic look. "Don't think like that. While you're there, you could pop over to Leipzig. The Order of the Resplendent Dawn has a temple there. They have one in Vienna, but Leipzig is a bit closer."

I grunted and stabbed my lamb. "I'm not joining. I don't need training. I can learn enough magic myself. I just need to buy myself some time."

Destiny shook her head. "No one doubts your ability, Sam. You're smart enough to learn this on your own, yes; however, proper training will reduce the learning time. It flattens the curve, as one might say. And let's not ignore the biggest benefit from pledging the ORD—you'll piss your father off royally."

Destiny was correct, as usual; I nodded. The Hermetic Order of the Astrum Argentum and the Order of the Resplendent Dawn had been rivals since Victoria sat on Britain's throne. The Astrum Argentum's High Council refused to grant a talented, intelligent, and outspoken magician whose real name was Andrew Edward Carrolton the title of Magus because of his homosexuality and his incorporation of sex magic into his ritual practice. He left, published the order's primary rituals, and then founded the Order of the Resplendent Dawn in protest.

Arch Magus Donal Hain's lesbian daughter joining this rival order would create a scandal. I smiled.

Destiny snapped me from my train of thought when she said, "You could try a car bomb."

I raised a puzzled eyebrow. "We've done shots together before, Des. What?"

Destiny set her fork on her plate and blinked at me. She kept her face blank, which always meant the next sentence was coming from that special place in her mind where she kept her weirdest ideas. And then she said, "If you still had your Civic, we could rig it to blow right next to Faustus, which might scare him, make him retreat, and buy you some time."

My eyes shot wide and then blinked once slowly. That was not what I expected her to say. I expected a quote from some movie or anime— something like that scene in *Dogma* where Metatron says, "I say we get drunk, because I'm all out of ideas." An actual car bomb did not cross my mind.

"My Civic was a good car. She saw me through a couple of moves after college, a few too many breakups, Mom's funeral, and starting my own business. She deserved a better end than... ." My cell phone showed Craig Wellington called. "Wait, it's Craig Wellington. Shit. Back to work."

I took the call. "Hey, Craig. What happened now?"

Craig sounded confused and worried. He slurred his speech. "Miss Hain, you know we've got a week before we fight the devil, and you said I shouldn't talk to anybody about what's going on. Does that include professors writing a book?"

"Writing a book? I wouldn't have talked to them, but that's an oddly specific question. What happened?"

Craig belched. "Excuse me. Anyway, I was drinking the other day since I got fired. Not like I have anything else to do. And then these two men came and knocked on my door. They had on blue suits like TV cops, said they were from UNC and that they were writing a book on legends about meeting the devil at the crossroads. I turned them down, but one of them gave me his card as they left. I thought about maybe they could give me some money after I talked, so yesterday, I talked to them."

I glared into the phone but kept my voice level. "Do you remember their names?"

"No, but let me get the card from my wallet. Cheap son-of-a-bitch only bought me a Quarter Pounder meal for my help. Uh, one was named Jeffery Smith, and—oh!—the other was something Washington. I think his first name started with a D or a T or something like that."

"Jeffery Smith." I rolled my eyes and shot Destiny a glare that caused her to stifle her laughter. We've known Jeffery for six years. Back then, he was a clumsy rookie S-T field agent, but he's matured as an agent and a person. He's a credit to the badge, but that meant the feds were involved. This was going to be more of a challenge now. "Well, I'll check the UNC website and send him an email. Thanks. I'll see you in a week."

I ended the call, and Destiny guffawed and snorted. A pair of servers, the bartender, and a handful of other diners turned to see her rolling in her seat, clutching her stomach. She slowed her breathing and calmed herself after five minutes, lowered her voice, and said, "Okay. I'm good now. S-T involvement isn't a good thing, but Jeffery's becoming more subtle. Still, a professor? Him? That's funny."

I shook my head and chuckled. She was right about the humorous nature of the image in my head. "Des, isn't being a professor the standard M. O. for the Grimms?"

She snorted. "Yeah, but we dress the part. Do you think he

even bothered to hit up Goodwill for a tweed blazer? Come on, Sam, he has that one navy suit he always wears when he comes to the office, and that's what he wore when he talked to Craig. I'll bet you a double round of baklava if I'm wrong."

"I'm not taking that bet." I sighed and shook my head, smiling. "The S–T's are involved now, probably because Craig can't keep his mouth shut about what happened to him. I'm just hoping the fact that no one believes him will keep him and people safe from government *protections*."

* * *

Sandy Paws whined when Sam removed her from her new bed inside Sam's blue and green plaid weekender bag. This repeated itself three more times, prompting Sam to hold Sandy in one arm, snuggled against her chest and shoulder, while she placed her clothing, toiletries, and travel makeup kit into the bag. She zipped the bag and then held her cat like a baby and scratched her eyebrows. Sandy closed her eyes, purred, and drooled.

"Mommy knows what you like, you big baby. And I'll only be a teleportation away. Auntie Destiny will take care of you, and I'll call and talk to you nightly. Okay?" Sandy's meow suggested an annoyed acceptance. "Look, I'll give you a special treat when I get back. Mommy needs to clear her head before she has a showdown at the crossroads. Maybe next time, I'll bring you with me. You'd love wandering through 'Milla's castle.'"

Sandy purred and buried her face in the crook of Sam's elbow. Sam smiled as she stroked her cat. Tears formed as she remembered the Christmas when her mom's excitement reached new heights. She kept the tree surrounded by presents for everyone except Sam. And then on Christmas morning, a dozen presents for Sam appeared under the tree—cat toys, a cat bed, cat food, litter, a litter box, and a blanket. Sam's excitement grew until she realized there was no cat; her mom remained confident no mistakes were made. When Sam returned to her room, she saw an opened cat carrier on her bed and a four-year-old cat, Sandy Paws, sleeping on Sam's pillow. That was Sam's last Christmas with her mom.

The doorbell rang. Sam rolled her eyes, and Sandy whined. Sam released her cat, allowing Sandy to curl up on the bed. She smiled as Sandy curled up on the pillows. Sam descended the stairs as the bell rang again and then again. She narrowed her eyes, growled, and cursed. The bell rang once more as she reached the door.

"What?" Sam asked as she opened her door, glaring at the person who rang her bell.

Agents Jeffery Smith and Damon Washington blinked and froze. Dressed in their navy suits, they looked like boys wearing their fathers' clothes while being scolded by their mom for breaking a window. Sam rolled her eyes and shook her head.

Agent Smith swallowed and said, "Afternoon, Sam. Mind if we come in?"

Sam exhaled and relaxed her shoulders. She smiled. "Hi, Jeff. New partner? Come on in, but make it quick. I'm about to leave for Austria."

"That's a long flight, Miss Hain," Agent Washington said. "You think you'll make it to the airport in time?"

Sam rolled her eyes and said, "I plan to teleport. And before you say it, just so we're all clear, I'll be teleporting into the castle of my girlfriend, Countess Carmilla Karnstein, matriarch of the Karnstein-Bertholt vampire clan. So no international Veil Piercing. She should be having her first meal of the night, so can we make this quick?"

Damon Washington's face suggested he did not appreciate her response. Jeffery Smith extended his arm, holding his partner back. "Of course, Sam. We just have a few questions regarding an open investigation. Shouldn't take too long."

Sam shrugged. "Next time, maybe hit a thrift store and buy a tweed jacket."

"Excuse me?" Agent Smith asked.

"Your cover was folklore professors at UNC. I don't know what you majored in, but where I went to school, humanities professors didn't dress like businessmen. Or, as Craig Wellington said, 'TV cops.' So, yes, I know why you're in town, and Craig has reached out to me for assistance."

Agent Washington leaned forward, placing his elbows on his knees. "So then you believe he fought the devil at the crossroads?"

Sam looked over at Agent Smith, smiled sweetly, and said, "Jeffery, did you forget to tell your partner I'm licensed to handle such cases? Anyway, that's not the devil's style. Anyone who knows anything about the other side of the Veil knows that the devil is more likely to assault you with his razor wit or eviscerate you in a legal case than he is to punch you. He's a smooth, charismatic lawyer. No, Craig did not fight the devil. He fought a human who black magic has excised from Hell and into a new body."

"What?" Both agents' faces assumed flabbergasted expressions.

Sam nodded. "It's a long and complicated story, but the gist of the matter is this. A ceremonial magician performed a complex ritual that should not exist, but it does, that smuggled a soul out of Hell and into a corpse. Giving it a new life of sorts. I don't fully understand it, but that's what happened. The soul in question was the late medieval charlatan Doctor Faust. And I know this for two reasons. First, I examined the crossroads and found evidence of black magic, including a small poppet. Second, the devil himself told me about Faust's escape, and he found an identical poppet in Faust's place of damnation. So, I put two and two together, and there you go."

Agent Smith took notes and nodded. "So you have both Mister Wellington and the devil as clients?"

"Not exactly. Craig is my client. The devil called in a contract I took out almost six years ago now. So, it's my job to bring Faust back to Hell."

Both agents winced. Agent Smith said, "That's rough, Sam. I know you don't run away, so why Austria now?"

"Well, since my girlfriend lives there, I'd like to spend time with her in person and not over Zoom. Also, I need to practice a few spells so I can have a better chance of keeping Craig alive. Anything else you need?"

Agent Smith shook his head. "Don't think so, but I know how to contact you if we need anything else. You stay safe."

After the federal agents left, Sam spent a few minutes snuggling Sandy Paws before she grabbed her bag and teleported to Castle Karnstein. She emerged from the teleportation portal and saw Martin standing in the doorway, holding a coffee mug on a silver tray. As she opened her mouth to speak, Carmilla burst into the chamber, pushing Martin aside as she ran to embrace Sam. They kissed.

Martin cleared his throat as he set the tray on the desk. "Yes, it has been how many centuries since the two of you saw each other last? That look will not work on me, my Countess. I have survived your dramatic glare and that of your mother and your grandmother."

Sam laughed and said, "Thanks for the coffee, Martin. I just had a lovely visit with a pair of S-T agents, so I appreciate the coffee."

Martin bowed and smiled. Carmilla tightened the arm she wrapped around Sam's waist. She kissed Sam's neck and then said, "Martin, how can you blame me for bursts of emotion when this cruel world regularly denies me the physical presence of this ravishing woman?"

Martin flattened his lips and rolled his eyes. "I see you have been reading those bodice rippers again, My Countess. Miss Hain, please help her express some of her distance-bridled exuberance before she approaches the overdramatic level of the Marquis d'Auvergne's son. Excuse me."

He bowed, collected Sam's weekender, and left the dungeon chamber. As he left, he reminded the women that he would serve the next meal in two hours—earlier than customary, as the Countess has skipped her breakfast in excitement. Sam and Carmilla's lips danced in a series of sweet, tender kisses before they raced up the stairs, kissing, giggling, and groping, on their way to Carmilla's bedroom.

After three hours of play, Sam and Carmilla, their makeup in varying stages of disarray, descended the stairs and dined in Carmilla's drawing room. Martin ended the meal by bringing a bottle of wine for them to split as they sat before the crackling fire, perfumed with the bundles of rosemary that hung before it. Carmilla wrapped her arm around Sam's shoulders as Sam rested her head against Carmilla's chest.

"Tell me, dear one," Carmilla asked as she stroked Sam's

hair, "aside from obvious enjoyment and comfort, what did you hope to find among the grimoires in my dungeon that you did not find the last time?"

Sam nuzzled into Carmilla's neck and said, "Last time I was here, I remember finding some protection spells—not rituals like I learned—that I want to practice. Since I'll be squaring off against an infamous magician, I need to have some quick-fire spells I can use to protect myself. Just in case my gun jams."

Carmilla nodded. She brushed Sam's cheek with the backs of her delicate, pale fingers as she kissed her lover's forehead. "I know what you will say, but would you consider formal magical training? Please?"

Concern and fear darkened Carmilla's trembling voice. Sam closed her eyes, inhaling the vampire's scent. She sighed. Carmilla felt like home, comforting, loving, safe. Sam needed this; she would miss this when she failed to return Faust to Hell. Her breathing became uneven. Her muscles tensed. She exhaled and wrapped her arms tightly around Carmilla. The vampire held her close, feeling her heart pulse, begging for connection.

Sam shook her head and said, "It's not that simple, 'Milla. I don't have the time. Both my father and Mister Ronan said that obtaining the focus and experience to control magical energies takes years of dedicated study. I don't have the time, and I have to do this my way. This all started when my father..." Her voice cracked as tears started flowing; Carmilla stroked her back. "This all started when my father sacrificed infants to bring Faust's soul back from Hell. Sacrificing others for power seems to be his thing. I can't make sacrifices. I won't. He used magic, so I have to show him and everyone else that magic isn't the only way. I have to. Please understand."

Carmilla lifted Sam's chin so their eyes met. The vampire offered her human lover a comforting smile and a nod. Words screamed in her mind. She wanted to tell Sam she needed to stay alive, that *she* needed Sam to stay alive. She wanted to lecture Sam on safety, about protecting herself as much as she protected others, but Carmilla knew such lectures would lead to a fight. Did she need to start a fight? Would it push Sam to protect herself or just push her away?

Yet, Carmilla only said, "I do, my love. I do."

As with her last visit, Sam spent her afternoons studying in the castle's basement and her nights with Carmilla. On the first day, she found the quick shielding spell that the grimoire promised would block offensive magic directed at the magician. She copied the incantation into a blue and gold leather journal, scanned the meter to find the most natural speaking rhythm, and then repeated it until she had it memorized. She then practiced the gestures. With her right hand extended, palm facing forward, Sam slid her hand to her left shoulder, then back to her heart, and then brushed beyond her right shoulder. Essentially, she was to catch the magical energy and then throw it to the side while reciting the incantation.

* * *

The second day started with Sam practicing the shielding spell, working on keeping her focus strong by envisioning a large kite shield of white-framed blue light. The shield moved along with her arm. She ran her fingers through her hair, which felt frizzier than usual. Sam used a similar visualization for the mental shielding spell she used to protect her from Zozo; it failed when her focus lapsed. She could afford no lapse this time. She stopped when Martin brought her coffee, water, and a light mid-afternoon meal.

Martin surveyed the room, his attention focusing on Sam, whose ponytail floated and frizzed. "Perhaps I should have brought a brush for your hair as well. My apologies."

"You noticed it too? There seems to be more static charge in the air. It's making my hair frizz."

Martin nodded. "I'm an old soldier, Miss Hain, but I have spent enough centuries around scholars and mystics to know that such atmospherical changes are often suggestive of the presence of magical energies. Perhaps you are doing well."

Sam smiled. "I hope so, Martin. I don't have time to be anything less than perfect."

"That poses a problem, Miss Hain. None of us are, and the only person who demands perfection of you resides within the mirror. What we want, and I have confidence I speak for the Countess as well when I say, what we want is for you to be safe and happy."

Sam spent the next day and a half practicing this shielding spell and learning a quick spell to counter another spell and dispel another's magic. Her mind wandered as she practiced. She thought of her friends, Carmilla, Sandy Paws, her mother, her work, and whatever remained of her relationship with her father. Blood sped through her lungs, and her skin flushed. Her nostrils flared; her body trembled, and tears formed in her eyes. She screamed and threw her journal at the wall.

Martin entered with her mid-afternoon meal, noticed the book on the floor and Sam crying at the desk, and said, "Drink some water first. Sorrow, anger, and stress can dehydrate you."

Sam covered her face in her hands and growled. Her hands

muffled her words. "I don't have time, Martin. I need to focus. On the day after tomorrow, the confrontation happens. I can't afford to lose focus. Why can't I focus?"

Martin nodded and handed her the water glass. "Drink. Do you trust me?"

Sam sipped from the glass. He added ice to the water; she appreciated that. She nodded. "Of course."

He smiled. "Then I will suggest something that you may make an initial objection to; however, I promise it is to your benefit. Take a break from your studies and come with me."

Martin exited the chamber. Sam called out, "Didn't you listen? I don't have time."

His voice echoed through the dungeon as he said, "Then trust me."

Sam grumbled but followed, taking the water glass with her. He led her up the spiraling stairs to the castle's armory. Suits of gothic armor, swords, axes, and other medieval and now archaic weapons lined the walls. Caches of firearms hid behind them, a fact Sam knew from aiding in the castle's defense when the Order of the Dragon attacked last December. Martin chose two small swords, handed one to Sam, and took the other for himself. Without warning, he lunged at her left shoulder, but her parry was too slow. Sam winced.

"What the fuck, Martin? You didn't warn me!"

He bowed and then presented his weapon. "Nor will our enemies. As the Countess' champion, you need to prepare for such offensives. And I have long found a little sport can clear and calm the mind. Now, you were likely trained in the French style, so I will use their terminology. Sabre rules. I want you to defend against the following. *Tierce, prime, seconde, octave, quinte*, and across your nose. Ready? *En garde*."

Sam squeaked; Martin gave her no chance to object before his first lunge. He slowed his pace, keeping the initial rounds manageable for a human untrained at fighting vampires. He repeated the process, quickening his speed with each time, until Sam found herself able to handle his supernatural speed. Sam's breathing quickened; she panted as her heart thundered in her chest. Once satisfied, they switched roles. His speed proved more than she could handle, and when she overreached on her lunges, he tripped her. She glared at him above her flaring nostrils. Martin smiled and instructed her to repeat the pattern again.

Sweat stung Sam's eyes, even in the cool mountain air that permeated the castle. When Martin granted her a break, he instructed her to drink water. While she downed a tall glass of sparkling mineral water, he removed his blue blazer, rolled up the sleeves on his white button-down shirt, and then removed his tie. Sam stretched her arms and shoulders. Had she known she would be fencing, she would have worn jeans and boots instead of the blouse, pencil skirt, and stilettos she wore. Martin approached, the necktie in his hands.

"Will you permit me?"

Sam raised a questioning eyebrow. "I'm wearing the wrong collar for a necktie, Martin."

"It is not for your blouse, Miss Hain. It is for your eyes."

She blinked. "You want to blindfold me? And then fence?"

"Yes. You have mastered the defensive speed. You have memorized the routine. Thus, if given a verbal cue, such as the number three, you should be able to execute the pattern through focus and memory."

Sam sputtered and sighed. She shook her head. "If you say so, Martin. Alright."

He blindfolded her with his necktie. The earth and pine scent of his cologne clung to the tie. Sam's nose twitched, and she sneezed. When Martin had ensured both her comfort and her inability to see, he helped her stand in a balanced position, ready to defend against his attacks. He took his initial position opposite her and stomped his boot.

"Now, Miss Hain, on the count of three. *Ein. Zwei. Drei!*"

Martin's initial lunge interrupted Sam's questioning utterance, replacing it with a wincing hiss as the point of his blade touched her right shoulder. He paused and returned to his starting position.

"Again, Miss Hain."

Sam threw her arms wide and said, "Hold up, Martin. I don't know if you've forgotten this in your old age, but I'm not a vampire. I don't have super senses. I'm not even a fucking Jedi padawan with the Force on my side. Why the fuck are we doing this?"

Martin smirked. She was almost at the point. "Correct me if I am incorrect, Miss Hain, for it has been some forty years since I have seen this *Star Wars* movie, but was this 'the Force' not some mystical energy that those connected to it could tap into so they might perform great feats beyond their normal mortal limitations?"

"Yeah, but it's not real. It's just a kids' movie."

He shook his head. "Of that I am aware; although it is good fun for an adult of even my advanced age. But tell me, Miss Hain, how does your father's order teach aspiring magicians to understand magic?"

She narrowed her eyes behind the blindfold. What the fuck was he doing? Sam's cheeks reddened, and her heart rate increased again. She ground her teeth as a deep sigh growled through her lips. "Magical energy is a series of vibrations emanating from and connecting all living things from the highest, most abstract expression of the divine to the most basic monocellular organism. By recognizing, feeling, and manipulating these vibrational energies, a magician is able to...oh."

"Again. This time, focus."

Sam nodded. She took a single deep breath and focused on the energy vibrations. The room felt empty. Martin stomped his foot. Sam's heartbeat thundered in her ears. *Ein.* Sam inhaled and focused her attention on the sounds ahead of her. *Zwei.* Nothing. No, a low rumble, like the motor of an electronic relaxation fountain buzzed in the distance, close but still distinctly away. *Drei.* Sam readied herself and raised her blade. *En garde!* The rumbling motor roared.

Sam flicked her blade to her right shoulder, parrying Martin's initial thrust. He lunged. She flipped her wrist and pushed his blade away from her body. Martin spun his wrist to slash at Sam's right flank. She caught the blade with her guard, spun her wrist, and riposted. The point of her blade struck his abdomen.

"One," she said.

"Excellent. Again."

They repeated the exercise for another hour. As Sam attuned herself to the energy flows around herself and Martin, her speed at both offense and defense rivaled Martin's. An alarm alerted Martin that Carmilla would wake in an hour. He traded Sam the blindfold for a handkerchief, and she wiped the sweat from her forehead as he retied the eldritch knot.

Breathing heavily, Sam chuckled and said, "I felt your energy. I didn't think I could do that. How'd you know?"

Sam felt a twinge in the back of her mind, similar to a pin prick, but she shrugged it off.

Martin smiled. "Tradition has long held that a bit of sport can help clear and focus the mind. From there, it was a mere matter of convincing you to sense and feel without thought. By removing your sight, you had to focus on sound, touch, and energy. I need no knowledge of magic when I understand humans. Now, while I prepare the Countess' first meal, why not spend the hour in her bath?"

* * *

The Wulpert-Inger Motel sat at the eastern edge of Fiddlers' Ford. The "u" flickered and the lights behind "Mo" had blown earlier in the week and had yet to be fixed. Deep cracks fractured the masonry, and the yellow, orange, and blue paint had continued to chip since the 1970s. The fourteen rooms lurked in a single line, casting long shadows on the cracked concrete of the parking lot, illuminated by three flickering lights. Three cars sat in the lot, but none were near the four rooms with light peeking through the stained, beige curtain in the window. The sign by the road promised guests rooms by the week, the night, or the hour.

Johann Faust sat in the maple armchair with the ripped orange vinyl cushion between the orange vinyl card table and the bed. Stains of various bodily fluids adorned both the ratty orange and gold comforter and the gray shag carpet. Through the open bathroom door, he saw the shattered glass of the mirror lying on the tile floor. He propped his unwashed feet on the bed and, with a skeletal left hand, scanned the internet on the black cell phone the Order of the Dragon assigned him. He opened the YouTube app and scrolled through the suggested videos.

"Cats, more cats, everywhere cats," he muttered. "In the centuries since I have walked this earth last, humans have invented this device that connects them to knowledge greater than that fabled to be contained in Alexandria, and what do they do with such a tool? They share pictures and these videos of their cats. Can something be called a video if I have not yet watched it? The word suggests it cannot, but still they do. And they share them and fill other websites with the same—What is this? This fool claims to prove the earth beneath our feet is flat? In my day, we knew it to be round. In centuries prior to me, its roundness was both known to sailors and calculated by mathematicians. How can such advances in knowledge be paired with such ignorance? This world needs my *generous* benefactors to rule it."

General Amanar requested a video call. Faust sighed, but acquiesced. The Order of the Dragon general's rugged and well-groomed face appeared on the screen. He said, "Johann Faust, our agents show you are still in South Carolina. How much longer will you be in this location before you move on?"

"A few days more, Herr General. I have a bit of minor business to conclude before the full moon."

"Good. You have returned to this region of this one country regularly since your return from Hell. Might I inquire as to your reasoning?"

Faust laughed a deep but crackling and empty laugh. "After the two magicians freed me from my unjust torture, I stumbled upon a book telling tales of Samael's travels in the New World. Many of them focused on his work in the southern part of this United States. And so, I came to do the devil's work."

Faust laughed again. General Amanar closed his cobalt eyes and shook his head. He sighed. "So everything you have done when not directly performing the duties required to repay your debt has been to mock the Lord of Hell?"

"His work is a mockery of God's, and now that I am become a god and achieved life beyond death, my work will be a mockery of his."

A sigh growled its way through General Amanar's lips as he narrowed his eyes. "Be that as it may, I will repeat the directive we gave you earlier to not remain in one location for too long. Your actions have the potential to draw the attention of federal agents. We would prefer it if you were to not have any engagement with law enforcement. You, Faust, are still a man."

Faust slammed his fist on the cheap wooden desk. His eyes narrowed, and his nostrils flared. "A man? A *man*? I am become a god. Creation and destruction are mine to control. What can these peasant conscripts do to me?"

Amanar voided his face of emotion and said, "Given the state of your left hand and the deterioration of the right side of your face, it would seem you have not fed your little gem in a few days. While you are powerful, enough of them could destroy your current body, and you would neither be able to transfer your soul to a new one nor regenerate this current one."

"Then it benefits us both that I have a snack scheduled to arrive in an hour. Have you located the last soul so I may pay my debt?"

Amanar's face displayed annoyance and frustration. "We have located the family's holdings in Sorefoot, Texas. However, word on the street is that some rift has caused Quincey Morris' direct heir to flee the state. We have not yet learned if these rumors possess validity. That said, Sorefoot, Texas is as far from your current location as Madrid is from the city of your birth. Conclude your business here and begin traveling west."

Faust performed a mocking bow. "Is there anything else you require of me, my noble lord?"

General Amanar swallowed and took two deep breaths. "Be on your guard while in South Carolina. Your proximity to Samantha Hain, the daughter of Arch Magus Donal Hain, is troubling."

"The apprentice's daughter is near? Why does a child's presence concern you so?"

"She is not a child, Faust. She is plucky and stubborn, and she has caused two setbacks—one major and one minor—to our Great Work within the past six months. Do not engage her. That is all."

Amanar ended the call. Faust stroked his chin. This body had lost its ability to grow facial hair last week. This Samantha Hain seemed to concern General Amanar, but the concerns of mortals proved beneath his concern. Still, the thought of this woman proving dangerous intrigued him.

Faust reached into his padded duffle bag and produced a black silk cloth wrapped around a circular obsidian mirror. He set the mirror upon the desk and then grabbed a golden censor, a lump of coal, a clay churchwarden pipe and a leather tobacco pouch. He placed the coal in the censor, sprinkled tobacco on the coal, and lit the coal with a snap of his fingers. Faust tamped the tobacco into the bowl of his pipe and sparked it to life. Soon, thick clouds of ash gray smoke filled the room with the tobacco's warm, spicy, earthy scent. The magician focused on the name "Samantha Hain" as he stared into the smoke curtain before his mirror.

Peering through the curling smoke, Faust watched as shadows formed inside the mirror. The smoke and shadows coalesced, allowing the magician to see a room with a stone floor covered in elegant, gold-trimmed burgundy rugs. Weapons and armor lined the walls. Two humans, a man and a girl, fenced in the room's center. Faust surmised this young, attractive, overweight brunette must be Samantha Hain. Was she wealthy? Her weight and surroundings suggested that. She had skill, but the man proved faster and craftier than she was.

The two humans' sparring ceased, and their mouths moved. The man removed his coat and necktie. Faust leaned forward, focusing until the vibrational energies carried sound into his mind. He asked her permission? For what? Is it not his right to order her around? Samantha agreed to allow him to tie the cloth over her eyes. He planned to spar with her blindfolded. Faust leaned forward, his head cocked like a curious dog's. The magician laughed as the girl failed to parry the man's thrusts, lunges, and slashes.

Faust waved the smoke and shadows away as he leaned back in the chair. "So, the magician's daughter has no affinity for magic. Unsurprising, given a young girl's natural temperament is different from that of a man's. Skill with a sword was nice, but what could weapons forged to fight men do against me? I have transcended mortality and truly become like the god who cast down Samael. *She* would do well to avoid me."

A tentative hand knocked on the hotel room door four times. Faust set the pipe onto the desk; smoke curled and danced from the bowl. He removed the wooden box from his bag, opened it, and took his crystal in hand. A lanky teenage boy with pimples covering his pale face held out a square box bearing the logo for Burrell Bros. Pizza. The boys' knees knocked against each other as his eyes darted about the room and the parking lot. Faust smiled and placed the crystal atop the box. The young boy opened his mouth to ask, but he fell silent when the crystal glowed. He collapsed on the concrete outside. Faust collected the crystal and the pizza before returning to his room. As he closed the door behind him, the boy turned to ash.

Chapter 10

Tomorrow night, I confront Faust at the crossroads. My Walther lay on my desk, and I cleaned the barrel. Would standard rounds be enough? From everything I've seen and read, Faust wasn't faerie, so cold iron rounds would offer no added benefit. He wasn't a lycanthrope, so silver rounds wouldn't—well, silver has magical properties against evil, so maybe. In life, he sold his soul and earned damnation, so perhaps the blessed rounds I kept for fighting renegade demons would prove useful.

The deal was a fist fight against Craig Wellington, my client. My Plan A was to try to Wyatt Earp things, talk to Faust, and try to convince him to return to Hell peacefully. I didn't have the skills to take him on, so I hoped getting him talking would buy me some time to think through other options. If that failed, shooting the bastard seemed the only option.

Destiny carried a large Sal's pizza box, a box of garlic knots, and a two liter of A&W Cream Soda into my office. She spread the boxes and the bottle on my desk and said, "Lunch break, boss. The longer you stare at your gun, the more morose you're going to be. So, let's talk about shoes, ships, sealing wax, cabbages, and kings. Did you know, for the longest time, I thought sealing wax was wax for ceilings?"

"Did you have a bad translation?" I shot Destiny a quizzical glance as I put my gun away.

She shook her head and smiled. "Nope. Mom loved the story, and she read it to me at bedtime. She always read it in English, saying it sounded right that way. My dad, well, he read me the stories my ancestors collected and then *Der Struwwelpeter*."

Destiny rolled her eyes. I giggled. Mister Werther would be that dad who read dark stories to his kids and thought nothing of it. "At least it got you that date in sophomore year, right?"

She nodded as she poured the soda into the red plastic cups we kept in the office. "Yeah, Jonathan Walker. His dad read him Shakespearean tragedies as bedtime stories. He was a fun date, but, well, you know."

What would I do without Destiny? She was my right hand, my source of courage, and, at times, my brain. In her own way, she gave advice and hugs that I needed as much as my mom's. Sometimes I think Sandy Paws prefers Destiny over me. I smiled and sighed. I've had a pretty good life. Just hope I can keep it going.

"So drinking black coffee has been made illegal."

"What?" I asked, as Destiny's voice snapped me back to the present.

She smirked and shrugged. "Oh, there you are. I've been talking for five minutes, and you've just had this blank look on your face. It's like the look you got when you and Carmilla started dating the first time, but without the schoolgirl wistfulness and adult horniness. Are you okay?"

I shook my head, clearing it before I sighed. "I don't know, Des. Just thinking about everything. And tomorrow night."

Destiny offered me a concerned, understanding smile and nodded. Her hand stretched across the desk toward mine, but then she turned and swiped a garlic knot from my plate. Her triumphant smile met my annoyed glare.

"The price for lack of attention is the loss of delicious carbs. It's a grim law." Her face remained emotionless as she spoke. And for five seconds after she finished.

My eyes rolled as Destiny cackled and snorted. She was proud of that one; I let her have it. I chuckled.

"You've got to lighten up, Sam. Brooding may be all sexy in romance and gothic fantasy novels, but it won't solve any of your problems. Planning will, and I know you've got a plan. So, what is it?"

I took a massive bite of Sal's Quattro while I thought about how to explain my plan in a way that didn't sound like I've given up. I moaned into the rich but light crust of this sausage, onion, bell pepper, and jalapeno pizza. Donna Fucra's marinara is a seductive potion filled with fresh herbs and tomatoes. Destiny used the plastic utensils provided to cut her pizza. I swallowed and then exhaled.

"Okay," I said. "Hear me out. I know what everyone expects of me, but I'm going to try to reason with Doctor Faust. The plan is to convince him he's opening himself to problems from both Heaven and Hell, and no matter how powerful he is, he can't defeat both armies combined. If he demands I fight him in Craig's place, I'll do so. But I'll have my gun ready in case that fails. He died once; he can die again."

Destiny nodded and chewed as I spoke. She sighed. "I'm not a fan, but I know you're not going to listen to me and study that soul binding spell. So, this is the best I can hope for."

I ripped off a chunk of garlic knot and dipped it in the plastic cup of whipped provolone. "I don't have time to master magic that powerful, Des. Four days of practice in Austria helped me sort of master two defensive spells. Plus, all the ritual components seem too hard to obtain on such short notice. If Faust flees, then I'll consider the soul binding. But I'll need all the time Nick is giving me for practice."

She sighed. "Defensive spells, huh? I guess you haven't learned any offensive magic by any chance?"

I shook my head. Magic was something I hated learning; I refused for the longest time because of my father. When I agreed to learn any rites, I focused on defense and teleportation. Magic would protect me, but it was not going to be a major part of my arsenal. The front door of the office opened. Destiny rose and walked into the main room. "Welcome to Hain Private Investigations. How may I—oh, hi, Jeffrey. How are things going? How's the boyfriend?"

Hearing that name, I stood and walked into the main room. Agent Jeffrey Smith stood next to Destiny's desk. His partner wasn't with him. Destiny sat at her desk. He smiled and nodded, and I smiled in return. I sat on the corner of Destiny's desk and asked, "More questions on the investigation?"

He shook his head. "Going well, Des. We've moved in together." He winced as Destiny's squeal of delight assaulted his ears. "Not really, Sam. I just came by to update you on our investigation, give you a copy of the formal report, and see how you're doing with your case."

My right eyebrow shot up, and I tilted my head. "A copy of your report? In the years I've known you, you've only given me a copy of one case report. Why this time?"

Jeffrey Smith massaged the back of his neck with his hand. He shuffled his weight from leg to leg, and his eyes shied away from my gaze. He shrugged. "I'm not really sure, Sam. Something about all this doesn't feel like it's a case for us. So, short story is that the investigation is over and we have deemed Mr. Wellington to be legally clear of the crime of Veil Piercing."

Destiny and I sighed in unison. I said, "That's good news. He's had shitty luck since the incident. Anything else?"

Jeffrey nodded. "There's a lot, Sam. But we did as thorough an investigation as we can do, and while he technically pierced the Veil by telling everyone about his incident, the fact remains that no one believed him. We could take care of the matter, and Damon and I discussed that path. The main argument in favor of taking action was that it might be merciful to either throw him in an asylum or to kill him. No one else is in danger, because everyone we talked to or listened to thought he was crazy. The problem is that, since no one believed him, taking action felt unnecessary. He's all yours."

I nodded and smiled. "Jeffrey, you've come a long way from your rookie year."

He bowed his head. "You had a lot to do with that. You and Destiny showed me there's more to what I do, what *we* all do, actually, than the letter of the law. Look, when I took the job, I believed in ghosts, and that's it. I honestly believed my duty was to disprove claims of supernatural crime or human Veil Piercing. Then I ran into you, and watching you work, talking to you, and screwing up on cases and having you correct me—all of that opened my eyes. Our authority, our power, our duties all took on new meaning. Sure, I locked a few people away for honest mistakes, and I killed more people than I ever thought I would. Most of them nonviolent..."

Jeffrey's voice trailed and cracked. He shoved his hands in his pockets to hide his trembling hands. I knew what he felt. I walked over and placed a hand on his shoulder. My voice had the same trembling crackle as I said, "Hey, it's okay to feel things. What we do isn't easy, and you've been given authority to kill at your discretion. It's a heavy burden. And hiding behind duty or law or any moral code doesn't make it easier. High Bard Murphy of the Seamus Duilearga Bardic College once told me that's why they place themselves in the heroic role in the stories. The morality of heroism helps them cope. He admitted they also drink a lot. Taking a life is hard—even when you know without a doubt they're the bad guy. Life is life, and seeing it end as a result of your actions is hard."

He nodded. "Yeah. I know it's hard. You know it's hard. If our insurance didn't cover a shrink, I would've either quit or drank myself stupid by now. You two have helped keep me from that, too. Someone who gets it, who gets me, helps. So, thank you."

Destiny beamed. "Helping people is what we do. And you're one of those government employees who's actually a people. And if I'm being honest, you kind of struck me as a lost puppy when we first met you, but you had potential. And we saw your heart."

He chuckled, and I said, "But I'm glad we could help you. We've got jobs that we can't just talk about with other people, so having someone to vent to, to share with, and just to talk to really fucking matters."

"It does, Sam." He sighed. "That brings me to my last bit of business. Your little crossroads boxing match happens tomorrow night. This is an unofficial request, and I am invoking no governmental authority. But I have to ask. Well, I feel like I should ask you this. Will you permit me to accompany you to this crossroads—just to keep you safe and to keep others away so there's no further incidents arising from this?"

That was not a question I expected. I've only worked with

Watchers once, and that was in Bannagh. My mouth went dry, and my hands shook. I smelled the torches, my father's pungent incense, and the burning flesh. I clenched my jaw and ground my teeth, trying to drown out Zozo's bleating, brittle laughter. My hand stroked the burn I felt on my cheek. My breathing went fast and shallow. I swallowed hard, tensed every muscle, and exhaled. I can do this.

I shook my head. "I don't think it's needed," I said. "That crossroads is so abandoned, no one will show up at midnight. But I can't stop you from going, so the choice is yours. However, since I'm driving Craig, I don't think you sitting in the backseat would comfort him."

Jeffrey nodded. "I get it. But I can always do a stakeout. I have a bad feeling about this, Sam. I'll keep the Lincoln's lights off, so it'll be mostly invisible. If all goes well, you won't even see me. Well, let me go file the official report. Here's your copy, and good luck tomorrow night."

Jeffrey handed me a manila envelope, nodded, and left.

* * *

With one bare hour until midnight, Sam Hain and Craig Wellington drove away from Craig's modest ranch-style home with its torn screen door, chipped tan paint, and broken windows. Craig reeked of stale beer and urine. Blue Oyster Cult's "Veteran of the Psychic Wars'" haunting, echoing outro gave way to Alanis Morissette's "Reasons I Drink." Heavy, gray clouds hid the stars and the waxing gibbous moon. An empty highway stretched before them as they drove south to the fated crossroads of 178 and 76. Aside from Sam's Spotify playlist and the rumble of her Forester's engine, silence filled the car.

Florence Welch's haunting voice sang the chorus to "Addicted to Love" as Sam's phone screen illuminated from Carmilla's call. Sam smiled and answered, "Hey, 'Milla. You're up late."

"Samantha, dear one," she said. Carmilla's voice sounded terrified. "Is it done? Are you safe?"

She's worried about me. I bet she's pacing her castle with Martin trailing behind her and goading her to go to sleep. Sam smiled. "It's about twenty past eleven. We're on the way. I'll text you when it's done, and I promise to call you first thing after sunset tomorrow, your time. Get some sleep. We don't need Martin to worry."

Carmilla laughed and asked, "Can you hear him? He is alerting me to each minute's passing. Fine, Martin, Samantha agrees with you. I will sleep. I love you, my dear one. Please be safe."

"I love you too, 'Milla. I will."

Sam exhaled as she ended the call. Craig looked over and said, "I didn't know your mom was German."

Sam shook her head. "My mother was an American of British ancestry. 'Milla is Austrian, and she's my girlfriend."

"Oh." Craig rocked in his seat. "I mean, that's good. Look, I'm not trying to say anything bad, but I'm a Baptist. And well, we were always taught that you know, that's a sin."

Sam rolled her eyes and bit her tongue. After a moment, she said, "My father is an Irish Catholic, and I attended a parochial school with more than one dour nun who told us to kneel and thank God that new rules prevented them from spanking us for unholy disobedience, like asking questions in religion class. I've had clients hurl horrid insults my way for being a lesbian.

At the end of the day, I'm the neighbor going out into the darkness to find the lost lamb. I don't think I do 'the Lord's work,' but I do good work."

They arrived at the crossroads with two minutes to spare. The county had installed a new streetlight, but it offered little light. Sam noticed the outline of Jeffrey's black Lincoln Town Car a few hundred feet from the crossroads. She parked and stepped into the darkness. The pressure plummeted while they drove, and the air turned cold. Sam's choice of a blue and orange sweater, denim jeans, and brown leather riding boots kept her warm until the north wind ripped through her. She shivered.

Sam ran her finger along her Walther's grip as it sat in its holster. Craig's eyes darted around and beyond the area illuminated by the streetlight. He panted and asked, "So, do you think he'll forget?"

Lightning illuminated the sky; a thunder peal shook through them. Sam and Craig turned toward the sound, finding only darkness. She shook her head and sniffed the air. "Do you smell that? Sulfur. If he's not here now, he'll be here soon."

Craig gulped audibly. Sam turned as the sulfur smell moved. She grabbed Craig's arm, and they backed away from the streetlight, moving west. Craig's hand grew sweaty and clammy as fear overtook him. He cowered behind Sam, peaking his head out to stare at the darkness. She took a deep breath and braced herself. Craig's fast, heavy breathing pushed past her ears, rustling the few stray hairs her hairspray could not hold.

A buzz sounded from above them, faint at first but growing louder at a steady pace. The earth rumbled. Craig clenched Sam's arm; his heart pounded. Sam focused on her breathing and remained calm. This was no demon, no vampire, and no monster. This was nothing more than a human. The combined reek of burning flesh, feces, and sulfur filled the air. Sam's jaw clenched, and she tensed her muscles. Not again. The streetlight flickered and crackled. A hazy sulfurous fog formed beneath the streetlight. It flickered and flashed with blue and white flames dancing about it, and when the fog dissipated, the tall, gaunt, black clad form of Johann Faust stood beneath the light.

Craig screamed. Sam rolled her eyes, and Faust laughed. He said, "Oh, it strikes. It strikes, Craig Wellington. The hour is come, and I shall now deprive you of the joys of Heaven."

Craig's trembling index finger pointed at Faust, and he said, "See! I told you he was the Devil."

Sam snorted and rolled her eyes. "The Devil? Please, that's just a carny charlatan who claimed to be Doctor Faust. Whoever you really are, this isn't funny. Leave now before something bad happens."

When Faust narrowed his eyes, a pale green light overtook them. His nostrils flared. "Charlatan? Charlatan? I will not be insulted by an arrogant, uneducated little girl. Stand aside, daughter of Donal Hain, my business is not with you but with the weak man who cowers behind you."

Thunder crashed as Faust shouted at Sam. He threw his arms wide, causing a torrential gust of wind to buffet Sam and Craig. Sam assumed the *en-garde* position, dropping her center of gravity lower than normal. Craig fell back, and his head struck a rock. He grunted. A ball of pale blue flame illuminated in each of Faust's upturned palms. The balls spiraled around his arms and then up his torso; when they reached the crown of his head, they exploded into a shape similar to the head of a massive azure dragon, its mouth as thunder roared and lightning clashed. Craig assumed a fetal position, and Faust laughed.

Sam rolled her eyes. She focused her gaze and met Faust's glowing eyes with her annoyed brown ones. With her thumb, index, and middle fingers raised in a medieval Hand of God gesture, Sam waved her hand across her body and then away to her right side. "*Nihil video quod timean.*"

Faust coughed as a lump slammed through his throat. The wind stopped. The thunder quieted. And the flaming dragon head disappeared. He blinked, and his eyes returned to normal.

His first sight was Sam smirking triumphantly as she folded her arms across her chest. She flipped her hair and said, "I guess I'm not so uneducated after all, old man. If you know my father's name, then you probably know my name is Samantha, and I am far more than my father's child. Craig Wellington here is under my protection, and I believe the deal was a fist fight. So, you and me, no magic and no weapons. I hear Germans are famed for their honor. Care to actually show some?"

Faust nodded, a wicked, tooth-bearing smile slithered across his face. Sam assumed a defensive stance, her hands held in loose fists at the level of her shoulders. Faust approached with a speed that rivaled Martin's. His right fist slammed into Sam's cheek. She grunted and staggered. Her heart rate increased as she rubbed her jaw.

"Is that what you desire, little girl?" He opened his hands, taunting her to attack him.

Faust blocked her jab and dodged her cross. Her left uppercut pushed his jaw toward his skull. Sweat broke on her forehead. She took two deep breaths, feeling the aura of strange energy emanating from Faust's core. Sam followed up with a right cross, a left jab, and a side kick. Faust grunted and doubled over. Craig cheered.

Faust unleashed a series of jabs. Sam's blocks matched his speed. She riposted on the last with a knee to Faust's solar plexus. He grunted. Sam slammed the heel of her boot onto his toes. He cried in pain. Sam thrust her palm into Faust's nose. It cracked, and blood flowed.

"I warned you to back off, old man. Surrender and go back to Hell."

The air around Faust crackled and warmed. The green flames blazed once more in his eyes. His nostrils flared, and a guttural growl rumbled from his lips. Winds swirled around him, billowing his black trench coat. Thunder pealed, and lightning flashed in the black sky as he said, "Never again will Faust set one toe into Hell."

Faust thrust his left palm forward, his fingers curled in a claw. Winds buffeted Sam as lightning jolted her. She winced. He pressed his magical attack; the wind knocked her down. Sam grunted as the sweat stung her eyes. The lightning flew over her.

"Still think you that I, the sorcerer who did cause the Rhine to circle Wittenberg, am but a conjurer of cheap tricks? A pox-ridden quim could not possibly understand my—Ugh!"

Faust coughed from the handful of dirt Sam hurled into his mouth. She panted as she lunged toward him and landed both a jab and then a right cross. She kneed his stomach, but he caught her leg and twisted it. Sam screamed. Faust grabbed her hair and threw her to the ground. He stepped on the back of her head. Sweat and blood caked the dirt onto her face.

Sam hobbled to her feet. She winced. Her heart thundered in her ears, and her short, shallow breaths stampeded through her lips. Faust hurled three balls of blue flame at Sam. She deflected them. Craig screamed; one ball of flame singed his work boots. *Time to end this.* Her Walther's sharp, loud bag reverberated through the cool night air. Faust cursed and grabbed his right hand. Blood flowed. Sam fired again; Faust deflected the bullet and smiled.

White flame surrounded Faust's hand. Sam screamed as her gun glowed orange; she dropped it. Faust raised his hands, and piles of dirt and rock rose and buried Sam; only her head remained free. Sam struggled, grunting and panting. Sweat and blood flowed from her dirt-crusted face.

Faust stalked the trembling Craig. The young man begged for his life. The magician's fists pummeled Craig, and his boots hammered Craig into the ground. In a surprising show of strength, Faust lifted Craig and tossed him toward the bound Sam. She screamed, cursed, and struggled against her bonds. Tears pushed their way down Sam's mud-caked cheeks. Blood, tears, and dirt blinded Craig as Faust produced his crystal. Pale green light emanated from the crystal. Craig's face blanked, and then he became a pile of ash. Sam wept.

Smirking in the shadows of the flickering streetlight, Faust stalked toward Sam. A dark, mocking laugh filled the night air as he circled her. Faust stopped in front of her, lifted her chin with his palm, and said, "And now the wager passes to you. We'll repeat this little meeting in one month's time. Now if you'll excuse me, I have to make a stop in Sorefoot."

Sam cried and screamed as her left palm burned. Faust disappeared in a burst of sulfurous flame. The earthen bonds released Sam, who curled into the fetal position and cried. Thunder roared. A vehicle's engine drew near as a black Lincoln Town Car pulled into the grass beside Sam. Both Jeffrey Smith and Damon Washington stepped out.

Jeffrey Smith kneeled beside Sam and observed her physical wounds. He looked at Damon Washington and said, "Let's get her in the car. I'll take her to Butcher's Bend General, and you drive her car and pick up Destiny so someone can stay with her when she's released. I'll send you the address."

Agent Washington nodded.

* * *

Sam remained silent as Jeffrey Smith raced along 178 into Butcher's Bend. Rain poured from the sky. He tried making small talk, reassuring her things would end well, and validating her feelings, but Sam did not respond. Jeffrey sped through the mostly empty streets as the clock approached three in the morning. Jeffrey Smith activated his phone's wireless assistant and directed it to call Destiny Grimm. The call went to voicemail.

He called again, and then he called a third time. On the fourth ring, a sleepy German voice whined into the speakers and said, "Huh? Am I getting a free copy of *Elder Scrolls: Daedric Rites?*"

"Only if you pay for it, Destiny," Jeffrey Smith said. His words sped through his mouth. "It's Jeffrey. I'm taking Sam to Butcher's Bend General. She's hurt, and she's in shock. I sent your address to Agent Washington. Damon's driving Sam's car, and I'd like the two of you to meet us there."

Destiny yawned as he spoke, and then her eyes shot wide. "What happened? Jeffrey, what happened out there?"

"Long story. I'll explain in detail—oh, fuck! There's construction. I've got to take the back way. Sorry, long story short, Faust used magic, powerful offensive magic, and her gun didn't stop him. He turned Craig Wellington to dust, and then did something to Sam. I didn't hear what."

"*Scheiße.*" Destiny sighed and shook her head. "I warned her this would happen. Alright, I'll throw on something quick, chug a Monster, and be ready for your partner's arrival. Bye."

After turning down Seventeenth Street onto Monroe Drive, the Lincoln Town Car screeched as its driver turned left onto Mullaney Boulevard. He called the emergency room, identified himself as a federal agent, and said his partner was injured and in shock while working; he requested someone meet them at the door with a wheelchair. His heart thundered as he pulled into the parking lot. A tall, well-built orderly with short red hair, a face covered in freckles, and green eyes stood beside a wheelchair. The orderly helped Jeffrey wheel Sam into the triage station.

A middle-aged woman of Asian descent, her hair in a bun that had grown steadily messier over the course of her shift, sat at the triage desk. Sam's elevated heart rate and blood pressure concerned her, and she noted them. Sam had several lacerations and bruises forming on her face, neck, and arms. She asked questions. Sam remained silent, but she began rocking slowly.

The nurse grew frustrated, looked at Jeffrey Smith, and asked, "Will you tell me what happened?"

"Full details are classified, ma'am." He flashed his badge. "Details are classified. I can tell you we were investigating reports of multiple violent crimes committed by a foreign national in Fiddlers' Ford. While in the process of apprehending the suspect, we split up to corner him. He hid better than we thought, and my partner took the brunt of his attack. She held her own, though. Another agent is taking the perp into custody as we speak."

She narrowed her eyes and growled. A sigh slipped through her lips as her shoulders relaxed before she said, "That explains the lacerations and bruises. All of her other symptoms suggest a traumatic response except for these three burn marks—perfect circles—on her left hand. What happened?"

Jeffery Smith shrugged. "He had an incendiary device rigged to blow. Best I can figure from evidence at the crime scene is she tripped the wire, tried to shield herself from fire and shrapnel, and got burned."

The nurse shook her head. "I know you're not telling me everything. Federal rules, I get it, but an incendiary device does not explain why these burn marks are perfect circles in a triangle, where each side would be two point fifty-four centimeters in length. Is there anything else that—"

"I failed," Sam said. Her voice crept in whispers. "I failed. Craig died because of me. I failed."

Jeffery Smith and the nurse blinked, locked eyes, and then turned their attention toward Sam. Jeffery placed a hand on her shoulder. "We got him, Sam. Damon just booked him. You didn't fail; you're injured." He turned to the triage nurse and said, "Oh! I forgot, and I'm sorry; she's been struggling with PTSD after a rough case in October."

"Is she on medication?"

Jeffery thought for a moment. "She mentioned taking something for it. Prozac, Paxil, Pfizer. It was something starting with a 'P.'"

"I take Paxil," Sam said. Her voice had more strength, but was still soft. "I take Paxil, and I take Minipress for my nightmares. Two...two times...I take it two times a day, always with food."

Sam burst into tears. Jeffery squeezed her shoulder in solidarity. The triage nurse grabbed the gray phone and said, "Hold tight. We'll get her in the treatment area ASAP."

Less than ten minutes later, the hospital called Sam to the back. After her initial treatment, which included cleaning and bandaging her wounds as well as a mental health assessment, they transferred her to a regular room, where an elderly physician of Indian origin, Doctor Rathnam Indurthy, checked in on her and discussed the treatment plan. He attempted to get specific details of the incident, but Jeffery Smith refused to budge. Shortly after he left, Destiny burst through the door and hugged Sam.

Destiny asked, "Well, what did the doctor say?"

Sam yawned, and then she winced. "The cuts will heal up. I'll be bruised and sore for a few days. Seems there's a chance I'll be upping my meds or maybe changing them. I hope not. Otherwise, Doctor Indurthy will check on me at noon, and if I'm okay, I can go home. I should text 'Milla."

"You can do that in a bit," Destiny said. "What really happened? Agent Washington just kept saying it was 'the damnedest thing he's ever seen.'" Sam started to respond, but Destiny stopped her. "No, you need your rest. Jeffery, what happened?"

Jeffery Smith walked to the door, shut it, and stood in front of it. "I'm sure Sam can give more details, but I agree. She needs rest. You know the basic details. Damon and I used nightvision goggles, so some details are fuzzy. Faust showed up in all the pomp and circumstance one would expect. They talked, and I assumed negotiations went south, because a fist fight began. Sam held her own; I thought she was going to win, but then he started hurling spells at her. She blocked them, and then we heard gunshots. He bled, but he didn't stop."

"I shot his hand. If I aimed better, I'd have won."

"You rest, young lady," Destiny said. Her father's authority boomed in her voice, shocking even her. She softened her voice and said, "Go on, Jeffery."

He nodded. "Then he raised the ground around Sam and put her in like a dirt burrito, burying her up to her neck. Faust wanted her to watch as he showed Craig something shiny that turned him into dust. He then did something to her, and we heard him saying he'd see her in a month's time. Then he vanished."

"He's headed for somewhere called Sorefoot," Sam said through a series of yawns. Her eyes closed, and her head lowered as she drifted to sleep.

Destiny tucked Sam in as she started snoring. She looked over at Jeffrey. "Thanks for being there. I don't know where Sorefoot is, but we'll learn soon enough, I guess. I'll stay and get her home. You get some rest yourself."

He nodded and left.

Doctor Indurthy released Sam shortly after one o'clock; Destiny drove her home, stopping at Wendy's since the hospital meal proved to be worse than that of a public school cafeteria. Sandy Paws sat on Sam's chest, kissing and head-butting her, making eating challenging. While Sam ate and snuggled her cat, Destiny made tea, kept Sam hydrated, started the laundry, and tidied the house. Carmilla called, and Sam apologized for not texting. While Sam explained the situation, Destiny's trained ears picked up on Carmilla offering to fly over.

Destiny snatched the phone from Sam's hand and said, "Forgive the interruption, Countess, but there will be no flying. Give us two hours, and we'll meet you at the Four Winds. Sam's going to take a bath, and I think all of us could use a drink."

Destiny ended the call after Carmilla agreed. Sam's face displayed incredulity at what transpired. "Wait? What? You just hung up on my girlfriend."

Seated in one of Sam's larger chairs, Destiny sipped her jasmine tea. "I'm helping to distract your mind."

Sam crossed her arms, glared, and growled. She snorted. Her right hand ran along the burn marks on her left and, and she said, "I don't need distractions. I need to focus. I've got less time now that he's marked me like this. Destiny, I have to focus."

"And that is why you need distractions now more than ever, Samantha Blake Hain. Yeah, that's right, I full named you." Destiny assumed the lotus position and took a long quaff of her tea, allowing the floral notes to fill her nostrils. "You're stuck in your head. Tell me I'm wrong. You're replaying last night's events, and right now, that's not what you need."

Sam rolled her eyes and sighed. Tears formed, and she hugged Sandy Paws tightly. "I failed, Des. You don't understand. I failed. I'm going to lose everything I've worked for. Mom. How will others trust me if word gets out that I failed? And the Four Winds? I can't look Nick Scratch in the eye. Maybe giving up is the best option."

Destiny clenched her jaw and took another sip of tea. To have her best friend state she did not understand failure hurt. That hurt worse than the shock, shame, and failure after the Berlin werewolf incident. She understood Sam's hurt, fear, and anger, but the unfairness of that accusation stung. She took a deep breath and then said, "Sometimes life is like a dark tunnel. Perhaps it's filled with shadows. Perhaps it's filled with Zubats. Perhaps it houses our worst fears. But we still have to walk through it. Why? Because whatever it is that we're looking for is on the other side. We know, and so we go."

Sam scoffed. "Easy for you to say. Your soul isn't forfeited if this guy doesn't return to hell."

"And that is why we need to hit the Four Winds. Okay, so maybe only one being knows more about what's going on in the world than Nick Scratch, but no one has a bigger stake in this than him. Yes, I know your soul is a big deal to you, but think about this situation. If you fail to return Faust to Hell, sure, your soul is damned to Hell for all eternity; however, if you lose, the *big guy* gets involved. You and Mister Scratch have one big similarity, Sam."

"What's that? Horniness for our partner?"

Destiny bit her lip to stifle a giggle. "Okay, two, but I'm being serious. Neither of you wants your dad to be super involved in your lives. Yes, Mister Scratch wins either way, but his payout is bigger if you win. We can't trick him, but maybe we can negotiate a clue or an idea or something. He wants you to win as much as you want you to win."

Sam relented and agreed. She bathed, and during that time, Destiny washed their tea mugs and put Sam's clothes in the dryer. They would probably need another cycle to remove the wrinkles; Sam would forget they were in there. Destiny wrote Sam a reminder on a Post-It and attached it to Sam's French press. She spent the rest of Sam's bath time playing with Sandy Paws and texting Jeremy, updating him on Sam's condition while hiding the truth behind the facade of investigator-client confidentiality.

Destiny changed into a teal blouse and black jeans, one of the two outfits she kept at Sam's for sleepovers and emergency overnights. Sam donned a burgundy turtleneck, medium wash denim jeans, and brown riding boots. After giving Sandy Paws pets, kisses, a can of chicken cat food, and a treat, the two women ascended the stairs and entered Sam's ritual room. As the portal opened, the bar's din roared. They stepped through the portal.

Flickering candles inside floating tulips bathed the Four Winds in gentle pink, blue, and white light. A massive throng from Faerie gathered at the Four Winds to celebrate a wedding between two dryads. One bride, whose coloration and shape suggested a summer oak, wore a leaf-tailed morning coat of resplendent green and gold. The other, a winter fir, wore a dress of pale blue ice and snow. The guests, all dressed in clothing colored to represent their respective courts, toasted the couple with glowing shimmer wine served in crystal glasses shaped like stemmed roses and tulips, delighted each other with riddle games, and danced to the music coming from the stage as Lilith revealed her deep soul and sang "Make You Feel my Love."

Nick Scratch had donned a black tailcoat with ruby buttons, a red ascot, black vest, and black tuxedo trousers. A wistful smile slid over his face as he leaned on the bar and watched his wife perform. As they walked to an empty booth in the far corner, Niamh O'Cuinn, the banshee Sam helped in Bannagh, floated over and hugged Sam, thanking her again. Sam forced a smile and nodded. She sat in against the wall, in the corner, rested her face in her hand, and sighed.

Destiny walked to the bar, and Nick Scratch sauntered over, a smile on his face, and said, "Welcome, Miss Grimm." He looked over at Sam moping in the corner and frowned. "If I am reading your companion's body language correctly, the two of you are not celebrating a victory?"

She shook her head. "That's one way to put things. Looks like a wedding. Who's getting hitched?"

Nick Scratch smirked. He poured a rich, golden amber Märzen and a matching bourbon that smelled of caramel, vanilla, and oak. He pushed them toward her and said, "You know the price for drinks."

"First one's always free, I know. Here's what I got." Destiny lowered her voice. "You've probably figured Faust beat the crap out of Sam, but he also put some weird curse on her, said he would claim her soul like he's been claiming others with his magic crystal, and then mentioned he had to head out to Sorefoot, which my Google-fu learned is a city in Texas. Don't know why, but that's what we know. Oh, and the Order of the Dragon is using him to collect the souls needed to resurrect Dracula."

"So that's the direction they're moving. Interesting, given everything else. I suppose that's worth another round or two."

Destiny took the drinks and said, "I was hoping to trade the intel for a pep talk for Sam."

Carmilla entered and glided across the floor. She sat beside Sam and wrapped her lover in her arms. As Sam wept, Nick Scratch poured a glass of Sanguinovese and pushed it toward Destiny. "Give her a moment. I'll be there after a tick."

Destiny returned to the booth and passed the drinks around. Carmilla sipped her wine. Sam swirled her bourbon and stared into the glass. She sighed and said, "Go ahead and say it. I know."

Carmilla set her glass on the booth's table and clasped Sam, keeping her head against the vampire's chest. "You are safe, my dear one. Now, that is all that matters. Now is not the time for lectures or flirtatious chiding. In the morning, the formation of a plan may begin, but now, in the shadows of the night, take comfort in my love."

Sam sucked in snot as she continued weeping. Her trembling arms wrapped around Carmilla. "And I ruined that. I've only got another month, 'Milla. I can't beat him. And he's going to suck out my soul and send me to hell in his place. And everything was going so well."

"Hell is your final destination, should you fail to overcome Johann Faust," Nick Scratch said as he sat beside Destiny, a snifter filled with brandy in his hand. "And while there are limited outcomes in this endeavor, several choices present themselves to you, should you choose not to roll over and play dead."

Sam snorted and sniffed her bourbon. "Easy for you to say. You actually get to reign in Hell. I'll just become another tormented soul."

Nick Scratch sighed and shook his head. "Take the lesson and make the best of your situation. Or, you could learn from your opponent."

Sam sipped her bourbon. It was warm and spiced. "What? Do you really think Faust would train me so I could beat him? Some helpful bartender you are."

Nick Scratch pinched the bridge of his nose. "I never said the line John Milton attributed to me—well, not without far more colorful language than a dour Puritan would pen to a page. What I meant, since you began this little tête-à-tête by literary allusion, was that perhaps you could learn a lesson from a literary handling of Faust's narrative. Kit Marlowe's in particular."

Sam rolled her eyes. "What? Take out another contract with you? That's what got me into this mess, Nick."

He narrowed his eyes, growled, and bared the tips of his fangs. "Perhaps if Miss Grimm appeared in a white gown with a tinsel halo and feathery wings, and I revealed my horns and crimson skin, then you would make the connection. Marlowe's use of the good and bad angels to prod Faust's movement is where your lesson lies. At any point, Faust could have turned back—at least according to Kit's theology—but he refused to change course. Do not be like him. Be better."

Sam threw her arms up and gave an exasperated sigh. "And what do you propose I do?"

"You know the answer to that question. You may continue to bumble around in the dark on your own, or you may seek training from one of the esoteric orders in the west."

"What about your academy, Samael?" Carmilla asked. "Could she not study there?"

He sipped his brandy and smirked. Her voice trembled in fear as she asked that of him. "Had we more than a mere month before her next encounter with that wretched charlatan, that might be an option. However, a crash course would be..." He paused and grinned. "Hellish."

Destiny giggled. Sam and Carmilla offered synchronized eye rolls. Sam said, "My father always told me it took years to master magic to the level I'd need for this."

Nick Scratch produced a cigar from the interior pocket of his tailcoat. He lit it with a finger snap and took a single, deep drag. "And how does one reign in Hell if one does everything their father's way? Prove him wrong."

He snapped his fingers again, refilling everyone's glass. Destiny cocked an eyebrow and asked, "You're being unexpectedly generous with ideas, Mister Scratch. What gives?"

He puffed on his cigar a few times and shrugged his shoulders.

"That bloody charlatan has made a claim on a soul to which I have a claim. I will not relinquish what is mine unless the mortal in question completes the terms of our contract."

Sam sighed but remained silent as conversations continued around her. Her father was a master magician; one of the reasons his absence throughout her life hurt so much was his ability to access the international portal network. He should have been present. He *could* have been present, had he wanted to be. He should not have cheated on her mother and walked away from her at thirteen, only to return after her mother died. She wanted nothing to do with him, and that included not relying on magic. Sure, a banishing here or a mind shielding spell there was fine; she needed to be safe, but using magic as a primary means of closing her case was something else.

But this case was different. Her usual goal of keeping all humans and Non-Human Mythics safe no longer applied. Johann Faust had to be brought down and sent back to Hell. Sam was no longer investigating a case; she was hunting a bounty. And that demanded a different set of skills. Skills she did not possess.

Sam downed her bourbon and said, "I guess it's decided then."